BAY OF PERSPA
HALLAR PORT
EMDAR PORT
RIVER ELOE
HALLAR
SAN REAL
KINGDOM OF
AVEDAR
SOR-RE
KING'S SEAT LOMILLAR
KING'S W
PERSPA
TRENAR
COLLUM
HIGHLANDS
STAR PASS

the POETS
of PEVANA

Peggy, Thank you for reading! All the best,

Mark Nelson

Mark Nelson
7/12/13

HADLEY
RILLE
BOOKS

THE POETS OF PEVANA
Copyright © 2012 by Mark Nelson

Cover art © Tom Vandenberg

Cover design © Erin E. Turbitt

Map of Perspa © Ginger Prewitt

ISBN-13 978-0-9849670-6-3

Edited by Terri-Lynne DeFino

Published by
Hadley Rille Books
Eric T. Reynolds, Publisher
PO Box 25466
Overland Park, KS 66225
USA
www.hadleyrillebooks.com
contact@hadleyrillebooks.com

For Carol, always.

Acknowledgments

This book is in your hands because of the support and encouragement of a whole slew of people. First and foremost, my immediate family: my parents, siblings, my wife and children. Without them, I never would have even tried.

I owe a debt to my early readers Jessica Carter, Grace Gabriel (aka PB&J), Lynn Brant, Richard and Kim Ross, Nicholas Van, Linda Morris, Samantha Robillard, and Vanessa Garrido for enthusiastic and necessary feedback. An audience, however small, is a great motivator.

I owe even more to Eric T. Reynolds (publisher) and Terri-Lynne Defino (editor and author) from Hadley Rille Books, who managed to look beyond the 'worst query-letter of all time' and gave a chance to a story that otherwise might never have seen the light of day. I cannot emphasize my gratitude to Terri enough. She held me accountable with her unrelentingly positive feedback and brought things out of me I did not know I had. She is an amazing editor and friend.

I want to thank Ginger Prewitt for her marvelous map, (folks: pay attention to the compass rose, please!) and Tom Vandenberg for his awesome artwork that serves as the cover of this book. I hope the words within do justice to their efforts.

This book is also dedicated to the old crowd that used to populate the Styxboard.com message board: Rosemary, Jesse, Angie, Karen, Queenie, Zan, Mike, Shogun and especially Joey Barat, fellow poet and the real source for the character Devyn Ambrose. In amongst the verse and the flamewars, I found the seeds for this story.

This book is also something of an homage to JRR Tolkien, CJ Cherryh, Bernard Cornwell, Patricia McKillip, Rosemary Sutcliff, CS Lewis, Guy Kay, CS Forester, and the host of other authors whose works have punctuated my reading and writing life. For me, story-telling is like the short story "Stone Soup."

This is my first offering to the pot. Thanks for reading.

Enjoy!

—Mark Nelson

The Poets of Pevana

IN A MOMENT OUTSIDE OF TIME, *Renia shed her tears in a gentle stream over the land. She caressed the hills and they grew fruitful. Vines sprouted upon the slopes above the river that cut its way around a hill upon whose shoulders perched a city of white stone walls and red tile roofs.*

At her side her familiar, Minuet of the arrows, gazed down with intent. At a gesture from the Goddess she would take hold of her bow and let loose a shaft into the murk of fate that was the collected roil of destiny.

"Whomsoever your arrows smite," said the Goddess in a quiet whisper," shall be as one driven to follow one's heart's desire."

And Minuet nodded her head and smiled. "And whomsoever my arrows touch shall do your bidding in their quest to reach their heart's desire," said she.

"As like they will," responded her mistress. "But nothing is certain in these times. The world recedes from us, my dear."

"I have shafts enough in my quiver, mistress. I could pin them to their fates and call them back to you."

"Allegiance without love is empty worship, Minuet."

"Better that than the darkness."

The Goddess sighed, an ageless, immortal weariness, and smiled sadly. "Perhaps, my dear, but it were better to fall into the darkness with at least my dreams of former days intact than to coerce attention from a wayward people. My places burn, Minuet. They forget me."

Minuet's fair brows knit together in care and concern. Such resignation in her mistress's voice had never before been. "My lady," she whispered. "Surely there cannot be an end?"

"If they turn away, then comes the darkness."

"But not yet?" asked Minuet. And the Goddess Renia paused, took reflection and found she did not yet want to recede into her dreams.

She gave the smallest lift of an adamantine hand, and Minuet swiftly put shaft to string.

"No, my dear, perhaps not just yet. . ."

And Minuet loosed once, and again, and then again.

And so the gentle barbs hurtled earthward to snick the dreams of the Poets of Pevana.

Chapter 1: Talyior Enmbron

R ED MORNING LIGHT POKED THROUGH THE SHUTTERS, transversing the room to bathe the face of a young man slumped over a pile of papers, quill fallen from fingers in repose next to a candle that had just guttered out. On one of the pages, filled with scratched out efforts and flowing lines in neat handwriting, lay the results of a night's struggle with words and passion.

The light yellowed as it rose up through the gap in the shutters, further clarifying the young man's face, creaseless save for a faint scar on the left of his forehead that ran just beneath the hairline to fade into the blond hair at his temple. The room was rumpled, a mixture of clothing tossed over the other chair at the table, a bed unused last night but still an unmade tangle of sheets and pillows. A mirror with a diagonal crack sported several hooks on which hung a cavalier's hat with plume and a rapier in a moleskin scabbard. The room looked lived in yet still had all the signs of impermanence, as though the young man was not the first nor would be the last to toss his nights away and scribble his angst on broadsides by cheap candlelight. The room smelled like hopes unrequited by a washing or dusting. It was perfect. It was a tragedy.

Talyior Enmbron was twenty-two, and lost in a most exquisite dream. He was in love, fashionably, hopelessly in love, with a woman he had no right to claim: Demona Anargi, the wife of a rather wealthy merchant of Pevana: the jewel of the southernmost trading cities of the kingdom of Perspa.

Talyior had been in the city since the early spring, originally working for his father, a prosperous carpet trader, but that interest had faded away with the midsummer heat and the lure of Pevana's charms. His parentage gave him entrance to society and its endless rounds of balls, feasts and dalliance. Demona captured him more than a month ago, and he had been lost ever since. He was aware of his foolishness. He did not care that his father's last letter informed him he was cut off and dismissed as a disappointing degenerate. The old man just did not understand love! He did not care that Sevire Anargi had returned to the city and had set servants to watch over his wayward wife. He was an obstacle, nothing more. Demona was an intoxicating prize worth any risk. She was perfect. She was *his* tragedy.

This particular dream, exquisite as it may have been, was doomed to dissipate, for the sun, finding the line of his scar began to seep its warmth into his wine-addled brain as a draft of cold air chills the foot left outside the bedcovers. The beating of his heart that punctuated the dream-kisses Demona bestowed on him changed into the angry hammering of Sevire's fist on the bedroom door and then again, as he lurched into headache alertness, into the sturdy knocking of Lyssa the maid.

"Up with you, now!" she shouted, rattling the handle in warning. "I know you are in there! Heard your snoring awhile back! Up and get yourself decent or risk giving me a free look at those nice legs of yours. I've a plate and a pot for you if you've a mind, or even if you don't for that matter. Tal? Hear me boy?"

Groaning, Talyior lifted his face from the pool of drool, noticing the wetness had smudged part of the last line of what he managed to compose last night. The first lines were a blur as he scanned them. Then, for a brief moment, the pounding of his temples eased and the last stanzas came clear as he read:

Though the city sleeps,
Shutters closed,
A thousand secrets it keeps,
This I know—
Above all else she is the one I need.

With skin clean and white
She draws me to the light
Constantly.
She is the well from whence spring all my dreams
She is Demona.

Let poor men cry about their hopeless lives,
Let rich men lie about the power and strife
Of what they call the noble life,
And let wise men whisper behind wizened hands
Words that amount to grains of sand—
None of those fools could ever understand
What it is to love Demona. . .

Such is the minstrel's plight
Doomed to pursue his passion
Under cover of night.
I must not bemoan my fate in this pass
Doubts are poor counselors
In the things that last.

Such is the price I pay
For daring to love, Demona.

His thoughts ran away from him like the ink from the final letters. It was probably good enough to present at the hearings that night at the Golden Cup, might even earn him a few coins to appease his landlady's demands for payment, but was it good enough for Demona? The maelstrom in his head beat a steady, negative beat as he croaked a response to Lyssa's shouted request.

"Gods, help me," he moaned aloud. "Demona. She must see what she does to me? Damn her conservative prig of a husband anyway. He can't satisfy her—surely he must know that? Lock and key. Lock and key."

"Lock and key what, my young sot?" Lyssa called, entering the room much too briskly and with a voice several times too loud. Talyior's vision blurred appreciably, and he had to shake his head to try and clear it, which just made the pounding worse and brought little black spots dancing before his eyes. He sat back in his chair and sighed.

"Here, fool," Lyssa said, plunking a tray down on the table. "I'd have thought a rake like you would know how to hold his wine. Shame! I've some bread and cheese and fresh well water. Don't break the crockery, mind you, and no spewing! Use the window if you must."

"Oh, please, Lyssa, not so loud. I'm in agony."

"Oh the pain, oh the tragedy!" She replied, even louder and in more good humor. "My young lover of words and women is a sot besotted. Tell me, are the tales I'm hearing at the well true? Demona, still? You must be a fool to be so persistent."

Talyior could not answer her. It took all his concentration to manage a small sip of water. It felt like love to his desert of a throat, but his stomach found it particularly revolting. Finally, like the passing of a rogue wave, he felt himself in calmer waters.

"A gentleman never boasts, Lyssa," he whispered. "You should know that. Is this bread fresh?"

"It is fresh enough for the bile it needs to soak up in your belly. It is fresh enough for a man who has not paid his bill for nearly a month. Gania is getting restless—best you have some coin on you when you come down today."

Gania, a woman with a temper as vast as her behind, owned the house. She loved her ale and the bawdy gossip Talyior related to her, some of it actually true. Talyior liked her, but not when his purse was nearly empty. His father's funds, now cut off, had almost run out. So had Gania's patience.

"Tell her something for me, anything, Lyssa. I'll settle with her soon, really," he said in his most plaintive tone. Dealing with Gania in one of her fiscal moods would just make him feel worse. And he needed to be in fine form. Money could be had at the Cup tonight, if he were in good voice and the competition none too stiff.

"And why would I do anything for you, my dandy?" Lyssa scoffed as she set about putting the bed to rights. "Strutting about in your plumage, living above yourself. Sevire's wife no less! You're a twit! That's what you are—a twit!"

But Talyior knew she was only pretending to mock him as she finished smoothing the bedding and resetting the pillows. He liked her—in a vaguely carnal fashion. She loved the *idea* of love. As Talyior had grown to know the city, he found Lyssa to be a keen observer of prices for wares and a hopeless romantic when it came to tales spun in verse. Talyior knew he was good-looking and talented and that seemed to matter more to Lyssa than anything else. He suspected she felt he aimed too high regarding Demona, but such aspirations were the stuff of poetry. And in Pevana, poetry paid—at least it did during the High Summer Festival.

"Well," she temporized when she had finished with the bed. "I suppose I could fashion a small tale for you." Her tone softened in kindness as she moved back to the door. "But it might be best if you used the window this morning. Try not to break your neck. I'd hate to have my efforts wasted."

Talyior smiled, and despite the pain, managed a small laugh. "Thank you, my dear, dear Lyssa. You are a rose among the thorns of this place."

"Ha!" she laughed in return. "Save your poetry for Demona. Eat! I can't have you wasting that bread!"

An hour later, washed if not terribly refreshed, he escaped having to deal with Gania by climbing out his window, around the ledge of the upper story and down the drain spout for the gutter. He made a carefully considered leap over the refuse pile just beginning to add its stink to the city smells in the growing heat of the morning. The landing jarred his aching head, and for a moment all went fuzzy while the bread and cheese Lyssa had fed him threatened to come back up again. He managed to stifle his gorge with a breath and a clench. Checking his shirt pocket for the carefully recopied poem, and setting his hat a little lower over his brow, as much to hide his face as to protect his bleary eyes from the light, he made his way out into the street and found it already crowded with shoppers early to market and tradesmen ordering their stalls for the day's business.

"What a cesspool," he whispered to himself as he walked along, nodding to the maidens out on errands, smiling artificially at the better-looking ones. "If it weren't for Demona, I'd chuck the whole place and head south."

And yet it was precisely because of Demona that he found himself still in Pevana, with its maze of streets and alleys, its suspicious husbands and fraudulent society gatherings. She was too sweet to leave—just yet. He found he liked writing. Words came to him, whether spiced to lure Demona to her window or to place on paper to be judged at the hearings. Words worked a kind of magic on him. They had cost him his family, indirectly, and yet he still felt vital somehow, more alive than he ever felt around his father and the tasks he had been set to that brought him originally to Pevana. He was young and in love with an unreachable woman. His life was at risk, maybe. His talent was surely at risk, for to lose tonight would be a tragedy. To have to face Gania empty-handed could prove fatal. He smiled genuinely for the first time that morning, and a young lady, thinking his smile meant for her, beamed back at him. An upwelling of good feeling rushed over him, and he chuckled a little as he bowed in passing.

"All life is a risk," he murmured to the day. "And what a glorious gambit! It's all in the trying. Hey, that's good! I'll need to remember that for later."

He spent a leisurely few minutes making his way to where his father held offices and warehouse space on the wharves in the harbor. Talyior never quite gave up hope that his father might relent. It was not as though he did not care about the fine carpets his father imported from the East; he just had higher aspirations. He loitered just long enough to learn from his father's overseer, Espan Gale, that no such communication had arrived with the latest shipment.

"Sorry, lad," the old trader said, not ungently but still with a hint of judgment. Espan had but one eye. A snapped line in a storm had taken the other. The lone remaining orb fixed on Talyior in a squint. "You know your father. I'll never know a more stubborn, willful man—unless it be his son. He's not said a word about you in the last two letters. Perhaps if you'd write to him rather than spending your time composing skirt-lifting ditties to the doxies on the wharf, he might reconsider."

Talyior shrugged off the implied criticism. He and Espan had delivered several orders together to estates where Demona had been present. Even though Espan only had one eye, Talyior was sure the older man had taken note of Demona's charms.

Leaving the warehouse, Talyior made his way out the city gates and along the bank of the small river that cut the land between the city and the outer headland before adding its waters to the harbor. He walked for about half a league up river to a secluded spot with a huge maple tree that grew right at the river's edge. In a hollow space beneath a root he kept a line, pole, some flies, a rope and hook and a precious stash of paper and charcoal pencils wrapped in an old oilskin boat cloak. It was quiet here, and out of the way despite being so close to the city, and it was directly opposite the outer rear walls of House Anargi.

The grounds of the Anargi estate ran down the hill slope to the walls next to the river. When he climbed the tree, Talyior could gaze into Demona's own chambers. If she was there, and alone, he used the rope and hook. If she wasn't, he fished and wrote.

He considered climbing up to check, but his head and his reason made him decide against it. Besides, Sevire had returned to the city earlier that week, doubtless preparing for the Festival, and Talyior had no wish to catch a glimpse of his fat head with its thinning, graying crescent bent to Demona's breast. Even the mental image made him queasy. Sevire was an ugly man, tending to the corpulence that came from age and high living. Talyior thought him a greasy, wrinkled, saggy waste of flesh, a cactus that took a rose to his wife. Talyior hated him for his wealth, the man was said to be able to buy kings, and for the small sun he placed on Demona's ring finger that bound her to him in marriage. And that was a pill most bitter and grating. Talyior knew Demona loved him.

She tolerated the old man, granted him his fumbling pleasures, but it was Talyior's back she had scratched the last time they made love. It was his name she whispered as he met her at that point where the universe was nothing more than a cosmology of two. He knew it. He knew it, even if he could never get Demona to take off that ring. She was an elixir to him, as stirring as starlight to the soul. He wanted her. *Gods grant*, he thought as he turned away from the wall, *that Sevire dine well tonight and choke on a chicken bone.*

He sighed, as only the young perplexed by unrequited love can sigh, and knelt down to reach underneath the tree root for his gear. Today he would fish and think and write, for words were flowing in him today like a river. They flashed, swirling, eddying words, fast words, deep words, words whose silver meanings darted fishlike among the currents of his thought. He wanted to try and catch some of those meanings, for in them he sensed lay the magic to achieve his desires—or at least lunch.

He readied his pole and cast out into the channel. Sitting on the bank, paper and pencil next to him, he waited for a bite, a word, a meaning. He reviewed what he hoped to accomplish that evening, for tonight's hearing at the Golden Cup was vital if his plan was to work. If his poem were to win tonight, he would earn thirty gold pieces— enough to pacify Gania and purchase new clothing and other necessary things. But more importantly, winning tonight's readings would mean he would present his poem before the Prince and the judges in the finals at the Festival Gala. Everyone would hear it— Sevire, the Prince and his retinue, and especially Demona.

He let his mind wander, imagining all the possibilities of such a public proclamation. It was a pleasant reverie and yet tinged around the hazy edges with threat's darkness. The competition would give him his chance, and Demona was worth the risk.

21

The daydream set thoughts flowing, and he took up his pencil and began writing, following the words as they spun out their magic on the page:

By the swirls of the river current
I let loose your name on a boat made of leaves
And watched it spin away from me.
And all that I knew of you
Passed away, like stillness lost to sound.
Helplessly, I called your name—
Once, twice, a third time—
And the river heard me
And caught the leaf-boat in a backwater
And brought you back to me
Unchanged,
Like the memories of love
Found in dreams.

"Tonight," he said as much to the world as to himself, "it begins tonight."

HE RETURNED TO THE CITY later that afternoon with four fine trout and three poems, the beneficiary of an excellent nap in which dreams of Demona figured prominently. He walked back along the river with music running though his head and rhymes bounding about like favorite pets keeping him company. He had just enough time to wheedle Lyssa into helping cook the fish and brush any stains out of his best cloak. Then it was a cloth to the face, a brush through the hair and back alleys as much as possible to the Golden Cup for the evening's Reading.

He had a reasonably clear image in his mind how it might play out at *the Cup*. He had registered his name there for several reasons. It was close to his lodgings; he went there frequently and liked the atmosphere of the place, but his primary reason related exclusively to the competition. The Golden Cup had never been selected to host a Reading before, and Talyior wagered most of the more seasoned, known, local poets would gravitate to the older, more prestigious establishments, leaving the Cup to accommodate the rest. Talyior intended to be the best of *the rest*. He felt it a truth just waiting revelation. Part of his inner thought laughed at his presumptuousness, but even that small, cautious part of him could not deny the music that had replaced the pounding in his head. He thought he detected the definite cadence of destiny. Tonight he would rise to the sublime.

It was a risk, of course, to present a love poem about the wife of the most powerful merchant in Pevana. He would be safe enough in the alehouse, but surely word would travel like lightning to the Anargi Estate. When he told Demona what he might do, she urged him to reconsider, but he had smothered her protests with kisses and well-placed caresses. He had not written the piece yet at that time, but the touch and smell of her had charged his waking and resting hours ever since—and charged the words he committed to page and memory as well. Tonight he hoped to serve Sevire and Pevana notice.

"Perhaps I should have sent the fish to the estate as a gift for the old man," he said aloud to a yearling gull that landed just in front of him on the path. "For surely a fish bone would work just as easily as a chicken wing." But the gull didn't answer, plainly more interested in the lingering smell of Talyior's trout than the sound of his words. It hopped out of the way when Talyior kicked a stone at it as he passed.

"No alms for you, bird. Go try Sevire's midden heap upstream. I am sure it is bounteous. He only eats the heart out of things and throws the rest away."

The gull screamed once at him and then kicked into flight. Talyior turned and watched it for a moment. It was probably off to fulfill its belly's desires gratis of House Anargi, while he, so much the more needful of the two, was forced to make do with fish and sensuous daydreams.

In his nap by the river, he had relived the events of their affair. A careful dance at a feast thrown by the Sailor's Guild, a stolen kiss at another, a midnight tryst that ended in her bed. How she purred; how the sweat had plastered those magnificent curls to her temples! It was a glorious dream, all the more glorious for being true, and yet it ended as suddenly as the trout, after taking the bait, is brought up short by the hook. A cloud had passed overhead, cooling him, and he had awakened to the sound of Sevire and Demona's voices raised in anger coming from over the garden wall.

"And I tell you, wife! You will send a note saying you are unwell and cannot attend!" Sevire had wheezed.

"And whatever would I want to do that for?" Demona asked, at once petulant and defiant. Talyior fought the impulse to climb the tree to better observe the quarrel.

"You will do so because I order you to," Sevire answered. "I know you've a wandering eye. The servants tell me things."

"Don't be silly, Sevire. I'm much too busy running your house to take a lover. Besides, who could compare to you? You are my lion, my silver-haired lion. Really! All I want to do is attend the reading at Basil's Perch. I've been cooped up, like one of those silly songbirds you keep in your study, for over a week now. It's Festival! I want to go out! You should come with me. It would be fun."

"Demona! I am old, but I am not a fool! I do not trust you these days. The Perch is a dung heap. You would soil yourself by going there tonight. I forbid it."

"Ah! It is fine for you to go running to the Prince and his cabal of lickspittles."

"I keep my eye on that one for my own ends, woman. House Anargi has the need and the right, and I do not run!"

"No, you do not. Hardly ever. I have to let you catch me now."

And at that Talyior had had to dunk his head into the river to keep from laughing out loud. The image of those heavy jowls and sagging belly pursuing the lithe Demona around that spacious bedroom was too much for a sane man to stand. He had held his breath as long as he could, and when he brought his head back up out of the water their voices had calmed and faded as if they were walking back up the garden path through the trees.

"Do not tempt my anger, wife. I give you fair warning. There are rumors. Rumors of a most unseemly sort. You shall stay at home tonight or I will know about it."

"As you wish, as always, husband." And with that the voices were gone. The last words had floated over the wall as a whisper, joining the currents of air, connected to the roiling currents of the river to form a miasma of possibility that had accompanied Talyior on his walk back down river to the city gates. The words led him to poem number three:

Words run in circles
Like line around the spool of a reel
Making a mockery
Of all my attempts at explaining
How it is I feel
About the love I have;
Its expression is hidden
In the waters of my life
Flowing by in its deep cut channel,
Carving the truth of me
Ever more intimately into the earth.
If you would know me,
You must dive into the
Deep waters. . .

As he turned to go underneath the gate arch, he wondered if it might be possible to get from the Golden Cup to Demona's window before the news of his poem reached Sevire at the palace. The idea was brash. It was tantalizing. It had all the ingredients of tragedy. It was perfect.

After all, he thought to himself, *I came here looking for adventure.* He dove into the stream of people making their way up the street, anonymous among the currents of faces and thoughts.

Thirty minutes later *he* almost choked on a fish bone when Gania surprised him with a visit to the kitchen.

"Well," she bellowed, pounding her plump, work roughened hand on the table next to Talyior's plate. "The dashing cavalier! Eating his fill after a day's honest labor, no doubt! Or was it daydreams and fishing line? You look full wrung out, lad. Did you get enough sleep last night?"

While he attempted to clear his windpipe, Talyior stole a quick, sullen glance at Lyssa, who just grimaced and quickly returned to cutting her onions for that evening's stew pot.

"You're two weeks late, my boy," Gania continued, thrusting her fat, pug nose into Talyior's purpling face. "I know you've been cut off. You know you've been cut off. I happen to shop at the same butcher's as Dalia Bernali, your Espan's housemistress. How long did you think I'd hold off, eh? You owe room and board, boy! No money? Then let's have that fine sword of yours off to Gymmi's for pawn and you off to find a job!"

Mention of pawning his sword sent Talyior into renewed attempts to breathe. He briefly considered giving up the struggle and fainting on purpose, but the threat of losing his blade was too much to ignore. That sword was the last thing his father had ever given him beside scorn and abuse. The lessons in how to wield it were the only hours Talyior could remember enjoyably spent during the last half-year at home. He couldn't lose it. It was almost as dear to him as words . . . gods help him . . . nearly as dear as Demona!

He coughed forcefully, sending the fish bone sailing across the table, over Lyssa's shoulder and into the stew pot. Talyior wanted to laugh, but his throat hurt too much. Grabbing the water pitcher, he sloshed a mouthful down, all the while staring into Gania's baleful brown eyes. She drew breath, but instead of tearing him to shreds she laughed, a deep, throaty chuckle that, to Talyior, sounded very much like the grunt of a boar-sow. Talyior did not know whether to join in or bolt for the door. He did not have time to choose, however, for with a garlicky cough Gania finished, thumped the table soundly once more and sat down, leaning back in her chair, no longer baleful, but still with a stern countenance.

"Ha," she went on finally. "I don't know why I always wind up with fools like you. I've seen it before; young pricks come to the city, turn themselves into an absurdity, then fade away dreaming of lost days working the docks. Or worse, they end up stuck on the end of a better man's blade and tossed into the pauper's pit. What will it be with you, eh? Gut wound? The Pox? Doxy boy?"

"I'm not a fool, Gania," Talyior replied, attempting to sound decisive but failing miserably when his voice cracked.

"Of course you are. All men are fools, especially young men with no money, no family and no prospects. Young men who reach above themselves wind up impaled on their own aspirations. I've seen it before. I'm old, boy, you are not the first walking tragedy to choke on a fish bone in my kitchen, but you'll be the last. I'll not waste the space on the likes of you again. I can't afford it."

"But, Gania, I'll pay you. I promise! I'm entered in the Poet's Competition for the Festival. The first reading is tonight. Thirty gold coins to the winner at each establishment. The winners present before the Prince with the victor taking two hundred! I'm good, Gania. I know it. I will win."

She just stared at him, eyes reflecting a little of the glint from the hearth fire.

"A filthy little scribbler," she said in her customary growl that grew louder as she went on, gathering volume like a stormcloud gathered moisture from the summer heat, piercing the afternoon sky with the threat of rain or worse. "A mousy little fancy-boy pouring out his passion on pages of parchment! An idler, wandering around all the days dreaming of breasts and lips and thighs, whose every third word is a sigh, whose world consists of countless romantic definitions of love—all of them the same because they are all lies! A . . . a . . . poet!"

Talyior nearly wilted under her scorn, but not quite. The conviction of his youth smiled back at her unaffected by her ridicule.

He rose from the table. It was time to wash, change and leave for the Golden Cup. He paused at the door.

"That's right, you immense mountain of a woman," he said in his best voice. "A poet, a scratcher with a quill. You'd best clean my rooms with care. Those wadded up efforts in the corners will be worth something someday."

"Don't try your sweet words on me, boy, or I'll crush you like the bird you are."

Talyior had to admit—she probably could. "Gania, Gania, my love," he intoned. "I would transport you. I would immortalize you."

"I had a husband once who got transported. You owe me five and six."

"I'll get you your money."

"Get it, or don't come back."

Talyior left, Gania's derisive laughter spurring him up the stairs.

Chapter 2: Devyn Ambrose

SWEAT RUNNING DOWN FROM HIS BROW AND POOLING into his ears woke Devyn Ambrose from a nightmare of falling masonry and burning gods. He sat up to wipe the perspiration from his face and the images from his mind. Not all the moisture was due to his dream.

It was high summer in Pevana, and he had fallen asleep with his work clothes on, again, after a late night with the horses and a fierce struggle with pen and parchment. He had been trying to write with little real success—a page of scratched and smudged lines of little worth. Frustration had tossed him to bed fully clothed despite the heat. And in the night came the nightmare of flames and falling faith.

He was familiar with the dream, for he had it often. He was just as familiar with his failures with words, for he could not get them to come at need. He knew the two were related, but he could not find a way to reconcile them. The heat of the Pevanese summer burned away all his ideas.

Dawn just began to brighten the stable yard outside his cubbyhole where he had his pallet and other private things. They did not amount to much: a small altar, charred on one side with a cracked bowl, a small chest of clothes, a mended writing stand such as cavalry commanders used on campaign and a sword with a well-kept sheath hanging from a tack hook on a post.

Devyn did not have much in the world, but what he had he treasured. The writing stand and sword had been his grandfather's. The altar he had earned himself, paying for it, as it were, with the burn scar on his left forearm. It still ached if he over-used it when working the horses or laboring amongst the crates and piles of tack made and sold by his employer, Malom Banley, horse trainer to the blue bloods of the city. He kept their extra carriage stock and trained their racers.

Devyn peeled off his sodden shirt and stumbled over to the water trough to wash. The water eased his scar a little as he splashed and washed the day into his soul. His auburn hair, the color of the sweet Pevanese grapes burned ripe for the vintage, sent rivulets of water down his back as he walked back to take up a towel to dry off. He flexed his arm. It did not hurt. Maybe today would be a good day. Maybe today the words would come. They had to, for tonight was the beginning of the Poets' Competition—the most important three days of the Festival of High Summer. He was entered. He did not have a poem. Yet.

He set about his morning tasks. Malom had him feed and water all the horses in the stable, and rub them down. He derived pleasure from the contented rucklings of the beasts as he went down the line. In his life, Devyn could count few close friends, despite being a native born son of the city. In fact, he found himself liking the beasts he tended better than most of the people he knew; and for a surety, he liked them better than their pampered owners. They deposited them with Malom, rough broken and untrained, expecting to take them up again later as conditioned and groomed racers and show horses. And yet he was scrupulous in the way he kept his feelings bound inside. What bitterness he felt about his role in perpetuating the reality of class stratified Pevana never reached the end of the bristles on the brush he lovingly passed over their flanks. It wasn't their fault, after-all. They were only simple souls. They trusted him to be gentle, so he was.

He finished early enough to use the found minutes to practice forms with his grandfather's sword. He stripped down to his underclothing and began the series of stretches he ran through before every session with the blade. He felt a shadow cross his back as he bent over to work his hamstring.

"Oh, love, now there's a pretty sight," a voice whispered sensuously.

Devyn straightened up slowly. "Sanya," he said. "How good of you to time your visits so precisely."

Sanya, the eldest daughter of Arno the baker, spent her mornings delivering daily orders to patrons and had taken to stopping by Malom's stables as long as Devyn had been working there. She plied her father's trade assiduously and mixed her own pleasures into the bargain. Work-roughened hands and strong forearms, the result of years kneading Pevanese summer wheat into dough, made her lovely in Devyn's eyes. Flimsy, powdered women did not appeal in the way Sanya, with her flour and perfume scent, did. Sanya had pursued Devyn for the better part of a year before she managed to break through his orphan's bitterness. Neither of them spoke of love. Devyn carried too much pathos around with him to ever see a way to settle down. And so it went on, for the several years to the present, a physical friendship, no ties knotting him in place.

Sanya's pleasant distraction did nothing to assuage the dark memories of youth or fill the hole left by his parents and grandfather. In truth, he did not know how to fill it. There was no room for love during his life as one of the children of the Maze, the labyrinthine slum that covered the southeastern parts of the city. He had survived, but came through the ordeal hardened, husbanding what little softness he retained for the horses placed in his charge. He questioned the truth of all feelings, and kept the troubling answers at arms' length. The physical aspects of love, like sword practice, allowed for the release of tensions. Devyn simply did not know how to let it become more; and he was fairly certain he did not want to learn how.

Still, he had to admire Sanya's pluck; most would have given up a long time ago. He wasn't being fair to her, and yet she didn't seem much troubled by it. She was a bawdy, baker's bitch, and for that more than anything, Devyn was grateful for her company.

But not today.

Sanya's ample bosom filled out her bodice; he noticed the top laces strategically undone to draw his and everyman's attention. And even though he found the fleck of flour dust left clinging to her left cheek in her haste to time her delivery of the day's bread particularly fetching, he could not let himself be drawn in. Not today. Today he felt the need for exercise and time and space to think. Sanya's charms would have to wait.

"Sanya, my dear, my loaf," he began. But her lips swallowed his next words as she grabbed his hair and pulled him to her. For a moment he almost lost his will—tantalized temporarily by the attentions of her tongue. He gently extricated her fingers from his hair and won back control of his mouth until, finally, with a last gentle brush of the lips he hoped would take away the sting of rejection, he pushed her away.

"Sanya, please, any other time, perhaps," he said quietly. "But I have to practice and compose today. Tonight is the first Hearing, and I've nothing solid prepared."

The look Sanya gave married both surprise and disappointment. She took a breath as if to speak but closed her mouth again. Her shoulders slumped ever-so-slightly, only enough to let Devyn relax. Stepping back, she smiled, ran a finger through the laces of her bodice and loosened their weave and exposing her breasts almost to the nipple.

"Words?" she asked with exaggerated huskiness. "You'd rather chase a sword point through the morning and words in the afternoon than chase these?"

Devyn laughed. "Sanya, please!"

"I'm trying to, but you won't touch me."

"I have to order my thoughts, understand?"

"I understand, all right," she retorted. "I understand I am third behind a row of horses' rumps and a pile of silly parchment. What will you do if I stop coming?"

"Then I would pursue you to the ends of the earth. You would weep in fear of the ravages I would enact on your person, wench."

"Promises, poet, from you are like unfinished poems. I don't believe you."

"Then run away and test my resolve."

"I'd find life on the world's roads lonely, I'm afraid."

Devyn's laugh deepened to a mock-growl. He gently caressed Sanya's cleavage before taking up the laces and setting her bodice aright. "Lonely?" he mocked. "Sanya, with such as these to lead your way, I find it hard to imagine you alone for any length of time, on any road."

"Don't tease me."

"Don't try and seduce me—not today, pet."

She gave up, and moved to pick up her basket of loaves. She paused before leaving. "Tonight, wordsmith—after the Cup, then. I've other deliveries to make. This lot is for Captain Avarran and the garrison down at the landward gate.

"Please give my regards to my old fencing master if you should see him."

She fixed on him eyes that flared flame-like defiance.

"Stop putting me off, or bread won't be the only thing I deliver to him."

"Ah! You wound me, girl. You wound me deeply!" And he bowed to her departing back.

"Tonight!" she cried over her shoulder as she flounced out the stable door and disappeared into the day.

Devyn stood for a moment, staring at the patch of sun brightening in the yard outside.

"Tonight," he murmured aloud. "May the Gods grant me the words."

He took his time with his practice, moving through the forms slowly at first, as if walking through the steps of a new dance, taking care to check his balance and point position. First his grandfather, and later the affable but dangerous Captain Avarran, had been sticklers for precision. "In a battle," his grandfather had been fond of saying, "brute strength often suffices, but in single combat a man often has to rely on his speed and skills. He has to be precise: point, blade, pommel, hand, arm, and shoulder. All must be connected and move as one. To be imprecise is to be dead."

Devyn had applied himself, seeing in the moves a rhythmic pattern that he later applied to his quest for words. As he moved back and forth across the stable yard, he saw himself constructing a set piece, a poem as it were, of steel and movement. In the flash of the blade, he saw beauty and purpose. In the arc of defense he saw cadence and motif. In the ending thrust he saw resolution. He saw in the movements a parallel to the need of the poet to be precise and graceful at the same time. Words without grace grated on the ear. Words without precision risked going unheard. Devyn, perhaps too much the perfectionist, always kept those thoughts uppermost in his mind. Blade. Pen. To be precise meant life.

His life had taken on some semblance of refinement since his days as a gutter rat in the Maze. Words and his gentle touch with horses had saved him. Vestiges of that rough survivalist lay at the core of all the words he composed or sword forms he practiced. Living in a stable with his charges did not preclude a desire for improvement in all things.

He knew such focus was not completely productive, but such was his way. He knew he needed the muses' benison or nothing would come, but open worship was now a thing of the past. The temple arsons had changed everything, and so he found himself shackled by doubt. All he could do was pray to his Gods with as much passion as he could muster.

After a time his moves became unconscious as he surrendered to the rhythm. Post, riposte, defensive arc and lunge until the sweat beaded anew upon his brow. In his mind's eye, Devyn was years and miles away. His parents' faces, first smiling in joy and life and then altered, twisted in death by pestilence, loomed before his inner vision. Bitterness informed Devyn's thrusts with his blade, as if he were trying to slay the past and its loneliness—as if he could bring them back—as if he could defeat death at sword's point. And then the images of his parents faded, replaced by the flames of his nightly dream as they consumed the carved oaken images of his people's ancient beliefs. Leering priests in red garb fanned the flames. City guards held back the reckless while the heat mounted. Cornices fell and smoke billowed up into the spring night as if trying to mask the sacrilege of their houses on earth from the Gods above. The flames grew, filling up Devyn's distracted vision. There was heat, shouts of alarm and clutching hands; and then a race into the darkness and smoke, the acrid stench of smoldering clothes and hair choking, choking, and blackness. And there, just discernable in a corner, the remains of a stone altar.

And so it came again, Devyn's dream repeated in the waking day. Flames and shouts and clutching hands, and there in the heat and smoke of the sanctuary a cracked minor altar, its stone bowl heated enough to burn a hole through his shirt sleeve. Breathless and in pain, Devyn had lurched through the smoke in search of a way out. And then a last clutching hand gripped firmly on his arm; a black-gloved hand and attached to a black-swathed arm. Devyn saw again the cloak billowing out to cover them both and the rasping voice bidding him come. The main roof of the last Temple of the Old Ways in Pevana crashed behind them as they escaped into the night and over the low place in a back wall to the silent alleyway beyond.

In his present, Devyn paused his practice. Dream and real time fused as the images took over: coughing and a growing, painful throbbing, and a quiet voice admonishing his temerity. Devyn relived the moment, his rescuer's face hidden by shadows and a fold of his hood so that the voice rasped out at him as if from a faceless darkness.

"That was foolish, and you know it. You are too young to trifle with the designs of the Prelate and his bunch. Surely you can see that?"

"But I had to do something," Devyn had managed to gasp out; his lungs ached from the heat and smoke. "I *felt* something. Maybe the Gods needed me to. I had to do it."

"So you risk your life for a stone bowl? Will that bring back your Gods? Open your eyes. The times are changing. Folly misinformed you, I think."

"Then why did you come after and help me? Aren't you a believer?"

And Devyn remembered then how the shadowed figure stiffened momentarily and drew away from him further into the darkness.

"Flames or candles, it's all just light to me. Say I'd rather not see a young life ended in a foolish adventure. Pevana has need of all her sons. Understand me?"

Devyn's answer had fallen beneath a wave of coughing as his lungs struggled to clear themselves. The spasm racked his body; he sank to one knee. When the fit finally left him, weak and teary-eyed, the shadow-man had gone. He found himself alone in the night with his rescued altar bowl, a burned arm, and a mystery.

Devyn brought his blade to rest with a last flourish as he returned to his waking self. A season ago, early spring it had been. And now, in the heat of Pevana's summer, in the midst of her Summer Festival, he stood in the dust of his exercise and wondered at the strangeness of it all. His arm was for the most part healed. The little stone altar graciously accepted his small ablutions and offerings. All that remained was the mystery. The thought punctuated Devyn's days: *Why would the Prelate order temples to be burned when he could order them rejuvenated for the King's Theology? Why? And who was the strange, terse man who had saved me?*

And that, really, was the catalyst for his dreams. More than grief, more than loneliness—there was the question. He had heard the Gods set mysteries in motion to be found and solved by the Poets. And so Devyn found himself doubly perplexed.

He went back to his sleeping place, wiped his blade clean on a cloth and returned it to its sheath and replaced it beneath his cot. "One thing is certain," he said aloud to the stables. "When I find the answer to my mystery, I'll find the words to my piece for the competition."

The horse in the stall next to him nickered; Devyn wasn't sure whether in agreement or derision.

BECAUSE IT WAS SUMMER FESTIVAL, Devyn worked fewer hours. Malom cut back on training and special tack jobs so his help could get out and enjoy some of the daily and nightly revels. There were races;

small fortunes were won and lost at the track outside the city walls during the week. Devyn liked to spend some of his free time down there watching his charges. He never wagered, only observed the races with a slightly proprietary air. He found people-watching fascinating, seeing within the ebb and flow of washed and unwashed humanity an odd sense of order, punctuated by the rise and fall of the mob's emotions as the races unfolded.

Pevana was noted for its horse fairs. Situated as it was on the southern border of a country famed for its cavalry mounts, it received visitors from all over the region. Just the day prior, Devyn observed three galley's warping into harbor, their pennants hailing from three different fiefdoms up the northern coast. The southern city-states also sent representatives. The most powerful and decadent of them, Desopolis, sent its agents north every year to buy new breeding stock and spy out northern secrets.

Spying didn't concern Devyn half as much as what happened to the horses. Despite being a native born Pevanese, his patriotism left something to be desired, especially since the run of temple arsons and the growing presence of red-clad Priests proselytizing in the ways and squares of the city. Let folk spy as they would. The Southerners were predominantly Old Ways believers anyway. But even that did not make much impact on Devyn's point of view. He felt like a boat cut adrift from the dock, awaiting canvas, course and conviction. He walked the streets and alleys of the Maze, a poet in search of a line, a soul in search of his faith, a penitent fool, begging for a meeting with his muse.

Today his feet took him down near the market stalls set up every morning by the outlying farmers come to the city to sell their produce. They set up their wares in the square outside the Golden Cup, run by his sometime acquaintance, Saymon Brimaldi. Devyn took his ale there when he felt the need. Saymon always found time to share words with him.

The Cup, ideally situated on the edge of the Maze's northern boundary, loosely defined the barrier of the warehouse district and the street that crisscrossed the city from Land Gate to Harbor Gate. The inn was just off the main thoroughfare that ran from the Southern Gate up the slope to the Citadel on a side-arterial that connected at an angle with Harbor Street. West and South of the inn lay the heart of the Maze, framed by the ruler straight width of the Southern Avenue, bounded on the north by the Harbor Street that passed out through the landward gate on the west. To the south and east of the Cup, the Maze spread in a semi circle of twisted streets—a cornucopia of life and the true wellspring of the vitality of the city. From its mixture of poverty and prosperity, its industry and despair, came the bodies for the shipping and fishing fleets, the tradesmen and laborers for the wharves and warehouses, and the servants and lackies of the Great Houses up on the hill.

The Maze was familiar ground for Devyn; its smells and noises were home to him. He drew the alleyways and clustered hovels of the place around him like a cloak. He had learned how to sup on dust and find shelter where none seemed obvious. He made despair a bedfellow companion and still lived to examine the memories. Even as he knew he could never allow his fortunes to lead him back to its cloying misery, he still maintained an interest in the life of the Maze and in one life in particular.

He found himself passing by the Golden Cup without stopping, his steps wending off the main street, away from the racetrack outside the southern gate, plunging into the heat and shadows of the human warren in search of that one particular life.

Kembril Edri, soldier, poet, called variously Edri One leg, or Kembril peg leg. He had lost the leg in a cavalry charge. A southron sabre severed it as neatly as a butcher slicing through a carcass, taking his leg just below the knee. Invalided out of the service with honors but little hope for advancement in a trade, he was a disregarded hero by everyone but Devyn, who worshipped him.

Devyn thought of the old poet as he wound his way through the narrows of the Maze, chewing on a heel of the bread Sanya had earlier left. Kembril had taken to drink to ease the pain of his maiming. In younger days, Devyn had worn a new path back and forth to the Cup bringing him the dregs from Brimaldi's barrels. The pestilence that took Devyn's parents had left the old man a consumptive wreck kept alive by the kindness of neighbors and the power of his own words. In the end, words sustained them both. Devyn found something intangible and fine in the wheezing magic of the old poet's voice. Kembril taught him to read, scratching out lines of verse in the dust to give the boy his letters. He had even arranged for Devyn to go to work for Malom Banley—a last favor from a former colleague. Devyn owed Kembril Edri more than loyalty; he owed him attention.

Such thoughts and reminiscences ran coursing through Devyn's mind as he wove his way deeper into the Maze. He knew all of Kembril's old haunts, and on a day as hot as this, the old man would station himself in the coolest place he could find: in the shade of the ancient oak tree. It spread its great canopy over the main well for that part of the city. None of the local denizens would touch living leaf or bough of the Tree, holding it Old Ways sacred. As an unwashed urchin, Devyn had played there with his companions swinging from the limbs like a troop of untamed monkeys. Those had been good times—all the more bittersweet for being book-marked by far longer periods of want and fear. But still, good times, and firmly cemented in his memory. Such are the vagaries of youth. Kembril and the Oak: two variables. Such things composed life, perhaps.

He rounded that last corner and came upon the Tree. Instantly, the air felt a little less thick, heat a little less intense. He murmured a brief thanks to Renia for the grace of the sight, for here a living Temple to the Old Ways endured as yet unnoticed, or at least disregarded, by the phalanx of Red-cloaked pruners and reformers. He took a deep breath, whispering as he let it out," May the Gods grant that stench and poverty be shield enough to keep you safe."

Beneath the bole of the Oak, sitting with back against the trunk and maimed leg propped on an up-thrust root, Kembril Edri held a ragtag audience of children entralled as he wheezed out a tale. Devyn stuffed the last of the bread into his mouth and sidled up to the back of the group, drawn by the familiar tones and recognizing the bits of the story itself as one of the handful he had loved the best. Kembril did not notice his arrival, for he spoke with his eyes shut tight as if seeing the tale unfold on the inside of his eyelids. Though he reposed at his ease, he held his head just forward and tilted somewhat upwards as if he were speaking as much to the heavens as to his human audience. Devyn smiled at the memories sparked by the uplifted aquiline nose, and then he let the stream of words catch him in their fluid current, and like the others there he plunged into the story.

"And then Minuet took her slender bow of carven yew and her quiver of arrows straight and true, and she let fly a shaft that flew, guided by Renia's will, straight into the Giant's left eye. Bitter the point that pierced that mighty eye, passing through the orb to sever nerve and evil fiber incarnate. In pain and wrath the giant swung his massive hammer with more than devilish speed, seeking to dash the fair Minuet. But she, hart-swift and protected by Renia's Grace, leaped aside ere the blow could strike, and with divine speed sent yet another shaft through the Giant's right eye. And happy the fate! Oh, glorious that shot, for it slew the Giant, passing through the flesh to shatter the twisted, tormented brain of the spirit possessed creature.

"And so it fell, even as its hammer smote the earth beside the intrepid Minuet. And such was the fury of that final blow that the earth itself was rent asunder and the seas flooded in. The Giant crashed to the ground, and over his bones the slow passage of time piled up a lofty height. And from his shattered eyes blood flowed that cut a deep channel on its way to the sea. And that, my friends," Kembril rasped in closing, "is how Pevana got her river, her harbor, and her hill."

Awed silence greeted the end of Kembril's tale. Devyn shook himself, laughing, out of the reverie as the children erupted with shrill cries for more.

"Tell us..."

"What about..."

"And then what happened?"

Kembril let it go on for a moment, his aged eyes bright as he took in the praise. Then he held up his hand, and as he did so he noticed Devyn for the first time. If anything, his smile deepened. He returned his attention to the smallest child in the group.

"I will allow just one question today! It is hot and I am old and I miss my rest. So, young mouse, one question."

The child, a little blonde-haired girl dressed in dusty rags stood up so that she looked Kembril in the eyes. Unabashed and saucy, she thrust her face close to his.

"What happened to Minuet? You didn't tell us about Minuet!"

Kembril leaned back in mock fear as the other urchins took up the cry, "Minuet the Huntress! Minuet! Tell us what became of Minuet!" They only quieted when Kembril held up his hand yet again.

"Minuet?" he said. "What happened to Minuet?" And then he looked up and caught Devyn's eye. "Well," he asked, "What did happen to the fair Minuet?"

Twenty pairs of eyes stared up at Devyn in expectation. He knew the answer. Kembril taught it to him years ago. Imitating the old storyteller's tone, he gave it.

"Minuet the fair, the intrepid huntress, Renia's agent on earth, plucked her arrow shafts straight and true from out the giant's eye holes whence they flew and placed them in the ground side by side as pillars of adamant and a warning to all who passed by. And so it was that Pevana gained her towers at the southern, landward gate. And Minuet then passed into the wild; ever mindful of the tasks Renia had set before her. Many trials she faced, but that, my friends is another story for another time."

None of the children recognized him. Perhaps the five years at Malom's, regular food and more fastidious bathing had worked too great a change on him. He knew several of the older kids, and questions rose in his mind about several faces that were missing from the throng, but he kept his silence. The children gazed intently at him, partly in awe of his ready response, partly suspicious of his presence so deep within the Maze. There were no more calls for stories, and like a receding wave, the mob swiftly disappeared into the shadows and alleys that opened off the area, leaving Kembril and Devyn alone in the mid-morning shade of the Oak.

Kembril moved his maimed leg, offering Devyn the root for a seat. "You've risen above the dust, my young friend. Sit you here and keep yourself free of the dirt."

Devyn did so, brushing the last breadcrumbs from his shirt and smiling wanly. "No amount of water or linen could ever remove the touch of this place, Kembril," he said. "You of all people should know that."

The old cavalryman cackled. His eyes took in his former ward in survival like a father would observe a son. Devyn noted their clarity, but he was dismayed at the decay that appeared to have set in over the rest of his mentor. The face looked more seamed and weathered than the last time the two had met, just under a year ago outside the Cup. The skin of his neck hung down in folds crusted with the summer-seasoned dust continuously coating the air. Everything about him spoke of an accelerated sagging, as though he were a tough old tree whose taproot had finally withered. Kembril coughed, wet and tired. It came to Devyn that his old teacher spent himself during his tale-telling, holding back his fading mortality with the pride of an artist determined to finish his piece. And the price increased with each performance.

"You look like one who is well taken care of," Devyn lied.

Kembril didn't answer at first, postponing his response behind a genuine smile. Devyn noted the absence of several more teeth.

"Ah, yes," the old man answered finally. "I am indeed well taken care of these days. The Maze is full of lonely widows. I used to think it was because of the power of my tales, but more and more, I think they like the notion that, once they get my peg off, I can't run away! Scandalous! I wonder what the Great Houses would think if they knew?"

"You might ask their horses. They spend rather more on the care and feeding of the animals than they donate to the poor."

"Ah, well, I do not suppose I would want to bother the beasts with my trials. Truly, however, I am fine. The locals feed me for tales. The wine is second rate, but what is an old man to do?"

"Come back to Banley's with me. I know he would take you."

At that Kembril's eyes darkened. "Not that old argument, please, Dev. I'm for the Maze. This tree and I," and he swept a thin hand and arm in a gesture still graceful, "are like wizened old bachelors—too set in our ways to uproot and seek new soil. Besides," and he brought his arm down to pat the ground next to him, which caused a small puff like talcum to rise up and coat his fingers. "The dust and I are old companions. I wear it like a wrap. It warms me. Let the doxies have their rouge and unguents; this works for me."

"If you were to bathe, you would make the water run brown until next spring."

"Probably, but then that might ruin my mystique."

"You would smell better."

"That never used to bother you. I smell of the Maze, boy, always have. I'm afraid if I were to bathe, more of me than just dirt would wash away."

"You aren't well. I knew it. Your cough is worse."

Kembril's eyes grew serious for a moment. "Yes," he answered. "I'm not well. My cough is worse. But I am still here. This tree and I, we remain. By next spring—who knows? Perhaps we both might be gone."

"You are speaking in riddles, old man."

"You came to find me, you—my walking riddle, my student. You come here to find me, your teacher, perhaps. Or maybe you come for the Oak. If you came for the wine, you've wasted your trip. It's vinegar anyway. And I finished the last drop just before you showed up!"

Devyn shook his head ruefully, hearing the resignation behind the old man's jest.

"I came to see you, although I didn't leave Malom's with the notion. Now I see otherwise. Old man, don't die on me just yet. I've too many questions yet to ask!"

"Funny," Kembril wheezed, "to enter a maze in search of answers to unasked questions. I'm sure philosophers from the college in the Citadel would argue against the wisdom of such an action. Me? I'm too tired to bother. You are here, now. Ask."

And so Devyn told him of the competition set for that night and his perplexing lack of a finished poem to offer for the reading. He told his old mentor of his frustration, and as he spoke he noted a growing sense of anger in his words as he related his adventure at the last temple burning. Kembril said nothing, just listened, eyes half closed; but at the mention of the temple, he sighed and shook his head, bringing Devyn's tale to a stop.

"What, what is it?" he asked.

His voice as quiet as dust, Kembril murmured, "So, yes, I see it now."

"See? What?"

"I see now why you've come to the Oak. And in a way, I see now why I spend most of my time here. Sad, really, I never. . ." And he had to pause while a fit of coughing took him. When he finally mastered himself again, his voice had a raspier, almost forced quality.

"Excuse me, my child. One of the hazards of my close relationship with this most sacred dust, I'm afraid. Please don't ask what you can do for me—we both know the answer. What I was trying to say was I think I understand your problem. With lights going out all around you, you find yourself faced with the need to find expression. None of the old tales and patterns will suffice. Correct?"

"Yes, yes, I think that must be it," Devyn said pensively, testing his own feelings. "For some reason, pastoral pieces to the beauties of the time just don't seem appropriate. My mood has grown darker. I start things, scratch around on parchment, but I get the feeling I am lying. Nothing seems to work."

"That is the way with lies, endlessly convoluted, eminently unsatisfying, and ultimately fruitless."

"So, what am I to do?"

"Tell the Truth. That is what real poets do, and if you would be a poet you must find your truth."

"But how?"

"You are sitting on it. You bear the mark of your faith in it on your arm. Doubtless, you placed some flowers and herbs in its altar this morning. Come, my young poet, sometimes one must look up from the parchment, put away the quill and observe how everything is rooted, how everything connects."

Devyn stared, speechless, as illumination spread to him as though it were sap flowing from the Tree to his veins. He saw his days over the last few months with new eyes, a new appreciation. With each temple burning his frustration had grown. Despair and anger mixed like ill-fated pigments to darken his creativity. No wonder all the fits and starts during the spring came to nothing! Light-hearted verse was useless to a heavy soul. He had been lying to himself, had been angry and helpless against the changes that went unnoticed, or at least unchallenged, by the masses. And there lay the source of his failing: he saw the need to challenge but lacked the power to act or so he fooled himself into believing. His desperate gambit at the last fire was a vain, personal expression. Bad dreams and light-hearted words: a lie. Anger, frustration and vacillation: a lie. He wasn't a Prince to order policy and dictate; he was a poet. All he had were words, and if the words he tried to use were lies, he was lost.

Devyn looked up into the canopy of the Oak and saw in the spreading boughs a tracery of how the Old Ways knit the stones of Pevana together. He sensed all that was at risk with every speech given by some red-cloak mercenary priest, with every proclamation issued from the Prelate Byrnard Casan and his cabal at the College. So fragile—and yet so strong. With every Temple closing, a limb of that tracery was lopped off, with every fire, a root severed, and so the decay proceeded apace. To write he had to find his truth, and in his truth he realized he had to act. The Old Ways needed a voice: *his* voice.

A little golden finch alighted on low-hanging branch and fixed Devyn with a cocked eye. It hopped down to the crumbs of bread he had brushed off earlier, a feast for a creature so small. It trilled its song to him in a quick scale of notes as if to thank him before taking wing and disappearing from view.

"Now," the old man whispered. "Wasn't that odd?"

"Odd? For a bird to peck at crumbs?"

"You wound me, boy! Old Ways believers hold that the finches bear messages from Renia to her huntress Minuet, and sometimes, though rarely, to the ears of Man. Were you not listening? Did you not hear?"

"It was a bird."

Kembril shook his head, smiling somewhat sadly. "Perhaps it was at that. I'm an old storyteller. What do I know of such things, eh? You need a poem, not finch-twitters."

Devyn shifted on the root. "I don't know if I have the courage."

"You had the courage to survive the streets and the Maze. You need a poem. It appears Renia needs a voice. I think you already have the courage to meet both ends."

"But during Festival? In the competition?"

"Destiny has a bad habit of not asking if one has room in one's schedule before complicating one's life. Destiny is. You can use it or be used by it. That is the only choice you have in the matter, I think."

"To do, or..."

"Or let axes be taken to this holy Oak without at least an eloquent protest. Do it, my friend. Look at it this way; think of the effect you could have on this place. Might make for an interesting fall!"

Even as he grew aware of the risk he ran under the present climate in the city, he found himself enraptured of the possibilities for adventure. He had had too much of rich men's horses and sweaty labor and shallow loves. It was time to speak out and tweak the noses of those who would change his world. The sheer audacity of the idea overwhelmed Devyn's reluctance, and he laughed a deep, cathartic laugh such as he had not known for many days. The sound of his mirth grew and spread, reverberating against the shutters and walls that framed the small square, floating upwards to wend amongst the leaves and limbs of the Oak's canopy. And so a bargain was made, and to his mind there sprung images wholly formed that promised words at need later. His laughter ran out in another sigh.

"All right," he said. "I'll do it."

"Of course you will. I can hardly wait to see the ripples of response from our northern guests. Such loud voices, but with so little skill! Is this the way of the King's Theology? To pummel adherents with sound until they tithe?"

"True, there may well be consequences, especially if I win, but how can I? It would never be allowed."

"Ah, but winning is not as important as being heard. Gold is but one reward. You've been adrift in yourself for too long, my son, time to set a new course. If the Maze or I have taught you anything, I expect you'll come out all right in the end. Keep your wits about you! The world is wider than Pevana's courts and alleys. Think on it while you scratch on your parchment."

Devyn had to be off—perhaps to Saymon's back room at the Cup for a glass and some paper. The first hearing was tonight, but strangely, he did not feel as frantic as he had that morning. He could feel the words percolating, sounds forming, rhythms stretching. By the time he actually reached the Cup, he would have his basic shape set. He rose and swiftly fished out one of his few gold coins, carefully husbanded wages from Malom, and pressed it in Kembril's palm, forcing the old man's fingers around it before he could reject the offer.

"I know better than to ask you to come along with me," he said, tightening his grip on the worn, dusty old hand with surprising intensity. "But this should get you a nice cup of something better than vinegar with enough left over for a bath and a clean shirt. If you want to see ripples of response, then get to the Cup tonight for the First Hearing."

Kembril's aged face beamed. "A bath!" he cackled. "Oh, the novelty! I rather think I'll risk it, just to see the show. Well met, my young poet, and may Renia's Grace go with you."

Devyn left his old mentor, making off in search of a mug of Saymon Brimaldi's finest brew, a quiet corner, and a quill with which he would construct a pathway of words to his destiny, whatever good or ill that might be.

Devyn emerged from the Cup, squinting into the late afternoon sun beating down on the tavern, with three rolled copies of his poem for that night's reading. He had worked feverishly, his mind inflamed more by the topic than the heady brews Saymon kept bringing him. He closed his eyes against the glare, and it seemed as if he could read the words of the poem in the inside of his lids:

Lost as the Night

In the last faint flickers of the last candle lit
For glories long loved but now faded,
Is the key to the clue to find wisdom true
That the red-clad hordes have degraded.
"Proselytize! No Compromise!"
Words shouted from pulpits and benches—
Such is the aim, to make the Future the same,
And toss the Past into the refuse trenches.
We have become lost as the night without stars,
And all questions seeking answers
Disappear in the great black and never return—
We wander witless and beguiled
Altars thrown down, temples defiled,
Fearful of shadows and mutterings foul
Bespeak us to our confusion.
And so we lose our Way.

Where are you Renia Fair?
Anoral, the rock of the world, gone?
And little Sorali, soul of all things bounteous,
Where have the winds blown you?

All are lost as the night whose lights have fled
From the heat of the flames
Of reformation and change
Images blackened

Forgotten names
Lost to the lives of Men.

Brave Boriman, stouthearted defender of Faith,
Who would defend you?
And Toparen, woodland nymph,
Your sacred groves have been hewn for fuel
To feed the final fires.

Such is the emptiness of loss,
For when we reach into the purse of faith for the reckoning
There is naught there to tally the cost
All consumed by the fires and fumes—
Reduced, rebuked, and replaced.

The smoke brings tears to these eyes,
For the soul of Man is a charnal house.
It is lost as the night. . .
The stars have fled
Taking answers and wisdom with them:
The great retreat from the lives of Men.

He took a deep breath and opened his eyes to survey the square. He had four hours yet before the reading, time enough to prepare and brush up his best boots. But a commotion made him pause.

A crowd clustered about a wagon used to haul wine casks and beer barrels, two draft horses still harnessed to it. A sallow-faced, red clad priest in full flaming flower screeched down at the mob from it, his foot propped on the tailgate, one hand grasping his staff and the other poised as if to bring down vituperative wrath on the group arrayed before him. Off to one side, Devyn noted Sanya, an empty basket on her arm. Captain Avarran, Devyn's friend and sword-mentor, stood nearby in full uniform. Guarding? But whom? Interest pricked, Devyn moved over to lean against one of the posts that held up the awning sheltering the Cup's entrance, crossed his arms around his rolled poems, and listened.

"Yay, all you malcontents!" roared the priest, sweeping fervent eyes over his audience. "For too long you have looked to lies for truth, errors for wisdom and found nothing, been given nothing, been gifted with nothing! For the illusions of the past did naught but delude you. And yet your lord has seen a new way, a new faith, one that answers those deepest of questions. And we come among you, my brothers and I, simple men with a simple message, urged quietly in the streets, offered to all who would listen."

Devyn stifled the urge to vomit. He wished he had a tomato, a big one left over-long on a windowsill and grown too ripe and squishy. He looked about quickly for anything close that would serve to shut the priest up. Ale-addled wits did not dismiss the risks of taking such action, but the provocation came too close on the heels of his afternoon's impassioned drafting to ignore. The old burn on his arm tingled, a mixture of warning and ware, a call to hurl physical opposition against the sanctimonious fool before him.

"Just one, one beautiful red tomato," he murmured. "What harm could it do to such a simple man? His robes are already red."

But he did not have a tomato. All he had were his three copies of his poem, and himself.

The priest roared on. Even from across the square, Devyn could see his neck muscles distend with the effort of making his voice louder and more insistent. Perhaps he felt the truth he so stridently tried to push into the hearts and minds of his listeners. Perhaps the fervor of his calling actually filled him. It did not matter. Devyn was done feeling like a refugee in his own city, for it suddenly seemed to him that an enemy force occupied Pevana. He had encountered too many of the red-robed fools in the last few months. He took to moving about the city by back alleys, even resorting to rooftops on occasion just so he could avoid having to listen to the endless sermons and propaganda. His adventure with the altar might have been an act born out of an unfocused frustration; this time, it would be deliberate.

He pushed himself away from the post and wove his way through the crowd, feigning drunkenness and jostling people as he went. As he passed Sanya, he reached out and gave her a firm pinch on the buttocks. She yelped and whirled around in search of the culprit. Devyn ducked behind a fat tradesman to elude her and moved quickly to the side of the wagon near the front wheel. Sanya's cry broke the priest's rhythm, and the man paused to scan the crowd for the source of the disturbance. The sight of Sanya's ample bosom swinging around made his eyes bulge even wider and rounder. He leaned out over the tailgate.

"What ails you, woman?" he asked. "Do you feel the spirit come upon you?"

"Not likely!" returned Sanya hotly. "But if I find the fool who pinched me, he'll feel the spirit directly!"

The people in the crowd laughed, which brought an angry glare from the priest that quelled them to silence. He straightened up and took a deep breath to pick up where he left off. Devyn took his chance.

He burped a long, loud, noxious smelling beer belch with the strong taint of the sausage he had consumed along with the brew. It was a divinely inspired burp, worthy of the god Boriman himself whose belches were thunder and whose farts were earthquakes. Instantly, all eyes turned toward him. The priest stared down with a look that would turn wine to vinegar.

Destiny's wheel turned as his burp faded to a fraudulent giggle.

"B-B-Boriman's balls but that felt good! Tha's the bes' one today that was! Whew!"

"Guards!" the priest shouted. "Take this drunken fool!"

Several of the priest's attendants moved to apprehend him. Devyn faked a stumble and rolled underneath the draft horse hitched to the wagon. The beast skittered aside but was held by the traces. Scrambling up on the tongue, Devyn jumped up to the driver's seat.

"Old Ways Brothers!" He held the copies of his poem in his upraised hand as if they were talismans of great power. A rush of good, wrathful energy flowed through him. All eyes centered on him. He

51

noticed Captain Avarran and Sanya in the back of the press, mouths agape, fingers pointing. Meanwhile, the priest, quick to gather his wits, grasped his staff in both hands to aim a mighty swing at Devyn's head.

"Pray for Renia's Grace!" Devyn shouted and leaped clear of the wagon, barely avoiding the blow. As he flew through the air, he twisted and landed a kick on the hindquarters of the second horse. Both beasts thrust forward against the wheel chock placed as a brake. Devyn hit the cobblestones and skinned his knee. The wagon lurched heavily, over balancing the priest, causing him to topple out the back of the wagon bed to land with a *plop* and a *thump* in a pile of freshly deposited manure.

It was perfect. It was laughter, anger, fear and chaos all rolled up like a sticky-bun. The square became a melee of bellowing guards, screaming women and horses, and people running every which way and all of them looking for Devyn. Just before he ducked down an alley he knew would take him safely to the Maze, Devyn caught sight of the priest being helped to his feet, his red cloak stained with horseshit.

"The King's Theology stinks!" he shouted into the chaos. Chuckling to himself, he lengthened his stride and sped down the alleyway.

THE CHAOS IN THE SQUARE continued for some moments before handlers soothed the horses and mollified the priest. He never did get to finish his sermon; the crowd melted away, taking advantage of the confusion, perhaps motivated by the unknown champion of the Old Ways. None were there to see the black-clad man step out from the shadow of the alley down which Devyn had fled.

He surveyed the mess in the square then spared a glance over his shoulder, down the alley. Picking up a piece of rolled parchment that lay, crumpled and dirty on the cobblestones at his feet, he scanned it briefly before rolling it up and tucking it in a small pouch tied to his belt. He moved out from the alley entrance and surreptitiously made his way around the edge of the square to disappear up the street, heading for the citadel.

DEVYN SLIPPED OVER THE TOP RAIL of the back corral at Malom's. His knee bled a little and the leggings would need stitching, but he didn't mind. Whatever the aftermath, his adventure had been worth it. He exulted in the image in his mind's eye of the spastic priest tumbling out of the wagon.

Life felt energized and dangerous, reminding him of some of the darker days he had spent in the streets, days he had been forced to the extremity of his wits. And tonight he would complete the journey by presenting his poem at the Cup.

Kembril was right; his was the voice for the task. He did not harbor any illusions about winning. The afternoon's escapade, the flames he hoped to fan tonight, was the prize. He would be lucky to live through the night let alone the week. Tonight would be about presentation; one, last, eloquent protest before the darkness took the old faith. The tragedy of it was the stuff of epic romance, almost heroic.

He turned the corner into his cubicle and came face to face with Captain Avarran. Devyn's good cheer popped like a soap bubble. His friend and sword master glowered at him with a look he reserved for his more worthless troopers.

"What were you thinking," he rasped. Each word brought him closer and closer. Devyn retreated until he came up against the watering trough.

"What do you mean?"

"I almost believed you were drunk. For a minute there your act took me in, damn you! Are you out of your mind? Those guards could have skewered you and no one could have done anything about it! I would have had to arrest you. No, don't smile, you young fool. One of them almost got you, but I tripped him up before he could stick you with his pike. What possessed you?"

Devyn didn't reply at first. His mind whirled. He could see the fear and anger in Avarran's face; hear the concern in his voice. "I had to," he whispered finally. "I just had to."

"Had to? Had to? Explain yourself or I will arrest you, friend or no friend."

"I had to . . . because . . . because," Devyn stuttered, and then his passion returned to him in a wave of feeling. He raised his chin stubbornly. "I had to because I've grown sick and tired of seeing those fools lord it over our people and our ways. They are like lice, but no matter how much I scratch I cannot get rid of them. Every time I see or hear one of them, I just couldn't take it anymore, Av. They are false."

"Then the people won't listen to them."

Devyn scoffed. "Right! Armed guards, Av, temple burnings. Why the need? What's being done about them? We aren't being given a choice. And yet I don't see anyone questioning anything."

"Perhaps they don't care."

"Perhaps they don't, but I do. I do."

The Captain made a quivering fist under Devyn's nose. "I know how you feel, you mixed up, morose fool, and if I could knock some joy into your head with this fist I would do it. You cannot change the trend of the entire city. Ever since you showed me that altar you filched—"

"Saved."

"Interfered with and stole! Don't temporize with me, boy! I never told you, but we were told by the Prelate's assistant to look for a youngish man with dark hair who was seen breaking through the cordon of guards keeping the people back from that fire. You were noticed then, but no one made the connection, so I let it go."

"Noticed . . . by a bunch of scabeous priests."

"Who are here with the King's grace and authority—and spare me your vocabulary, boy, or I will whip you. You have to understand. I have been in meetings with the Prince, Devyn. He is in a spot with little wriggle room. Do you think it is easy ruling a city like this, with its past? And I will tell you, my ignorant friend, his cousin the King has questions and doubts. Doubts! Think you the Prince needs his city in turmoil—with the Prelate in attendance and *observing* the workings of the place and putting into effect his royally decreed reformation?"

"The Prince doesn't care about us."

Avarran drew breath as though to dispute Devyn's claim, but then let the breath go in a long sigh.

"How would you know?" he continued quietly. "You've been wallowing in your own personal sty of despair since your grandfather passed away." He tapped his index finger firmly on Devyn's chest. "Don't argue; you know it is true."

"How would you know?" Devyn retorted, but even as he spoke he knew it was a weak effort. Avarran just stared at him with a mixture of affection and disgust.

"It's in your eyes, boy. Even that chit Sanya has seen it. And it has grown more noticeable these last few months." He grunted. "You think you are a zealot. All you really are is a misdirected child."

Devyn flinched. "Maybe I was. Maybe I just now found my course."

Avarran frowned and cocked an eyebrow. "Stealing condemned property and tippling the King's priests out of wagons is not a *course*—it's a straight road to the gallows."

Devyn sagged a little at that. He liked Avarran as a friend and teacher. He respected him. Seeing the disappointment in his eyes troubled him. He bowed his head. Avarran put an arm around Devyn's shoulder. And then both of them started laughing—a gentle chuckle—and the tension of the moment burned away.

"I must admit," Avarran said finally. "Seeing you appear on that wagon, the look on your face, the look on the Priest's face—priceless. The poor fool had to try and recover his dignity with a huge shit stain on his robes. Ha! Not even a glass of Saymon's best house wine would calm him down. He stomped off toward the citadel after a search for you came up with nothing. If it wasn't so patently dangerous, I'd say it was almost worth it."

"Then you—"

"I said *almost*. You need to take care, my friend. Your drunken act might have been convincing, but your hair is still dark and your face is still young and both attributes were in full view. *Renia's Grace! Perfect!*"

Devyn laughed with him, and yet inwardly shuddered. His intentions for the night at the Cup would make his escapade in the square look like child's play. Opening his mouth in a public forum made everything official. Word would spread, Avarran might actually have to arrest him, and the thought saddened him, even as his resolution held.

"I'm for the Cup tonight," he said. "I'm entered in the Competition."

Avarran smiled. "Good!" he exclaimed. "I was wondering about that. Sanya mentioned you put her off to go write. That was a move even more reckless than interfering with the Priest. She is a formidable girl, that one."

"Unless she managed to get you to ignore your duties this morning," Devyn responded, smiling in return. "You have no idea how formidable. She is relentless."

Avarran took a step away then turned back. "Speaking of duties," he said. "I'm sorry I'll miss it. I have patrols till dawn." He shoved Devyn backwards into the water trough. "Luck to you, my friend!"

"Wha . . . what!" Devyn sputtered, sitting up and shaking his wet hair from his eyes.

"You're a drunken sot and you need a bath!" Avarran shouted over his shoulder, picking up his hat and sword. "Luck to you again, and stay out of trouble!"

Devyn stared at the stable door after Avarran left, his mind a mixture of consternation and good humor momentarily at war. Then he sighed and decided to at least take part of his friend's advice. He peeled out of his shirt and dunked his head.

After washing, as he stood dripping before his camp table, he noticed two of his poem copies were missing. *Avarran?* he thought as finished drying off. *What would he do if he knew? But he couldn't know or he would have done something, more than just warn me. Then where were they?* In the end, it was only a minor mystery. He hadn't signed either of the pages. It wouldn't matter after that evening anyway; everyone would know.

While toweling his hair, he heard several horses ruckle as if in greeting. Before he could wrap the cloth around his waist, he felt a light pinch on his left buttock. He turned around.

"You should never pinch a girl's ass unless you mean it," Sanya said seductively. Her hand tickled around to his front.

"Sanya," he managed to get out before giving up the struggle and kissing her. He was not due at the Cup until true dark at the earliest. He wanted to be the last to register and speak. This time, he had time, and her tongue was doing such interesting things to his.

Chapter 3: Byrnard of Collum—Lord Prelate of the King's Theology

THE OLD MAN SAT BEHIND AN ORNATE DESK set in the center of a well-appointed room with a pen poised above an inkwell next to a small sheaf of papers. Red vestments, an ornate yet light cloak and a red silken over tunic lay folded on a chair off to one side of the desk. The old man, dressed in close-fitting black garments, sat, ramrod straight in his chair. His discarded clothing and the medallion hanging from his neck spoke of the priesthood, and yet his bearing and the cut of his other clothing attested to something far, far more martial.

Byrnard Casan, the former Lord of Collum, despite his appointment as representative of the new King's Theology, still thought of himself as a military man at heart. He approached his duties as Prelate with all the tenacity he had visited upon the King's enemies when still active in the field. He readied paper and inkwell on the desk and stared at the blank page for a moment before rising and walking over to the window, his movements still cat-like despite his age, to take in the view of the southern parts of the city. He occupied spacious rooms in the residential wing of the Avedun Palace and rather enjoyed the notion of working his will, as it were, from underneath Prince Donari's nose.

He surveyed the view as though it were a game board and noted with satisfaction the various blackened spots that marred the red-tile uniformity of the spread of rooftops. He traced them with his eye, seeing in the pattern the growth and success of this most recent endeavor. He smiled. Flames had served him well during his northern activities and this southern translation looked to be similarly prosperous. He rather enjoyed the incongruity. Ostensibly intent on saving *souls* rather than inflicting carnage on a foe, he found he still enjoyed the effect of a good fire. To him, all those charred stains were gaps cut in the ranks of the ideas against which he moved. Piety was the elixir of fools. A campaign was a campaign, and the victory that lay at the end of it was motivation enough.

Casan and the King had framed the policy years ago as a means to cement the restive northern fiefs closer to the crown. The King claimed a dream had led him to the notion of using superstition along with spears to achieve control. Casan let him have his fantasy as long as it meant *he* would be the instrument of its application. Power worked for the lordly classes, but the commons needed a further prod. Casan liked the practice of using faith as a weapon. Its northern expression had been particularly effective.

Byrnard turned his gaze to take in the shadowy ridges of the hills that separated Pevana from the north and recalled those campaigns. Combining the fire of religious zeal with the careful application of the sword, he managed to suborn the north to the point where he felt secure of their allegiance to Roderran. And when Casan came south he continued his good works; all for power in the guise of reform. Roderran wanted the south, and to get it he needed Pevana's wealth and people, its cavalry and location. The old ruler of Pevana, the present Prince's grandfather, had been recalcitrant ally. The wily old man refused the north's will. His vigorous personality kept the south unmolested, but the Uncle was his nephew's first teacher, and Roderran knew all his tricks.

Byrnard turned away from the window and returned to his desk. He recalled the current Prince's grandfather with some asperity. They had been contemporaries, vying in their youth for military status—a contest Casan knew would have ended with himself in second position if not for the untimely death of Avedun's father that called the man to his crown. In the absence of competition, Byrnard had flourished. And now, nearly forty years later, he took some measure of revenge at sitting at the desk once used by his former adversary.

Underneath his royal charge to reform the south, he also felt as though at a fulcrum point in the process of revenge. The old man was dust; Casan was not—a significant difference that brought a slight sneer to the Prelate's shriveled lips as he settled himself in the chair.

The time was ripe. Donari was but a shadow of his grandsire. He was weak and pliable. The old warrior-turned-priest dipped his pen into the ink well and began to write. The flourish of his pen made small air currents that caused the candle flame at his elbow to dance slightly. After a few moments he paused to read over what he had composed, his face an emotionless mask of cold objectivity.

To: Roderran II, King of Perspa
From: Byrnard of Collum, Lord Prelate in the King's Name
Sent from the Avedun Palace, Pevana, on the first day of the High Summer Festival

My Lord:

I hope this missive finds you well and in good spirits. Our arrival here was met with requisite acclaim by those elements we spoke about ere I departed your august presence. Houses Anargi and Hollaran are solidly yours in all matters. Sevire Anargi, in particular, seems most fervent in his good offices on our behalf. He has folk planted all over the city that will now report to me. He has been most helpful in all matters related to the changes and reform we have enacted throughout the season. There have been but few incidents; and those I will look into personally after I send this off to you. I must confess myself pleased and yet disappointed at the state of affairs here in Pevana. I expected more from Prince Donari; he does little credit to his grandfather's memory. Please understand, my liege, I mean no disrespect to your family. I admit it, I was rather looking forward to a challenge, but apparently none seems forthcoming. He is rather more malleable than his forebear.

He has done well, I must say. Pevana is easily one of the most prosperous of your domains. The merchant classes gather wealth and ornament their lives; some even have visions of reaching for noble status. I have received gifts my lord, which are on their way north as I write this. Hopefully, this missive will pass it ere it reaches the capital. I think you will be pleased. And yet what I send is but a trifle that awaits your indenture should you have need. As a staging ground, Pevana is perfect. The harbor is more than adequate, and the available shipping more than meets your needs. The city is brimful at present with revelers, and my informers tell me the levy here would indeed be sizable and healthy.

My lord, from Pevana you could take the south in a season's campaign...

Byrnard paused then replaced the pen in the well, rose fluidly from the chair and walked over to a sideboard and poured himself a half-measure of wine in a silver goblet. Sipping the wine, he left the study, moved down the length of his sleeping chamber and went outside through an open balcony door. He leaned his elbows on the railing and surveyed the view, his mind working like an accountant even as he took in the panorama of Pevana's elite sector of stately homes. *So much affectation*, he thought to himself. *So soft. Workable— like clay.* His eye passed over the nearer homes to settle on the domed and pillared mansion that belonged to the eager Sevire Anargi. From his vantage point he could see the Anargi estate was one of the largest, with the top of a high wall just visible. Behind the upper galleries, Byrnard could see the tops of trees that spoke of a large garden or grounds that ran down to the main city wall abut the riverbank. The setting sun glinted off a golden rooftop in a flash of red-gold splendor.

"Pretentious," he scoffed under his breath as he turned to go back inside and finish his missive. When he was done he sanded and blew on the page before rolling it up and sealing it with candle wax. He rang a small bell that had been placed for the purpose on the corner of the table and stood as the door opened. Immediately three men walked in and approached the desk. Two sat down. The other, dressed in clothes befitting a messenger-rider, bowed to the Prelate, took the missive, and hastened from the room.

When the messenger departed, Casan turned to consider the other two gentlemen. Aemile, the discommoded priest from that afternoon, scowled and wilted by degrees under Casan's cold stare. The other, Jaryd Corvale, younger, neatly trimmed, returned Casan's look with one of his own that spoke of darkness and suppressed ferocity.

He sat, motionless save for the slow, measured tapping of his be-ringed right index finger on the arm of his chair. Byrnard noted the finger, looked up and held the younger man's gaze for moment before smiling and sitting down. *Like knows like,* he thought to himself.

The Lord Prelate took a sheet of paper from the top of the pile and pushed it over to the priest. "Is this accurate?"

The priest's scowl deepened in answer. "Yes, my lord."

"Aemile," Byrnard said succinctly. "Do try to smile once in awhile. You'll win more converts that way. That face of yours would sour a bushel of apples. A smile, my friend, might also keep you from ending up in the dung heap!"

Aemile's face blanched, and his features softened somewhat, abashed, but he did not smile.

"I will try, my lord, but these . . . these people," he muttered sullenly. "They try my patience. They won't listen."

Byrnard allowed himself a small smile. "Yes, yes," he soothed. "I know. I've read your copious letters. I know of your tribulations, my friend. If your face is any sign of how you've gone about things, it's no wonder you've been ignored in the squares. So, tell me again about this afternoon. All I had was a message before I went into the meeting with the Prince's Council."

"I was assaulted! And the useless city guards did more to hinder my men than help when I set them after the drunken fool who tipped me out of the wagon."

"I understand he got away. What a pity."

"The lower third of the city beyond that square is what the locals call 'the Maze,'" Jaryd offered. "He was gone down an alley and into the mess too quickly to follow."

"You have sent in groups?"

Jaryd looked to Aemile, who lowered his head. "Yes, several times," the priest said shamefacedly. "We've tried to be a presence there before, but it doesn't work. Brother Inar was pelted with nightsoil just last week."

"We cannot have the King's Clerics going about smelling like excrement," said Byrnard, his voice rising. "The place is obviously the center of your troubles." He turned to Jaryd. "Do you have measures in mind?"

"Of course, but this is Festival, and untoward flames might do more harm than good. The place is a den of the lower classes. They hardly matter."

"Except as a source for dissent."

"They will follow their lord, in the end."

Byrnard paused. If he were correct about Prince Donari, then the minor irritations he had report of ere his arrival would cease to matter. He laughed inwardly at himself. In the north, resistance had been short but bloody. There had been some malcontents who had chosen martyrdom over reason. They had been forced to do some real killing—it had felt like the old cavalry times, riding down the fools who put their hope in iron rather than change their faith. Such a simple thing when set against the complexity of politics and dynastic intent. It had been different as Roderran's program had flowed south, less violence, but more resistance of a passive sort. Pevana was proving to be something different yet again.

The temple fires, set so assiduously by Jaryd and his team of incendiaries, had not elicited the kind of virulent response that usually identified figures of resistance. No one stepped forth to lead—and thus become a target for removal. The Prelate had hoped Prince Donari would show himself such a one. Byrnard did not trust his loyalty to the crown; he questioned Pevanese ties to the northern scepter altogether. They seemed more interested in their vines and festivals. He found the behavior self-absorbed . . . soft somehow. And yet was it so? He took up another sheet of paper. This one, written in a flowing hand, with scratched out words and corrections, was torn and soiled.

63

"You may be correct," he said aloud, scrutinizing the words on the page. He had read them through a dozen times already since Brother Aemile's messenger handed it to him on his way to the initial meeting with the Prince and his council. It had taken all his reserve to keep from bringing up the subject of the poem—for it was a poem—during the interview with Donari and the merchant leaders. He finished reading and pushed the paper over to Jaryd. "Or you may be mistaken. What do you make of this?"

His apprentice read the page over quickly and returned it without comment.

"Aemile found this afterwards," continued the Prelate. "I assume it was you? From this green stain—horseshit, I suppose. Indeed, this smells of something other than passive ambivalence, don't you think?"

Jaryd's nonchalance slipped away. "You say he was a young man? Did he have dark hair? There was one incident at the last temple *cleansing*. Some fool broke through the cordon of guards and dashed into the flames. I don't think he made it out again. At least, neither I nor any of mine saw him."

"Didn't you post watchers?"

Jaryd's face turned dark. "There was a lot of smoke," he grumbled. "I had people out asking questions for days afterwards—nothing. For all I know or care, he could be buried under the pile of masonry and ash. That's all that was left of the place."

"Do you see a connection?"

"The incidents are months apart, my lord, I doubt it."

"And you?" Byrnard asked, turning back to the hapless Aemile, who seemed to visibly shrink further into his chair.

"It was a young man, dark colored hair, I think," he said. "There could be a connection, I don't know, my Lord Prelate. Perhaps . . . the last temple to go was dedicated to Renia. The goddess is also mentioned in the poem. Perhaps?"

"Exactly, maybe you aren't worthless after all, Aemile." Byrnard sat back in his chair, his decisive attitude drawing his agents toward him. "This is what we shall do. You," he addressed Aemile, "will send out more groups into this *Maze*. Tomorrow. Festival or no Festival.

You," he addressed Jaryd, "will make sure trusted eyes make their way to every alehouse in the city that will be used for this so called *Competition of Poets.* Perhaps your last little fire flushed out something."

He let himself smile a bit more grandly than the one he had allowed earlier, and more heartfelt than the one he had offered Prince Donari in farewell. "Let us see if we can find a pretext during this festival for our purposes. Roderran is getting impatient."

The others returned his grin and departed quickly to set about their tasks. Byrnard took up the paper, leaned back in his chair and scanned the lines one more time.

"Who wrote you? Eh?" he muttered. "Who among all these sheep crafted you? Hm?"

Byrnard had never had much use for poetry. Life was predicated on clear, terse, military communication. Even the Precepts of the King's Theology, which he had helped to compose, had little of the ornate or symbolic about them. They were concise statements of power and guidance, not elaborate parables of confusing interpretation. Even so, Byrnard could not help noticing the poem had a language and rhythm that would have to be called beautiful, despite its excessive sentimentality.

"'Where is Renia the Fair?'" he scoffed. "Brave Boriman and Sorali? They are nothing but smoke easily dissipated by a breath of air or the wave of a mightier hand." He held the paper up to the flame, dropped it into a bowl on the table and watched it turn to ash. Sweeping a hand across the bowl, he scattered the ashes and left them where they lay.

THE ORNATE OPEN CARRIAGE SAGGED VISIBLY as Sevire Anargi heaved his bulk onto the cushioned seat and tapped his cane on the footboard, alerting his driver to proceed. He sighed, a wet, wheezing noise of contentment, a sound that only the overfed and jaded can make.

It had been a good day, so far, he thought, staring vacantly at the palace as the carriage trundled away. Even the jarring of the cobblestones on his overworked kidneys could not take away his good feeling. He always took pleasure, although careful never to show it, at seeing Prince Donari nonplussed. The look on the Prince's face as the Prelate laid out his program was worth a year's profits.

Why, the man practically stuttered trying to find words to respond! his inner voice tittered. *And he called himself a leader? A disgrace, more likely. He's a fop with neither backbone nor vision. Comes from never having to work for anything. Ah, me, but I could have shown him a thing or three, but he's a royal. A royal fool! But still a royal.*

And so his thoughts bounced along, keeping time to the measured paces of his team of matched bays. And such thoughts! The last week had seen such a rise in his prospects. What had been nosed about the meeting halls and on the docks, as a business journey to his outlying properties had actually been an embassy of sorts to meet with the Prelate Byrnard as he marched south with his retinue. Sevire had felt the need to clarify certain *arrangements* agreed upon before handing in messages. Said arrangements had thrown a sizeable amount of wealth his way in the months following the first temple burning. His harvests had been good. Certain of his competitors had not fared so well. The thought of the grief and hard times attendant to the Hollaran ship fires made him chortle. Flames! And no one was the wiser.

Those memories added spice to his good mood. It was altogether a fine thing, to be so happy, to have spent such a day as this, despite its weary travel and onerous state functions. He felt like the little boy in the peasant folktale who got lost in the woods and called upon Blessed Renia for aid. She sent Minuet of the Arrows to lay out a pathway of stars to lead the child to safety. The boy walked along, picking up the stars and putting them in his pocket. When he got home, he discovered he had a pocket full of diamonds and was never hungry or lost ever again.

Sevire had no need of old, impotent goddesses. His pockets felt near to bursting, all by his own cunning, and not with useless baubles given to him by a deity whose last temple he helped destroy by fire, whose dedicated silver now adorned a shelf in his kitchen. Sevire never let such small nusances cause him worry. Self-doubt made for small profits, and he currently connived after nothing less than true hegemony in Pevana. He chortled happily; pretty fools like Donari cut the image of the hero to the masses with youth and high-minded ways, but the real power lay with types like Byrnard and himself: factual dispositions with minds of accountants. The boy was nothing like his grandfather, thankfully, or else Sevire would never have dared plot as he had. When King Roderran came south to stage his expedition against the city-states, he would reward those who prepared the way.

Let him see Donari for the foppish child he is. Yes, let him but see, then he would perforce look to other, more sage, like-minded men to rule Pevana. Someone like me.

Sevire rather liked the notion of becoming Prince Sevire, of founding a whole new and glorious extension of House Anargi in the annals of the realm. His mind jumped with each small lurch of the carriage from point to point of his plans as though he were reviewing the moves of an already completed chess-match, one crafted as perfectly as a spider's web. And to think all he had needed were a few ill-timed accidents at sea, several loyal fellows with oily rags, and the chaos of Summer Festival.

The extravagance of good cheer allowed only a tiny spark of fury over the afternoon squabble he had with Demona to infiltrate, but the spark still smoldered. The few whispered words about Demona and a certain young cavalier son of a northern rug merchant had set his overburdened heart racing, reminded him that while his wealth might please Demona, his sexual prowess never could. His ambivalence to the casual flirtations that were inevitably part of Pevana's elite social circle was an indulgence, and his choice; but the rumor cut too close to the quick.

He had rushed home in spite of the lumpy, roadway abuse to his heart and backside, and came upon her trying on yet another new dress to wear to the Initial Readings in the Poet's Competition. Sevire enjoyed watching Demona dress, and undress, knowing that her ample bosom and shapely thighs were his for the taking. She was a beauty, no question, with a spitfire's temper not easily banked. Controlling it was nearly as laborious a task as pleasing her in bed, but necessary. Independence led to unpleasant things, as far as he was concerned.

Sevire took deep, wheezing breaths, doused the smoldering down again. He recalled images of her flaring, cajoling, pouting and spouting that stirred his loins as it confirmed his suspicions. If he had been a younger man, he would have taken her there beneath the lilac bushes and thrust away her personal desires. He was expected at the council meeting, and he wasn't a young man anymore. And neither could he afford to have her running about town unescorted, especially during the wild times that usually attended the Summer Festival. Too many plans lay in the balance, dangling in webs of intrigue, to allow any sudden upsets.

In the end, his demand she stay home that first night of the festival had been met by the slump of shoulders and downcast eyes that signaled her defeat, and his control maintained. Sevire would make it up to her later.

Princess Demona sounded almost as good as *Prince Sevire*.

His carriage turned in through the estate gates and passed on down the driveway of crushed white rock kept wet, despite the rumors of drought, to keep the dust down. He gazed fondly at the grandness of his house as the carriage drew near. There was to be another social fete later that evening to honor the Prelate Byrnard. Enough time remained for a glass or two of wine. Perhaps Demona might try on her new gown for him again. . .

Chapter 4: Eleni Caralon, the Saddle-maker's Wife

ELENI CARALON SUCKED ON THE FINGER pricked while working on the hem of a dress meant for Demona Anargi. She leaned back in her chair, wondering how she could have fallen asleep mid-stitch, and realized dawn pinked the horizon outside her window.

Unbelievable.

Well, she was awake now even if her husband, Tomais, gently snored in the adjacent bedroom. She looked around her workroom cluttered with nearly a dozen gowns destined to grace the shoulders of some of Pevana's finest. To her tired eyes they appeared a profusion of sparkles and lace hanging from frames or pinned to lines attached to the ceiling, each of them a work of art, and Demona's outshone the lot of them. Hers had been the most difficult, and the requested alterations taxed Eleni's talents as never before. But she finished it, finally. The last stitch in the hem of that dress claimed her finger.

She rose from her stool, the crook in her back rivaling the throbbing of her digit, and left the room. The Summer Festival always provided her with a windfall of business, but this year seemed unusual in the extravagance of the requests. The constellations she left behind her in the other room represented nearly a half-year's wages for her. She let herself smile a little; Tomais would be pleased. She knew she should be pleased, too, and might have been, if not for yesterday's act of desperation.

What were you thinking, Eleni Caralon? Presenting yourself at those doors!

Three times since last winter, she made written application for admittance to the college at the citadel but never received a reply. Nothing left to lose, or so she believed, Eleni determined to find out why. She asked to see the headmaster. The clerk who took her request returned with the man himself, an aging, rheumy-eyed priest dressed in the red robes of the King's Theology.

"Get yourself and your insane notions gone, woman." His words came back at her again and again. "Go home to your husband or father or brother, who will surely have more appropriate tasks for you."

Eleni had been too stunned by the whole scene to get angry. It had all been so casual, so dismissive, as though she were a bug unworthy of the attention needed to swat it to eternity. She walked home in a daze, and it was not until she reached the citadel gate that the rage welled up like the violent burp of a volcano. She erupted, exploding in fury, shoving the poor gate guard who came close to wish her good day. And then she had stalked off, her feet beating a rhythm of disgust and umbrage at the unfairness of the world. She did not hate men. She just despised the ones who made the rules that kept her from her dreams. No woman had ever attended the university; as things remained, none ever would.

It was no wonder sleep eluded her, her husband's attentions irritated her, and she had sent him to bed confused and chastened. Eleni's solace was to get lost in her work, a trade allowed her sex, and one she was good at. She turned those pretty gowns into expressions in fabric and bead and floss. It should have satisfied, as it should have pleased, and yet. . .

She went downstairs, took a roll from the bowl on the kitchen table and sat munching while pressing her finger against a cloth to stop the bleeding. Pain was already fading to a dull ache. *If only all pain were thus easily appeased.*

The sun, from that angle just clearing the headland to the east, sent its first beams in through the kitchen window to warm Eleni's shoulder. The rising light spread like fingers across a small pile of cut paper—a gift from her husband—she sometimes used to keep track of orders or to make grocery lists, most times not.

The topmost sheet bore a handful of lines scribbled in her hand, an attempt to wrestle some of the images that came to her at odd moments into some sort of form. They were a curse on her calm and they were her calm; a baleful reminder of her expressive impotency and the only venue in which she felt truly content. Eleni wanted words. She wanted to use them, write them, weave them into patterns the way she stitched the cut cloth into the dresses. Lines of poetry were a beckoning magic, but useless to complete the spell.

She finished the roll, pressed the finger no longer bleeding, and decided life would never be fair; it would just be. She would have to find her own way and took a small measure of hope. It was Festival. Anything could happen.

She contemplated sleep while morning grew around her and decided against trying. Tomais rumbled, still abed, and she was not quite sure she deserved his warmth after the way she snapped at him. She went to the house door, opened it and leaned against the frame breathing in the cool air. By mid-day the summer heat would turn everything tepid and stale, but for now it was pleasant.

The street outside held familiar morning bustle with carters on their way to market, workers on their way to their employment, and women off to the local well. Folk greeted her as they passed, their voices quiet and genuine. Eleni chastised her discontent. She and Tomais were well-matched in all ways, love being the best way of all. He, a noted saddle and tack-maker, and she, a skilled seamstress, they were prosperous and well known in their circle. She had known darker days.

Eleni lingered on her doorstep, exchanging pleasantries and gossip with those who stopped to talk. Her finger stopped hurting, the crick in her back faded, and her anger receded somewhat. She smiled at the day, pleased to find she actually meant it.

A discordant noise up the way drew her attention. Several priests and their attendants turned off the main way onto the street, moving purposely behind the late market-goers, sermonizing before they ever reached them. Eleni ducked back inside as they passed, her carefully nurtured good mood evaporating in the unrhythmic stomping of their progress. They were altogether indecorous for her taste, just like the headmaster back at the college, and she wondered if it was universal amongst the creed.

Frowning, she closed the door and retreated back upstairs. After checking the final stitches of Demona's dress, she collected her basket of tools and put them on the worktable. On the corner lay a piece of paper crowded with her rage finding purchase in the long night of her sewing. The ink was dry; one letter in the middle was a blot, smudged by the last of her angry tears as she composed. The words had come in a spurt as though jettisoned from deep inside her spirit until released by some unspoken need. She scanned the words, at once pleased and afraid.

I watch my life progress
Like thread spun off my spindle.
Woven into a timeworn theme
By tradition's heavy shuttle.
And as the pattern grows
My heart knows
The finer points of pain. . .
And no change.

At times it feels like I'm
A clue awaiting discovery.
So much seems to go into the cloth
That there's nothing left for me
To do but count the days,
Weave my cage
And gather up the ends
Dreaming then—

Of a day that will surely come,
These trials cannot daunt me
Because I know I can conquer this.
I am a journey waiting to begin.
In time the threads will tell me
My destination.

"I will define myself," she said aloud, the determination rising up from that same deep space inside. "I will be who and what I wish. Somehow."

Setting the paper down, she poured herself a glass of water from the jug on the table, and strolled out through the double doors to the balcony outside. Tomais added it the year they were married. It faced south, overlooking the lower two thirds of Pevana, with the harbor and its roadstead to the east and the slope of the hill falling away toward the landward gate on the west. They decided to keep the shop after they were wed for the perfect view, and besides, Tomais liked to leave his sheds behind him when the workday came to an end.

Eleni moved over to the railing and breathed deeply. A small breeze teased the ends of her blonde tresses and cooled the perspiration beginning to form between her breasts. She stretched, imagining herself a divine specter, perhaps Renia herself, or her maiden, Minuet of the Arrows. They were women, were they not? No one dared hold them back, tell them *no*. She fixed the image in her mind—Eleni of the Words—and laughed softly, sadly at her own folly.

But her earlier thought returned to her: this was the week of the Summer Festival. All Pevana would take to the streets to dance and sing in excess. Nearly anything was possible, even the sort of miracle she needed. And yet even miracles needed a spark to light them. To be a poet of Pevana demanded a poem. She would enter the competition of poets. How, when women were forbidden to enter?

Eleni settled herself into her chair, cut to her size, yet another gift from Tomais. Her husband, her love. The thought of him distracted her, reminded her of harsh words given to his kind ones. His sweet face, his calloused, entreating hands, his deep, rich voice as he asked her forgiveness when he had done no wrong...

His voice.

Eleni bolted upright in her chair. Tomais' voice, one of the finest in all of Pevana, would be her emissary to the world; he would speak for her in the competition. The beauty of the idea blossomed for her like a hothouse flower. True, it might not mean anything to her grand designs on attending university, but her words would be heard. It was a start.

Turning to go inside, to tell Tomais of her brilliant plan, her dress billowed in a sudden breeze, the draft tickling up between her legs as though they were her husband's fingers gone exploring. Eleni grinned, and then she smiled grandly. Tomais was always at his randy best in the early hours of morning; perhaps she would wait to tell him afterwards.

"NO!" TOMAIS SHOUTED IN FRUSTRATION. "You cannot be serious! I can't, I won't... it's ridiculous!"

Eleni collapsed back onto the pillows in frustration. "Really, Tomais, I don't understand, why not?"

"Because I am not sure it is right, that's why!"

"But is it right to deny half of Pevana's population a chance to do something new and exciting, to deny them opportunity, just because it is tradition? That's absurd, and you know it!"

She watched him mulling over her words, a deep frown pinching his brows together, and held her breath for hope. His eyes held hers, fixed, as they had been fixed since the day he first professed his love for her. The moment lengthened. She took a breath in fear and matched his sigh in exhalation. Poets have often written about the unwisdom in love, the blindness that precludes sense, and yet there was something to be said for love's power to engender understanding, and through that connection support and reason.

"Love," he whispered. "I do not make the rules, but even though I think it absurd that you want me to break them for words, I see your point. But, words? Eleni, it is impetuous!"

"I can't help it! You know how I am and you married me anyway. More fool you, I suppose." And as she finished, her voice caught, stalled by her admition. Tomais paused in mid-breath, exasperation forming on his brow like a thunderhead and then gentled.

"E, come now, why must you say that?" he said softly. "You are a stubborn woman, granted, a pernicious, stubborn, headstrong, opinionated . . . beautiful, caring, sensitive, perfect . . . woman. But, honestly, must you?"

Eleni stared up at him as he ran out of words. They had been going at it since she whispered her request to him as he held her, half-asleep, while their commingled sweat cooled them into full wakefulness. She searched his face while their silence grew to a moment.

"Tomais," she sighed, releasing the tension. "I have to try. Please?"

"But—"

"Please? Just be my voice this once. No one needs to know. The worst thing that could happen would be no one would listen."

"Could you handle such a thing?"

"Better to at least try to be heard, than admit defeat before hand."

He smiled and Eleni knew he would do it, urged on by his love for her. She knew she perplexed him. She also knew he mesmerized her with those blue eyes of his. She reached up a slender hand and began teasing his chest hair. At her touch she felt his pulse quicken.

"Aye," he murmured, lowering himself to kiss her gently on the lips. "I'll do it for you, wife, if you teach me the words."

She reached up to cup his face in her hands, smiling through the tears that formed for the first time in the corners of her eyes. She kissed him deeply and drew him down to her, arching her hips, just so, as he rose to meet her.

"Aye, husband," she whispered into his ear as he entered her. "We've time to learn the words . . . *ungh* . . . after."

Mid-morning was well on its way to mid-day before Tomais left her to check on his work teams at the tanning sheds. Together they had sat down to go through her collected works, looking for the one to use that evening at the reading. It was not an easy choice. Eleni wanted to be different. She had attended readings in the past. All too often the poets let their words run away with them into long-winded epics of meter and rhyme. Eleni wanted to be daring. She wanted to make a statement, even though no one would know it came from her.

One by one, they reviewed them until they were left to choose between two. The first was a condemnation of the college and the men who had chosen to ignore her applications. She looked over Tomais' shoulder as he read it out loud, trying to recall its cadence:

Truth

Truth, I spin in a circle
May I be unbroken
You can't get in.
Doesn't that anger you?
In your pompous ploy
To judge and analyze,
To make yourself seem
Superior and sensible
And the rest of the world
Weak and will-less—
To be exposed,
Burnt away like
Mist after rain
On selected Sundays,
You forget that Truth

Is just a mirror
Showing the Self
To the Self—
Like to Like
Uncluttered by deception.

Lies, like weeds, wind
Their way into the cracks
In the defenses we rear
To protect us from ourselves.
Words, miss-spoken and miss-heard,
Breaking codes, unknown, like
Trip wires that ambush
Relationships, which then
Lay like bloated
Corpses, victims of
Disasters unnatural
To smell and taint
Even Truth.

And so love dies
Faith . . . fades
And options disappear
Like youth in middle age
To be replaced by remorse
And resignation,
A bird, earthbound
That used to soar
To all the high places
Light and laughter used
To take us.
Are they just

Disconnected memories,
Or do they add up to
Something?
At what point,
In this quest to label
All the shades of
Darkness,
Do you lose your
Hold on Light?

Tomais had fallen silent when he finished. He reached around to hug Eleni's middle to him.

"Why do you have so much anger in you?" he asked. "Aren't you happy?"

Eleni stared at the words on the page for a moment before kissing Tomais on the forehead. "I am happy, darling, with you, because of you. I live in joy of that part of my life," she said softly. "But I know there is more, always there is more, and I want it."

"Am I not enough?"

She smiled. "More than enough, on days like this. But not all days can be spent in bed, in your arms. There is more to me than domestic joy. It is a part of me that I keep for myself. You know that. I cannot let it go because of some spoken decree or unspoken taboo. There will be children some day. My chance to follow these words is now, and I cannot stand the idea of being barred from following where they might lead."

At her mention of children his hold on her tightened briefly. "Aye, a babe or three would change things."

"So, you see? You might have already planted the seed that will force me to choose."

"Eleni, you can always write. Babes or no. Is this worth such temerity?"

"Absolutely! I want an audience to hear! Words scribbled on pages or screamed at the corners of a room disappear into silence. Ink can fade."

"But *you* will have them."

"That is not enough."

He took a deep breath and let it out slowly. "All right. But not this one. I don't have your anger, my dear. It would sound false. This one," and he picked up the last paper. The poem was the shortest one in the pile. "This one I could manage."

Dust

Dust,
Hangs in a sunbeam
That misses me and
Covers the torn pieces
Of all the promises you made.
I watch particles collect,
Obliterating
All that was you in them. . .

His voice trailed off dramatically and he finished reading in silence, Eleni looking on over his shoulder, knowing which poem they would choose.

AFTER TOMAIS LEFT, Eleni made her way down the hill to the market near the Harbor Gate. The late hour meant poor fare from which to choose, but she did not mind. She felt boyant, inflamed, and excited for what the night might bring. She had just enough time to pick up a few things, go by the Cup and register her husband for the competition, and get back to her workshop to make any final adjustments to Demona Anargi's dress. She intended to spend the late afternoon cooking Tomais's favorite meal. They would celebrate the adventure together and then go early to the Cup. She laughed inwardly at her temerity. It was a risk she was taking, despite all her high words to Tomais that morning; what if, after all, her poetry was ignored?

"At least it won't be because I am a woman," she whispered to the bunch of carrots she held up for inspection.

She made her purchases and turned back toward the center of the city, walking easily down the wide avenue that ran from Harbor Gate to Landward Gate, stopping at various shops along the way. The summer festival was always a boon to tradesmen in the city, and Eleni had brought several garments she had completed for the proprietors with her. She passed the better part of the early afternoon making deliveries and checking fittings. On the way she encountered Gania Landare, mistress of a pension that catered to sailors and warehouse workers. They were friends, of a fashion. Eleni's mother had sewn dresses for Gania when Eleni was a child, and after Eleni became her own mistress, Gania steered such orders as she could to Eleni's shop. In her bag she had two newly mended and altered shirts for the son of a northern rug merchant and something of a rake, according to Gania.

Looking up from scrutinizing the quality of some pots displayed on a table at a tinker's booth, Gania waved a meaty hand to Eleni, the scowl formerly adorning her face replaced by a huge, toothy grin.

"Eleni!" she bellowed, startling several shoppers nearby. "Well, young miss, and how is your man and yourself today?"

"We are both splendid. Who could be anything else during summer festival?"

Gania's smile tempered somewhat. "Aye, as to that, I agree and then I don't, but I can see you are in fine spirits. There are others, rumors and such, you know, that tell a different tale."

"Truly? In truth, I've been so shut in the shop these days—a dozen gowns!—that I've quite missed all the gossip."

In answer Gania looked back up the avenue to where it intersected with the main north-south street. A procession of red-robed King's Theology priests was thrusting its way through the bustle and turning down a side arterial: the Street of Lamps. A crowd followed them. Eleni felt her interest prick. She wondered it they were the same ones she had seen pass by her door that morning. Glancing back at Gania, who still stared at the disturbance, she heard her speak in a small voice at drastic odds with her girth.

"There's some who whisper prayers in alleyways and ask questions. And others who wonder aloud in support and ask why not? I've heard various things about the old temples. And I've seen more of those red-berry boys. Two days ago one screeched at a mob for an hour from above the Harbor Gate arch."

Eleni had heard something of the same thing from one of her patrons, the chatty wife of one of the more well-to-do merchants, had mentioned the imminent visit by the Prelate Byrnard and his priestly retinue several days ago. Eleni had been so busy concentrating on her tasks, and later stewing over her rejection by the college, that she forgot about it completely.

"Ah, yes," she said. "I remember now. Myhra Saldani mentioned something about it during her fitting last week."

The column of priests and the following crowd disappeared down the Street of Lamps, and Gania, with a dismissive grunt, turned back to Eleni.

"Did she now?" Gania groused. "I suppose there's some as would worry 'bout it more than others. As for me, as long as it don't affect my business or my boarders. . ."

Eleni smiled. "I trust both are going as you would wish, Gania."

The older, larger lady smiled down at her, her ruddy face twisted into a semblance of good humor and sardonic disgust. "Oh, such a time I've had with the fools I've let rooms to this season. Drunkards and wastrels, loiters and doxie boys. I've half a mind to boot the lot of them and start over. But be that as it may, Lyssa and I are doing fine in spite of it all. Have you summat for me? I'll be heading back to help Lyssa finish with the evening's cooking. Will you and Tomais be out? It is festival, after all!"

Eleni reached into her bag for the shirts. "Yes, as a matter of fact, we'll be going to the Cup tonight." Part of her wanted to tell Gania of her plan, but she had never shared any of her dreams or writings with anyone except Tomais. She held her tongue and handed over the shirts. "These are for your rug-merchant's son, what was his name again?"

"Ha! That one! I'll take them, but I may not give them to the wretch. He's behind to me, but I'll beat some coin out of him for both of us. That boy, Talyior's his name, is getting himself into deep waters lately. Miscreant."

Eleni laughed at that. Myhra Saldani had also mentioned the latest gossip about a clandestine affair between a young cavalier and Demona Anargi. Woe to the fool who tried threading that one! Her husband, Sevire, ancient though he was, was known to have a vicious, vengeful nature.

"You mean he's. . ."

"So I've heard, once again just now! Mistress Demona must be feeling the lack, as it were . . . ha! The lad's a fool. I just hope he pays up before Sevire has him skewered. He snuck out of his room this morning to avoid me, or so Lyssa tells me, and goes fishing and writes, if you can believe it, poetry, when he should be down seeing to his father's affairs at that warehouse on the wharf. The overseer, Espan one-eye, told me the old man has cut him off. I wouldn't look too eagerly for payment if I was you."

As she finished speaking, Gania looked up suddenly, her face clouding over with saved up wrath. As if called by Gania's words, the young owner of the mended, unpaid for shirts materialized from the center of a crowd at the mouth of the Harbor Gate. He had a string of fish dangling from one hand and a jaunty air to his step.

"There he is," rasped Gania, making shift to leave. "D'you want to come pummel him with me?"

Eleni had followed her gaze and noted the blond hair poking out from underneath a light cavalier's cap. She had only met him briefly, and only to get measurements. They had scarcely spoken, and if rumors were true about him, he surely would not have remembered Eleni. She had barely taken notice of him herself. Now, however, even from a distance she could see his good looks. Gania's scathing observation about how he spent his time gave her reason to pause, for young Talyior was not just a patron; he was competition. She watched him turn at Gania's gate and go in the front door.

"No," she said, turning to head off to the Cup to register Tomais in the reading for that night. "If you wouldn't mind, I'll leave the pummeling to you, Gania. I've other stops to make and a meal to prepare afterwards. You keep the money, if you get any, and I'll get it later. Good day."

"And you, Eleni. Enjoy yourselves! Word has it that the Cup's been chosen a site for the first reading! Enjoy!" And with that she stumped off towards her house, her hands clenching into fists as she walked as if anticipating the carnage ahead.

Eleni walked on, grown aware at the size of what she had chosen to involve herself. Even though she was going to be anonymous, she still felt the pangs of pressure suddenly perceived. "We will," she whispered to herself. "By Renia's Grace, I hope so."

Chapter 5.1: Evening of the First Day of the Summer Festival
To the Golden Cup: Devyn

*D*ESPITE THE SLOW RETREAT SHE SENSED IN THE MATERIAL *WORLD, the goddess Renia retained love for her city, still held it in her celestial bosom, and on this first evening of the Summer Festival she bent her gaze downward with a mixture of sorrow and joy. She noted how sunset cast its fading glamour over Pevana, bathing all in a red glow as night spread outward from the remains of the day.*

She gestured and a skeen of clouds dispersed, their thinning mists deepening the colors so that they matched the tartan of tile roofs in the city below. Renia bent her gaze downward and sent her will to test the emotional currents in the lives flickering there. Action wove itself among the intentions of the innocent and guilty, the moral and perverse, and the hapless and hopeful, twining all within its great web with strands silken yet unbreakable. Destiny walked the streets. In the city a thousand thousand rhythms cadenced out their patterns: words and meter to the poets, heartbeats of lovers, the tramp of the watch on the cobblestone streets. Everyone and everything moved toward a night of great event and Renia lent her grace as a pervasive element among the shadows. It was Festival, and as the night deepened it was as if the city herself took note and stretched forth to take the great breath before the plunge into the chaos of carnival.

What Renia read in the souls below brought her sorrow, for few among the masses below noted the time's import. So many did not care, but that, too, was part of the pattern, or so she consoled herself. Man needed help to understand, and so Renia graced him with a gift: the poets who sought with word and rhyme to bring order to at least a portion of those things open to Man's ken.

With a thought Renia sent her minion, Minuet of the Arrows, called Fate by later men, to set about her business. The well of Pevanese faith was drying, cruel logic advanced in the guise of red clad columns, burning, suborning, taking the very stones of her temples so that hope flowed out to be swallowed by the desiccated, indifferent earth. At her lady's command, Minuet sent her barbs into the night to prick the fancies and ambitions of men in one last gambit before the darkness took them.

Of those few who felt the stirrings of grand design, five souls felt it the strongest: a prosperous rug-merchant's son, the young wife of a fine saddle-maker, an orphaned horse trainer, a Prince and a spy. Perhaps Minuet's arrows touched them all. Perhaps all were merely unlucky or fortunate, to be at large during such a juncture in Time . . .

DEVYN EMERGED FROM HIS CUBBYHOLE in the stables pressed and dressed for the evening's adventure. He and Sanya spent the fading afternoon hours searching and finding new ways to expel energy. She had chided him heartily for his foolishness outside the Cup, and then just as heartily ravaged him. He surprised himself by the ardor of his response, as though something had broken through in him. Was it gallows humor? One last jest before the final drop and the eternal dangle? Or was it something else entirely?

He awoke alone, but strangely free of the loneliness that had haunted his days for so long. For once, he did not feel like an orphan.

"Whatever may come from this night's work," he murmured, smiling at the mirror as his mind wrapped itself around the memory. "At least I can no longer say I haven't lived. Kembril was right. No defeat without one last, eloquent protest."

Devyn made his way out of the stable and through the outer gates of Malom's establishment. He checked the status of the evening and drew encouragement from the light; he liked the twilight hours the best. He found inspiration in the changing color of the heavens and the first shine of the stars as they made their appearance. Full day revealed too much of the stink and stain of life exposed as stark and unlovely, a business deal bereft of art. Full dark masked too much of the sublime and beautiful, creating shadows within which lurked humanity's fears, thus defeating art again.

Devyn found his words most often in the early stars; in the diffused illumination of twilight he sensed the best of both extremes of the day, and so found there his art.

He paced down the side street to where it intersected with the main avenue that ran from Land Gate to Harbor Gate. Crowds milled about already, getting an early start on the night's revelry. All over Pevana, inns and taverns, private homes and brothels would be thronged with people bent on eating, drinking, groping, singing and laughing as much as they could. In the chaos of carnival, every man had an equal chance at sloughing off the dross of his life and thumbing his nose at responsibility. In the week's excess class lines blurred somewhat, and the people mixed together to form a unique vintage of washed and unwashed souls, of pale, water-fat skin and sun-roughened shoulders. It was a week during which love was found and spurned, hopes raised and dashed, lives saved and lost. It was a week during which the stocks of wine and beer fell to almost nothing, as though the Pevanese were honor-bound to drain everything to the dregs. And from the looks of some of those that jostled Devyn as he walked along, it appeared no few of the locals had succeeded in at least numbing the pain.

"And that is my greatest fear," he murmured to himself as he sidestepped a fat fellow who was already reduced to a stumbling hulk. "What if everyone is too besotted by wine and the time to hear? What if no one cares?"

Devyn crossed the main square that served as the intersection for the southern avenue and the landward avenue. People swarmed the space, some moving with purpose to the alehouses that were to serve as the sites for the first reading in the competition of poets. Crowds surrounded street musicians and dance groups. Near the ornate fountain set in the middle of the square, an open-air kitchen had been set up.

The smell of roasting meat and fowl made Devyn's mouth water. He purchased a blood sausage to nibble on. He climbed up on the edge of the fountain and leaned back against the side of a water-spewing dolphin to survey the thickening sea of movement spread out before him. Above, true dark descended, and the faces of the revelers took on surreal aspects as they moved from shadow to light. The open fires of the camp kitchen and the great lamps set about the fountain served to cast a faint but jolly glow about the proceedings.

The falling dark spurred more currents of activity, as if the collective multitude suddenly realized the festival proper was well and truly begun. Voices rose in a wave of sound, cheering, singing, screaming, a cacophony of noise bent towards the need to vent. Part of him wanted to scoff at the resident hypocrisy; where was such energy when it was most needed? Where was the joy and vitality that would preserve Pevana and its faiths? How could they celebrate while Renia's gifts retreated into the night?

And yet another part of him wanted to laugh along with the crowd, to exult with strangers, to dance and share the convivial chaos. In between bites of the sausage, Devyn weighed his choices: despair or joy? What would be compromised? The notion hung before his mind's eye while he tackled a piece of gristle. If despair and anger, what purpose? If joy and laughter, what use his protest?

He looked around him once again, taking it all in. Even during the bad years on the streets and in the Maze, he had loved the week of festival. Perhaps it, too, was part of the Grace of Renia. Perhaps there was a deeper purpose to the week's mayhem than to distract the multitudes from the control exerted on their lives. Perhaps joy was part of the pattern, too.

The moment lingered an instant longer like a boat poised above the falls and teetering over the edge. He stopped trying to worry the gristle apart and swallowed, took a deep breath, and sent forth a barbaric howl to join ranks with the tumultuous din reverberating around the square.

Devyn leaped down from the fountain into the mob roiling in the square and fought his way through the human current to the far side where the avenue recommenced on its way to the Harbor Gate. The Cup lay at the midpoint of a side way, the Street of Lamps, a diagonal that ran from the main thoroughfare to connect with the road from the harbor. He smiled as he walked at the memory of his afternoon's adventure. Part of him felt like a lover returning for more delight. Every step brought him nearer to that point where he would have to give voice to his truth, and in so doing make all things after irrevocable. He popped the last bit of his sausage in and chewed with relish; it was, after all, quite possibly his last meal. He made sure to wipe the grease on the back of a chattering fool who thought he was a friend and yelled a jolly greeting. Right here, right now, life was good.

Insight swarmed over him as though one of Minuet's arrows had pricked his conscience. As he observed the goings on around him, Devyn's mind reviewed the lines of he had written that afternoon. The cadence punctuated every stride. The rhythm modulated every breath. Everthing pointed back to him.

I am the poem.

The realization almost made him stumble, or else his foot found an uneven portion of the pavement. He made the turn down the Street of Lamps. A crowd jostled outside the Golden Cup. He would be one of the last in. His heart kept pace with his feet, tapping tympani to destiny.

"Renia, save me," he whispered to the stars as he neared the front. "Don't let me stutter."

Chapter 5.2: To the Golden Cup: Donari

". . .and so I tell you the people are deluded! They have lost their way. I have come to help them find the path again. Mistaken allegiances are an extravagant waste of time. Let them but see the value of the King's Theology, and they will put aside the childish myths of their forebears."

And so it had gone on for several hours. Donari, Prince of Pevana, had to exert the utmost self-restraint to keep himself from yawning. The Prelate's voice dominated the council. He sat there, his secretary at his elbow feeding him notes, as if he were giving a speech.

Hunched down in their chairs around him at the far side of the table were the heads of household for most of Pevana's elite families. Merchant lords, all—rulers in commerce, traffickers in influence and gold. Sevire Anargi and several others listened in rapt attention to the Prelate's peroration. Donari could almost see Sevire's lust for opportunity quivering beneath the folds of his third chin as he nodded his head sagely at the effluent spewing out of Byrnard's mouth.

"King Roderran expects us all to do our duty," the Prelate continued in that nasally, high-pitched voice that set Donari's teeth on edge. He could not decide which was worse: Byrnard as Captain of Roderran's Guard or as this red-robed pontificator.

"My brothers who preceded me here tell me there is resistance to the Word. There have been incidents at the *revisions* conducted at some of the Old Ways Temples. Priests ignored, molested! Just this afternoon, a drunken wastrel rudely discomposed Brother Aemile in one of the squares near the harbor. Guards chased the miscreant but he eluded them. I'm told part of the southern portion of the city resembles a rabbit warren. Hardly sanitary, Prince Donari. Such cesspools of sedition and disease ought rightly to be rooted out. But mayhap you know what is best for your city. Let you look to the sewage; my brothers and I will look to their souls. My friends, we must redouble our efforts. Pevana must be taken into the fold. Let us work together to unite her under the glories."

Donari let the noise flow by him like water gurgling by a bridge pylon. He could almost stomach the obsequious drivel if he let his mind wander to the bottle of last year's vintage waiting for him back in his sleeping chambers. Doing so let him attend to the growing concern of what to do with the nosey cleric and his royal mandate. He already knew about the incident from that afternoon. Senden Arolli, his eyes and ears about the city, came to him just before he left for the meeting and showed him a copy of a rumpled poem. Senden was certain the author was the same young man who had risked his life at the last temple fire a few months ago. A quick glance told Donari everything he needed to know.

His right temple began to pulse. He and Senden had spent several evenings mulling over the crown's intentions. Roderran wanted the south, and would go through Pevana to get it. His choice of Byrnard as Prelate had been a strategic maneuver, not a pious one, for despite the robes and ritual, the man acted in all ways like the conquering general he used to be. Beneath that conical cap connived the same, straggly-haired strategist who had made a career and a name for himself by outwitting the realm's enemies. He and Roderran made a perfect pair: creating new ways to exert authority and manipulate power in their quest to spread the political aims of the North. But what exactly did that mean to Donari? To Pevana?

What does it matter? Donari sighed inwardly. *If it is the south my cousin wants, it is the south he will get.*

The thought made him wince, though his face betrayed nothing. He had watched the growth of this new *movement* as it ran its course in the northern-tiered cities, but never gave it serious attention. Pevana was too far south to matter. The lands to the south were governed by loose, pagan federations and were, therefore, not a threat. He had missed something. He had been distracted. He should have seen it coming. He should have kept a firmer grasp on the aspirations of the great Pevanese merchant families.

Power was being gathered and manipulated, infecting the petty and the pious with its rank attraction. Senden had warned him, tried to stop the holes bursting apart the fabric of his city; until now, Donari had been too careless to care.

Every syllable pouring out from Byrnard's mouth hammered into Donari's mind the realization that he had let Roderran, his agent, and types like the gluttonous Sevire Anargi act with too much freedom around him. The thought made his pulsing temple flower into a full-blown headache that grew steadily worse.

"Quite right! Quite right, my lord Prelate!" Sevire gargled. "We here, we civic-minded elders, must look to our people and help our city find its way into the fold of the King's gift." And he looked around at everyone in turn, shaking his jowls emphatically. He turned his baleful, heavy-lidded glance last on Donari.

Quelling a sudden urge to vomit, Donari forced a smile and nodded in apparent agreement. *Help our city*, he thought as he searched for something innocuous to say, *the way you seem to have helped yourself, if rumor is true, to the temple silver.* He bit the inside of his mouth to restrain himself.

"My Lord Byrnard, doubtless, will see we enjoy the benefits of such a union," he said aloud in a disaffected drawl. "With so many eloquent voices preaching in every corner, well, I am certain the effect on the people has been felt and will most likely show dramatic results soon. But this is Festival, my friends. Passions run high."

Byrnard's eyes narrowed on him. "All the more reason to control and direct them, then." He smiled thinly, because he was a thin, hard man with edges sharp as flint. "And I'm sure with the visible support of Pevana's ruling elite, and the good offices of her Prince, the King's near cousin, we shall see the numbers of the faithful swell. And the grace spread to all men."

You bastard! You hollow appendage. If I can spoil your plans I will; and my foolish, power-swollen cousin's, too!

"I am the King's servant in this as in all things," he said instead, his smile as foppish as Byrnard's was thin. "And I am my lord Prelate's host. Please make free of the rooms provided you. I'm sure you will enjoy the revels. Have patience with my people. Perhaps we just need time to adjust."

"*If* they are his majesty's *loyal* subjects," Byrnard quipped, "Roderran's patience is more bounteous than the seas outside Pevana's excellent harbor. The Word of the New Theologies is beyond time, and so is patient. I, too, will be patient, my Lord Prince, but look you into these several *happenings* that have been reported to me this day. They smell of, dare I say, rebellion."

A nerve behind Donari's right eye began beating like a blacksmith's hammer on an anvil. Senden's warnings, all they had discussed pounded through his mind in time to that rhythm.

What ambition or threat breathes down Roderran's neck to make him trump up such blatant action in the name of piety? The South is no threat. Why risk Pevana's people, its culture, to get to it? Is it just because he can? Is power that cold a thing? Conquest and control that much a prod to action? For land? For treasure? Glory? Why?

Prince Donari let go a small sigh and rubbed his left temple. It was time to stop making things so easy for them. He would connive and manipulate with all his grandfather's wiles, as well as employ the realities of society he'd learned in the fleshpots and alehouses of places like the Maze. The combination had given Donari a unique perspective on his station: he, unlike most rulers, understood how expendable he was. His behavior had scandalized his mother, but it had brought him to a level of understanding he was only now coming to appreciate; Donari knew just how Pevana, the real Pevana and not the social salons of the wealthy, worked.

Donari was Pevana's miscreant son; it was about time he showed some appreciation. But too big a bite taken out of this vast mouthful of sludge would result in regurgitation of all his hopes. He needed a plan. He needed Senden. But for the moment, Donari needed something small and irksome; something that would give him pleasure, if nothing else.

"The temerity!" a high, nasally voice sneered, dragging Donari's attention back to council. "A woman! Not only did she dare *apply* to the college, but she had the unmitigated gall to actually inquire as to why her application had not been answered yay or nay. And she did not take kindly to my firm dismissal. I heard she shoved one of the college guards on her way out. My Lord Prince, if the women of Pevana are any indication of the ilk of citizenry, I should think your cousin-King might be wise to send more priests!"

Donari's headache eased. The priest, a fool recently installed as headmaster of the college, awaited a response. Donari quirked an eyebrow. In his periphery he spied Prelate Byrnard's craggy face and thin lips pinched in disgust.

"A woman you say," Donari obliged. *Minuet, your arrow strikes true. I thank you.* "The temerity indeed. My friends, I believe our business here is ended for the time. I will look into recent *happenings*, my lord Prelate."

"Yes, do." Byrnard sniffed, looked down his bird-beak nose. "Save me the trouble of doing it for you."

Donari froze as he pushed to his feet, his headache bursting like a melon dropped from a balcony. He held his temper in check, conjuring the image of the bottle of wine cooling in a bucket in his chambers, but the anger smoldered and then appeased burned anew. He held the Prelate's haughty stare, watched it dim so slightly it might have been a trick of light. Donari felt the corner of his lip twitch, his sneer became a smile so grand it would have fooled his mother. Eyes never leaving the Prelate's, he said, "I understand the kitchens have prepared an early meal in honor of your arrival. If you will follow the page, he will show you and these other worthies to the table. I hope you will not take it amiss if I am not present. I have a headache that seems fit to perplex me, and I fear I would be poor company. I trust you all will attend his lordship?"

Much nodding of heads and scrapping back of chairs attended his words, even a few murmured prayers, perhaps some of them actually meant, for his speedy recovery.

"Good, then. My lord Prelate, welcome to Pevana. I bid you good even' and good repast."

Donari, pinching his brow against the pain, walked with as much dignity as he could muster down the hall to his private apartments. Bursting in through the ornate double doors, he dove for the wine bottle in its bucket of water. The suddenness of his entrance disturbed the maids who were still laying out clothes for the evening's events.

"Out!" he shouted. His throbbing temples made him want to scream and break something. He took up the bottle, already opened, and heaved the bucket out the open balcony door. He did not care if it hit anybody. He didn't even bother with a glass. Two swallows left him coughing and nearly faint.

The wine burned its way into his gullet, adding a new pain to the aching pulse behind his eyes. He had not felt this much rage in years, not since the day his grandfather trapped him into adulthood with a coronet of silver and a golden ring.

He took another drink, more tenderly this time, letting the tannins play about his palate before swallowing. As the wine reached his stomach and began to warm him, the pulse in his temple receded, replaced by a sense of calm as his natural control overcame his distress.

He smiled as he poured the remains of the bottle into a large goblet. He would make Byrnard pay for his disrespect. He would see the man's sallow complexion burn as red as those fires he and his were so fond of setting. The plan roiling earlier in his head revealed itself to him with the suddenness of spring, and like that day when the world stopped holding its breath against winter and decided to live, Prince Donari Avedun breathed in the freshness, exhaled the stale, and silently thanked the brash young woman who had so annoyed the nasally Priest for pointing him in the necessary direction. Crossing back to the door he stuck his head out into the hall.

"Ah, Cryso! Good. Please apologize to Gisa and Anlise. I forgot myself for a moment. Have Cook send me up a cold plate of something would you? But before you do all that, find Senden and send him to me, thank you."

He went back into the room, and ignoring the finery laid out on the dressing stand, flung open the doors of his closet and rooted about in a chest of drawers. The garments he pulled out were somewhat weathered but still serviceable. He held up the shirt, examining the memories associated with it rather than the stitching. By the time he found what he wanted, Senden had arrived and stood by the closet door with a slightly sardonic smile on his lips.

"Your mother will be so disappointed at your sense of taste," he said, reaching out to take the pair of boots from the top of the pile Donari held in his arms. He sniffed the boots. "They say there are cheeses to be had in the north whose taste improves with age, even as their smell grows worse. I don't think the same holds true for these boots."

"Ha!" Donari scoffed, tossing the garments on the bed. "Where we'll be going tonight, I doubt we'll offend anyone's sense of smell."

Senden cocked a questioning eyebrow.

"You were right, of course," continued Donari. "The weasel Byrnard has a mandate from my cousin, and he's swayed Sevire and several other houses to support whatever it is." He fumbled with his neck cloth. "I have decided that life has been too easy for their ilk of late."

"And?"

"And get yourself back to your rooms, my friend, and change into something suitably scabby. Meet me on the balcony at true dark." He glanced outside. They had perhaps an hour. The red glow of sunset was now just a memory of color on the horizon.

"Am I to know where we are going?" his eyes and ears asked. "What about the state dinner you are missing? There's to be a ball afterwards."

Donari took up a rumpled, nearly shapeless hat and stuffed it over his curls. "I'm ill. They'll never miss me. They'll stuff themselves at table then spend the evening gossiping and scheming, and then they'll go home to scheme and plot some more. No doubt they will call the evening a successful beginning to Festival.

"I've had enough of those fools for one day. I need to spend some time with my people. I have a mind to try some of Saymon's ale tonight and hear some poetry. You and I are going to the Golden Cup."

Chapter 5.3: To the Golden Cup: Talyior

TALYIOR ESCHEWED THE DRAIN SPOUT and left Gania's through the kitchen door opening into the same alley. The swelling noise of revelers rose as the sun fell, replacing light with the burgeoning chaos of the festival. He chose to make his way through alleys quickly gathering darkness, adding to their shadows. For some reason he felt on his guard, as though to walk openly in the street in the fading light would be to invite trouble. Not tonight. Words called him. So much depended upon tonight.

Destiny's hand gripped his shoulder, guiding him through the turnings, around refuse strewn before him. He walked through the stench of animal leavings and the detritus of failed human lives like the heroes in the old stories who seemed to barely touch the earth as they paced their determined way into myth. He would slay his dragon at the Golden Cup; nothing would keep him from such an appointment. His hand strayed to his sword hilt, useless in the duel to come, but reassuring nonetheless in its solid, focused balance.

A tiny, breathless laugh burbled out of bravado. If all went well, he would need the sword shortly afterwards. Voices would carry his name, and the subject of his words winging through the night. By morning, even the yearling gull he had encountered on the way back to the city would know of his temerity. There was something in the air that was not the aroma of horse manure piled behind the blacksmith shop. Tonight, all over the city, people would crowd the selected establishments to listen and be transported. It was as if the city's buildings themselves paused in their gradual, groaning decay to pay attention.

He lingered at the alley opening to scan the square he had to cross in order to reach the Cup. Celebrants milled around in clusters of inside jokes and cheap wine. Doubtless the main city squares were full of people, but the area around the Cup seemed normal as yet. The Golden Cup was not a new place, nothing this close to the Maze was. It had a slightly disheveled look about it, a tired matron too busy with the business of service and spirits to bother with niceties like paint or an awning. Its owner, Saymon Brimaldi, a man of middling height and impressive girth, reflected the atmosphere of his place. His shaggy head and full beard, both complimented with bits of gray and scraps of food, led patrons to joke that Saymon would never perish from starvation; he could comb his face and dinner would fall out.

Saymon served good house beer with a smile and some of the finer wines, having conveniently fallen from careless delivery wagons, with a wink. The good, solid, over-taxed working class folk of Pevana that patronized the Cup proved it a local favorite. Talyior liked it well enough, though it lately had become a fashionable place for inferiors of society to mix with their moral betters. Even Demona and her friends had once or twice borrowed their servants' clothing to blend into *the District*, as they called the warren of streets and alleys. She fooled no one, of course, and neither did her friends. Homespun clothes did not hide such beauty, and neither did it alter demeanors. Luckily for them, wealth and class were great insulators against embarrassment or comprehension.

Demona came to him at the Cup once, reckless and daring, cloaked and slightly drunk in her abandon. He smelled her perfume before she even reached the room he had taken for the purpose. She laughed afterward when he offered to upend the contents of the chamber pot on her cloak and gown to complete the disguise. The memory steadied him, and he made his way over the open space of the square to the doors of the Cup, saying a silent prayer to whatever god who chanced to listen, for words.

The air inside smelled of pipes, pints, and sweat with hints of perfume that bespoke of cleaner skin. The place was full and boisterous. Talyior had dreamed about the Pevanese Summer Festival as a boy. Espan and the other shipmen who plied his father's trade mesmerized him with lurid tales, not all of them clean, of the events that took place during the hottest week of the summer. The affair begun out of the old Prince's political need had proven so successful that it quickly became a highly anticipated, and lucrative, event; and poets were an integral part of the proceedings from the first.

The old man had been sly. Pevana was already known for the quality of its shipyards and the liquid satin of deep, red wine pressed from the grapes that grew on the slopes of the hills above the river. His city drew the merchants, it drew the nobles, all it needed were the artists as coveted and fashionable as gold and wine. As the festival grew through the years, the competition among the verse mongers did as well, and Pevana became known as much for its poets.

Talyior learned from Lyssa that the clerical set, unrestricted by the current Prince these last few years, had begun appropriating parts of the festival to serve theological purposes. Proclamations and sermons mingled, irritating but tolerated, with the revelry, games and poetic competition. Talyior found something clown-like about the sight of priests, sweating profusely in their thick robes, shouting their sermons in shrill voices over the heads of people more intent on the prospect of tankards and a tumble than the contents of their spiritual ledgers.

Still and always, the Poet's Competition took residence in the core of the week's events, drawing hopefuls from far and wide as it had drawn Talyior down from his northern home. All it took was a convincing plea to his father to allow him to learn the family business up front in the marketplace and off he was sent with the skeptical hope of his sincerity. Talyior was sincere in the desire to test himself, just not at selling rugs. After a final good-bye, seven days' sail with a following wind delivered him up to a new world.

After checking in his blade with Saymon, he moved through the crowd to a table near the small stage to check in. Talyior noticed there were quite a few names already listed on the overseer's tablet. He would be the last to deliver his piece. He had timed it thus; his would be the last, and lasting, impression of the evening.

He signed his name and made his way back to the bar, stealing a few surreptitious glances at the five judges sitting at a table set off to one side. Two of them were grey-haired and finely dressed; the other three were younger, tradesmen probably and of them one had the look of sailor. Talyior did not recognize any them, but as Lyssa promised, when he spoke his fears of being judged by class not by talent, the cross-section of Pevanese society calmed him. These men had put their names in and were awarded places on the panels by lot: one from the nobility, one from the priesthood, one from the tradesmen's guilds, one from the shipyards, and one from the business owners. It was considered an honor, but one that carried with it some risk. Judges who had been involved in unpopular decisions sometimes met with unfortunate accidents.

The overseer rose and moved to the stage, displacing a pair of musicians attempting to be heard above the revelry.

"Welcome!" he bellowed. "To the first hearing of the Summer Festival!"

The roar of the crowd, attended by a massed thumping of hands and tankards on the benches, forced the man to pause. Talyior felt the hairs on the back of his neck rise. He took a short pull on his mug and nearly choked on it going down.

The noise subsided; the overseer continued. "Tonight's winner receives thirty gold coins! Let us thank the Prince for his generosity!"

The place erupted in a guttural chorus of boos and shouted insults.

"I've got his thirty gold coins!" screamed a toothless old man next to Talyior. "And I'd like to shove't, up his arse!"

"The Prince likes boys!" shouted another.

"He's got a leaky spigot!"

"Simpering doxy! Sleeps with sheep!" And so on for a good few minutes. It evinced all the power and passion usually missing from the daytime orations of the local priests. The patrons, fueled by the heat and good ale let loose their love for their sovereign with extravagant zeal until the overseer finally, laughingly, raised his hands to reclaim order.

What a place! A poem in itself. This was worth getting cut off by the old man.

When the uproar finally died down, the overseer called the first entry to the stage. As Talyior turned to see who it was, he caught sight of a man entering the Cup out of the corner of his eye.

One more poet? Or just a spectator?

Talyior followed with his eyes. The young man, for he seemed to Talyior of an age with himself or close to it, wore a battered but serviceable hat; at least the plume was new. Auburn hair fell between his shoulders, a moustache and a goatee, neatly trimmed, to match. His clothes were good but, like his hat, only just. He hesitantly checked his blade at the door, then turned to scan the crowd with a vaguely sullen set to his jaw. He met Talyior's gaze in passing, took a glass of last year's red from Saymon, and smiled a small smile that eased his look immediately.

And moved to the overseer's table.

Curses! I won't be last!

The newcomer bent to speak quietly yet earnestly to the man who shrugged his shoulders and handed the latecomer a pen. Talyior felt his shoulders slump as he signed the page, but he did not mope; his attention was drawn back to the stage where the night's first poet, an older, balding man with a high, nasal voice and apparently afflicted with the stutters, took the stage.

Oh, that Pevana should without your guidance be
Lost like a mastless ship upon a stormy sea,
We stand as one, a city united in trust
Under your wise rule both stern and just. . .

Talyior took a healthy pull of his ale, smiling into his cup. *No worry here.* He settled on a stool and leaned back against the bar. *Not tonight.* But all the same, he would keep half an eye on the auburn-haired latecomer sitting now by himself in the corner, who, by chance or design, had upset his plans to speak last.

Chapter 5.4 The Duel: Devyn, Donari, Eleni . . . and Jaryd

DEVYN ENTERED THE CUP in the lee of a loud and boisterous group; already well along in their celebrating and spoiling for the show. He waited as they settled in seats and booths before approaching the bar to have a word with Saymon and procure a glass of his famed red wine. He looked around the room. It appeared set to bring forth a loud and boozy night, rich with the aromas of beer, wine and food. Combined with the sounds of revelry, it made a heady perfume, indeed.

He took a sip from the goblet Saymon handed him and turned away from the bar, catching sight, as he did, of a youngish man leaning confidently against the counter, a pot of ale at his elbow. Something flashed familiar in the blue eyes that held his own and Devyn found himself smiling without meaning to; but no, just a trick of light, for the fellow broke the connection and turned away as if he hadn't seen Devyn at all.

Making his way to the overseer's table to register for the night's competition, Devyn looked at the page. He leaned low to ask the overseer, "Do you think it a good thing to speak last?"

The man shrugged, and handed Devyn a pen. Devyn scrawled his name just as the first poet made his way to the front.

Last. Just so. Yes, just so.

He found a seat in the corner, a pulse already beating in his temple. The first poet began to speak, his shaking voice making Devyn's temple throb a little harder. A poet needed courage and conviction! This man had none. He started to think that, perhaps, he might even win this competition, even if he lost his life doing so.

He scanned the crowd, trying to pick out the others who would speak, and again found his eyes falling on that confident young man. *Now that will be a competitor.* Devyn, sipped carefully from his wine, trying to pretend he was not scrutinizing the fair features, blond hair and well-tailored clothes. *A cavalier,* he thought, and caught himself snickering. At least someone in this competition would have some passion, however doxy it might be.

The first poet droned on. Devyn glanced about the room, watching faces and seeing heads come together to whisper, some chuckled. His pulse quickened. Laughter? Boredom, perhaps, but laughter? Would anyone dare?

He found his eyes drawn back again, as if pulled on a thread, to the cavalier, to the careful attention of keeping his posture just so, and the way his eyes darted about the room. The man looked enthralled and perplexed at the same time, and Devyn realized that was how he must look to anyone watching him as carefully. The awareness sparked a moment's empathy in Devyn, made him and the stranger kindred. *An untold story, that's what he is. And so am I; at least, until we speak.*

The adventure at the temple fire and the chaotic episode outside the Cup that afternoon were nothing more than preamble. His story began, or ended, tonight. He calmed his suddenly racing pulse with another, larger, sip from the goblet and settled back into his chair a little.

The first poet finished, the next took his place, and so on through the evening. Devyn sat, bathed by words, surrounded by the crowd's response to each competitor. The variety ranged from the sycophantic to the surreal, and all were delivered with the sort of underlying anxiety he found, strangely enough, lacking in his own pulse. Was it ego? His disdain for money, having gone without for so long? By the end of his first glass of Saymon's wine, Devyn realized the difference: everyone wanted to win, and he only wanted to be heard.

Habit or hubris, Devyn could not keep himself from quietly evaluating the poems. Some were good. Many were dreadful. One in particular caught his attention, for its final stanza reminded him of

Kembril and Avarran. The author was announced as Abel Soren, a city guardsman:

And there in the night the standard fluttered
Bathed in moonlight, splashed with gore.
Protected by shield and buckler
And valiant men placed to the fore.
"Hold, my lads!" the proud King cried,
As the last wave surged to the line.
"We'll sing of this in comfort yet
Back home or in halls more divine."
But in the morn, pale and forlorn
There were none left alive save one
To tell the tale of the stand in the vale;
Of the victory lost and won.

A fine piece, but not fine enough to win, in Devyn's estimation. He felt something akin to his own tastes when a young man, announced as Tomais Caralon, the Saddlemaker, shuffled up on the small stage, urged on by a small slip of a woman. The couple paused next to Devyn's chair and the woman smoothed the young man's collar, stretching up to kiss him on the cheek. Despite the room's rumble, Devyn overheard the small words of encouragement she gave him: "Deep breath now, love, and give them my words for me."

The love shining in her eyes made even skeptical Devyn smile. She returned to her seat. Devyn's eyes followed. There was something of her words, of that look, of her excited nervousness that combined with her whispered, *give them my words for me.* Devyn glanced back at the man on stage, recognized him; he had made several deliveries to Banley's in the last year. A man gifted in leathercraft, but poetry?

Tomais stood before the crowd mute for what seemed like minutes as the mob grew more and more restive. Devyn drew breath to join in the fun, but his whistle died on his lips when he saw the young woman move quickly out from the shadows of the corner next to the stage. She was dressed conservatively, tastefully—a wife, not a mistress. Her high forehead and blond tresses accentuated graceful movements that spoke to Devyn of rhythm and meter. The crowd whooped and whistled as she made her way up to stand before Tomais.

"Give him a kiss, dearie!" someone cried and various others joined in like a chorus.

"If he cannot talk, let us have a dance!"

"Show us yer leg, honey!"

"If he cannot get you home, I am your man!"

The woman ignored the crowd and took Tomais' face gently in her hands and whispered words only he could hear. *I bet I could guess the gist of those words,* Devyn thought, smiling into his cup. *A woman! Perfect!* The look of frozen fear left Tomais' face and he smiled. She kissed him once on the lips, drawing even more ribald response from the crowd, and moved quickly off to the side. Tomais faced down the mob until the noise subsided. Then he spoke in a high, clear voice at odds with his size, and as he spoke silence fell like darkness in winter. He was done in two breaths, and yet Devyn sensed in the words a whole lifetime of pain:

Dust
Hangs in a sunbeam
That misses me and
Covers the torn pieces
Of all the promises you made
I watch particles collect,
Obliterating
All that was you in them,
All that was light,
All that was necessary
And important.

Now they are shards
Rendered impotent
By a gray coverlet
That doesn't warm
But rather mocks
The memories. . .

Devyn found himself standing and clapping, his action spurring others to their feet. Tomais stumbled backward when his wife vaulted into his arms. They moved towards the back of the room to a seat in the shadows of the balcony, followed by a spate of saucy commentaries and laughter.

Returning his attention to his wine and the stage, his mind turned over his suspicions that the woman rather than Tomais had been the poet; the piece had a quiet quality to it, a feminine conceit. He looked around the room and realized no one else seemed to have realized it. *So terse yet so full of emotion.* He spared a glance at the couple, the fervency of their embrace, the look of pride in both their eyes as they ignored the crowd's hooted suggestions for what they should do next. He raised his cup for another sip, found it empty, and came face to face with the glaring hole in his life the scene communicated: he did not love—*anyone.* He cared for Kembril, liked and respected Malom and Captain Avarran. Sanya was a delicious convenience, but he did not feel the same kind of intensity for any of them he sensed in the clasp of the young couple.

They had a world.

He suddenly knew himself a debtor, his life nothing but a series of unfortunate accidents, moments; and none of which added up to the eternity he saw shining in the young woman's eyes. Regret welled up so quickly that he had to shake himself to toss it off, remind himself of the larger issues he had to deal with. He could not consider the prospect of love in his life, especially considering with what he intended for the evening.

Mark Nelson

He raised his glass as if to seal his decision with the wine's absolution and turned his attention to the stage once more as the young cavalier took his place to present his piece.

Demona

Who is to say when the light will strike?
Who can stay its penetrating might?
As though a mere man could dare understand
The power and passion, the soul's thrust
Of the first look from a lover's eyes.
Not I
Not I

What role would logic hope to play
In forming the words the heart must say?
As though it were easy thing to pause and think
And consider the elusive meaning
Of the first look from a lover's eyes.
Not I
Not I.

Better to ask the tides to retreat before your will,
The seasons not to change
For time to stand still
Than to demand a reason for love's first taste
Held in the gaze that takes
Your soul in a firm yet inexorable embrace.

And so it is with I,
For though close shuttered the city sleeps...

Devyn heard the first lines clearly. Then all the rest was a haze of syllables and sense impressions that hammered at his center. He was shocked, appalled, enthralled by the sheer effrontery of the poem. What lunacy! To openly profess love for the wife of the most powerful merchant-noble in the city! That Devyn had actually met Demona Anargi made the piece even more intoxicating. She was indeed a great beauty, altogether wasted on the aged, ugly, mean-tempered Sevire Anargi. Devyn remembered feeling a moment's pity for her that day Sevire brought her with him to Malom's stable. He had squelched Demona's interest in the training of their matched pair, tut-tutted and asked only after the price and delivery-date. That was nearly three years ago, and, as gossips reported, nothing at all had changed. Indeed, if the poem were any indication, it had gotten worse.

Devyn listened to the man draw his piece to a close, and the only thought that occupied his mind, besides the grudging appreciation of the poem's power, was that he listened to the words of a dead man.

The young man finished to uproarious applause of emotions unleashed by Festival and drink. Hats flew and crockery crashed. Sevire Anargi was the richest man in Pevana, but poorest in popularity. Hearing him cuckolded, even in verse, thrilled far beyond the average nose thumbing the less privileged indulged in. Festival or no, Pevana loved a scandal.

Devyn did not have time to surmise whose death sentence would be enacted first, the young cavalier's or his own, for as the shouting subsided the overseer rose and bellowed out his name as the evening's final participant. He swallowed a last mouthful for courage and forced his limbs to move toward the stage. He felt like a soul in two worlds: the criminal stepping up to his final moments at the gallows, and the prophet approaching the pulpit.

Devyn turned to face the crowd; a sea of features made stark and surreal by wine, want, and the moment. He took a breath; time slowed to almost nothing. He saw Sanya in that stilled moment, sitting with Avarran in the nearest corner to the stage. She looked back at him, pride and fear in her eyes, as if she knew he was about to cast his lot with his poem. Saymon leaned forward over the bar, wiping his hands on a rag; and there with him, the young cavalier looked directly at Devyn over the mug.

Impressions from the scene clarified for him in fits and starts: an old woman, snoring softly, the saddlemaker and his wife still cooing in a corner. Above, two shapes in dark clothing leaned a little further over the balcony fronting the upper rooms. Their faces were in shadow, but one a hand on the railing, a golden signet ring flashing on his finger. Faces Devyn knew. Faces he did not. He took them all in as time lingered, slowing as for a temporal breath before a cataclysmic plunge.

Kembril shuffled up to the end of the bar, hoisted a glass, and broke time's hold on the Cup. His old rheumy eyes shone with something deeper than pride. He seemed not to notice the man that followed him in.

Devyn took a breath, tossed his dice at Fate's table, and began:

In the last faint flickers of the last candle lit...

The words took him away. The timber and volume of his voice, as if Renia herself graced the moment, astounded him. Devyn closed his eyes and let himself go where the words took him. Each syllable acted like a stepping-stone on the pathway to history. Each word led him further on its course. With each stanza more and more of his old life sloughed off. By the time he finished to a stunned, then uproarious, response, Minuet's arrows had found his life, pierced his fate, and bound it beyond recall.

He did not mind. At least he did not until the Overseer bellowed for quiet to report the results.

"My friends! Take a pull and shut your gaps! We have a *tie*! Yes, that's right you drunken fools, a tie between Devyn Ambrose and Talyior Enmbron! A first! A first, I say, to ever happen in this competition! They shall split the prize!"

Devyn turned to look for Kembril, but the old man was already gone. So, too, was the man who had followed him in. He looked over heads, tried to get through, but Devyn was taken by the tide of humanity jostling him from all sides, calling, "A duel! A duel to decide the winner!"

Someone pummeled his back. Another thrust a wine glass into his hand, sloshing a portion of the contents over Devyn's sleeve. More voices joined the chanting. "A poetry duel! A duel! Let them have a duel!"

Devyn tipped back the glass, drained it in one gulp, and nodded to the overseer who bellowed, "All right, then! A duel it is!" The crowd urged him back towards the table set near the stage, pushed him into the chair there. Someone stuck a pen in his hand. Talyior Enmbron sat across from him, smiling and bleary as Devyn felt, and for the first time, face to face.

AFTER THE CLOYING PERFUMES OF THE PALACE, the trek to the Cup through the alleyways with their piles of refuse and smells animal and human had been like a tramp through a meadow after a spring rain for Donari. He had been cooped up too long amongst the courteous and coiffed. With every step, with every dust particle and pebble he disturbed on the way, he felt as though he were putting on an old and treasured shirt found once again at the bottom of a drawer.

"Ha, Senden!" he laughed, a little breathless from their climb up the old way to the open window on the second floor. "Remind me to get out more! Whew!"

He heaved himself up and into a darkened room at the end of the walkway in the rear loft of the Cup, once again using their old route from younger days when trouble was still fun and politics were folly. Donari paused, letting the memories of all those former beddings and nightly roils sluiced by wine and ale come back to him, while Senden finished his ascent, much more quickly and silently.

Senden opened the door a crack, surveyed the room below and was, apparently, satisfied, for he waved Donari through and to the table within. Senden ignited a wad of felt and lit a candle. As the light grew it revealed a decanter of wine in a bucket of still cool water.

"After watching the events of the afternoon," Senden murmured by way of explanation. "I figured I might need to observe."

"Shut up and pour the wine. This is not the first time you have anticipated me. I shouldn't be surprised. There was a time when folk who presumed to know their betters tended to disappear." Donari smiled into his cup. Senden chuckled softly.

"I do know you, but even after all these years I wouldn't presume to know you too well. In truth, I expected to be here, watching, alone."

"Then why two glasses?"

"Depending on how the night went, I didn't expect to be alone at the end of it."

"I'm sorry my curiosity has spoiled your plans."

"No plans. Just preparing in order to make the most of opportunity."

Donari took the wine and refilled his glass. "Can we observe the poets from the balcony without drawing attention?"

"We should have no trouble, my lord."

"Then fill your glass, man, and grab that chair, and let's get about our business."

They passed through the door and set their chairs next to the railing. They had full view of the common room awash in people and noise. Just as they sat down, the overseer of the revels stood up on the small stage and bellowed the rules and introduced the first poet.

Donari tried to keep his seat. He knew it would be more politic to watch unobserved, but as the competition progressed he found himself fidgety and restless. By the time the young tanner took the stage, he was leaning over the balcony. The spectacle drew him. His city's heart and soul lay within the words and rhymes of the competitors, reflected in the shouts of acclaim or derision from the crowd. Donari missed this, missed listening to the language of the streets and the passion. *Perhaps it is only the wine*, logic whispered. But his heart said no; it was truly the life of his city, and so, worth saving.

"Did you hear that, Senden?" he hissed. "How did that young fellow, the tanner, pack so much into so few words?"

Senden leaned over to whisper, "He is an excellent tack-maker, my lord. Several of the guards speak highly of his skill." The tanner left the stage accompanied by a pretty young woman. Senden made a small gesture her way. "But I know something you do not, and it ends with me wondering if the girl isn't behind the words, not the tanner."

Donari frowned, the ghost of a headache poking at his memory. "Was it she, then, who made a ruckus at the college?"

"You know?"

"I only heard something about that this afternoon. I assume you have more to tell me."

Senden grinned. "Don't I always? She is the daughter of old Streni Larossi, the tailor, and has petitioned the college several times for entrance. My man was one she took her . . . frustration out on as she left. I believe her name is Eleni."

"Interesting," Donari breathed. "I had an inkling of an idea when I heard of this at council, one I think you might—"

The overseer's voice boomed, startling Donari's thought from his head. A tall young man with golden hair and pretty features took the stage. Senden leaned over to whisper in Donari's ear. "Ah, see there? He is the one rumor claims is bedding Sevire's Demona. Talyior Enmbron, northern blood, a bit of a fop."

Donari stared down at the young man speaking his piece for the competition. The brazen honesty of Talyior's words appealed to Donari. They reminded him of his own youthful passions that the years and politics had jaded. Remorse churned in his belly, not simply for younger years but for those passions that made life worth living; and worth fighting for.

Talyior Enmbron proclaimed his love; a death sentence, if he knew Sevire. Donari admired the strength of the emotions even if he did not believe the subject worth the young poet's life. He sipped his wine, sighed and leaned towards Senden.

"What a glorious fool. I envy him his feelings, if not what will come of them."

"Sevire was absent for much of the spring and early summer. Since his return, the gossip has gotten louder. Now?" Senden drew a finger across his throat. The crowd roared, drawing Donari's eye back to Talyior. First the young woman to irk Byrnard, now this young fool to infuriate Sevire; it was as if Renia herself contrived to help him reclaim his city, humiliation by delightful humiliation. A smile began to tickle the corners of his mouth.

"Senden," he said, his signet ring tapping a tune on his cup, "let us see if we can contrive to keep this fool alive."

"I know that tone. Are you scheming?"

"Yes, I am, and you are going to help me. Do what you can to keep him alive. I have better use for him and his passions than a slit throat in an alley."

"As you wish, my lord," Senden said, just as the overseer shouted, "Devyn Ambrose! You're up!"

"Why do I know that name?" Donari whispered.

"He is the author of the piece I showed you this afternoon."

"That stripling?"

"He works for Malom Banley. You may remember hearing about his grandfather when you were younger. He was—"

Donari waved Senden silent as the dark-haired young man began to speak.

In the last faint flickers of the last candle lit
For glories long loved but now faded,
Is the key to the clue to find wisdom true
That the red-clad hordes have degraded.
"Proselytize! No Compromise!

Every syllable, the cadence and beat, drummed anger and frustration. Each line accused, "Listen you, lord! Why don't you take care of your people?"

We wander witless and beguiled
Altars thrown down, temples defiled
Fearful of shadows and mutterings foul
Bespeak us to our confusion
And so we lose our way.
Whence thou, Renia the Fair?

114

The invocation of deities struck him like a blow to the forehead, hammering him with the unescapable fact that while he contested with the likes of Sevire and Prelate Byrnard from his throne, he had allowed them to manipulate him and wrest the gods from the people and their city. In trying to do no wrong, Donari ended up doing nothing.

Well and truly chastised, indeed, shamed, he thrust himself away from the balcony and moved back into the room, heart racing, mind struggling to keep pace with the roil of his thoughts. Humiliating Byrnard and Sevire with the evening's poets was suddenly no longer a game; because of Devyn Ambrose, it was a maneuver.

"My lord?" asked Senden, following. "Is there something wrong?"

Donari turned his stricken face, his eyes drawn to the single candle on the table. He had indeed been Pevana's miscreant son; it was about time he became her Prince. It was time he purged his city of those like Sevire, who cared only for accounts and balances, profits and losses, control and dominance. Words spewed forth from mouths at a council table, agreeing to northern intervention into Pevana's internal affairs and such men saw an advantage in it.

And so temples burned.

They would burn no more.

"Did you expect this when you brought me that rumpled piece of paper this afternoon?" he asked Senden.

"You read the words—"

"But I did not *hear* them. I heard them now, and so did they." He jabbed a finger towards the cheering crowd. "Do you hear that?"

"They are the mob, my lord."

"They are Pevana!" The Prince began to pace. "I have failed them."

"You have ruled with skill and care—"

"Liar, Senden, and a terrible one at that. You're a smarter man than I. While I played, you planned. I have let priests and thieves like Sevire muddle their lives. I think it is time to do something. These two young men had some idea what will happen to them, but they tossed the dice anyway. And that young woman, the saddle-maker's wife, the tailor's daughter. She is a poet! A poet denied a voice, and why? I have let it happen, that's why. The way I failed her, I have failed my city. And now those two young fools could well die for the words passion forced them to speak, because Sevire is that powerful, and Byrnard that obsessed. That must change. We will keep them safe, for themselves and for Pevana itself. She needs her poets. I need their passion."

"A duel! A duel!" The chanting roared up from the crowd in the room below. Donari paused. Senden slipped through the door to investigate. He returned almost immediately, grinning sardonically and reclaiming his glass.

"It seems our two fellows finished in a tie. The mob wants a duel to determine a winner. It's getting rather odd down there."

Donari poured himself another small measure of wine. He raised it to his lips, whispered into the Cup, "Again your arrow strikes true, Minuet." Tipping it back, rushing thoughts adding spice to the vintage, he felt the fires of the spring rise up in his gut. Casan's smug arrogance and Sevire's fatuous greed collected as images forming a pattern. Ambition stalked Pevana's peace; he would have to for shame, for trust, for honor. He swallowed the last gulp down, setting his goblet down with a heavy hand.

"A duel of poets!" he said. "Could it be more perfect? They could be at it all night, which should keep them safe. It should give you time to set a few matters in motion for me."

"Such as, my lord?"

"Starting a new tradition, my man! We will ask our most wealthy and honorable Sevire Anargi to host a banquet of this first reading's winners. Pevana needs to honor her poets. We'll ask the Prelate to attend. It could prove a most illuminating evening, don't you think?"

"Illuminating, but dangerous for a pair of young fools."

"No more danger than they've already put themselves in. Not only will Sevire have his wife's lover castrated and quartered, by dawn every one of Byrnard's spies will be scouring the city looking for Devyn Ambrose. And that is where we come in."

"We?"

Donari laughed, the sound coming up from his gut, dizzying him. "And by *we* I mean *you*, of course! If our boys are to live to present their passions to the college in the finals, they will require some help. A feast to keep them in the public eye. We dare Sevire and Byrnard to act."

He moved to the window to begin the climb down into the night. Senden did not follow directly.

"Well?" Donari asked. "Have you honey in your shoes? Come on! We've work to do."

"I'm behind you, my lord," Senden said after a moment. "Never fear."

Donari looked up, one leg already over the sill. "Me, fear? Never, Senden. Never again."

Chapter 5.5: The Duel: Talyior

For Talyior, up until the final moments of the competition, the evening passed as an ocean of words, noise, leering, cheering faces, tears, joy, laughter, wine, beer and pipe-smoke. It fell about him like a well-worn cloak, snuggling up against his soul like a favorite pair of boots to the feet. He had been warmed and felt part of something much more sublime than a simple series of poems interposed between shouted orders for spirits and food. He had felt as though he were defining a dream, one of poets in the warm summer night sharing words and images that bathed the mob with light, masking the grotesquerie of human failing and, at least for a collective moment, ennobling all who listened.

All that changed when the overseer announced the results of the competition. Talyior felt his knees go weak and the blood threatened to rush from his face. After his poem he felt certain of victory. After hearing Devyn's, he felt just as certain of defeat. He forced himself to take a long pull from his mug to regain his balance as the Cup erupted into a chaos of thrown caps, shouted responses and huzzahs. He tossed off the last of his ale and made eye-contact with the auburn-haired young man he now knew as Devyn Ambrose, who quirked an eyebrow as he looked back at Talyior, as if he, too, were aware that something unusual had just happened, even if no one else seemed to realize.

He had to his raise his hands to cover his head as the crowd pummeled his back and shoulders, warmed to the notion of a duel. He recognized one of Sevire's bully-boys leaving as the crowd surged forward. He did not care. Not now. Not like this! His gambit had worked. He had not been last, but late enough in the evening. The crowd had been ready, no, they had needed, begged, pleaded, implored to hear about love; especially a daring, a tragic, a despairing love.

He had felt a thrill halfway through the piece, as though he were speaking to something beyond the sea of faces straining over the benches to hear his words. He was reaching out, beyond even Demona's isolated chamber, beyond Pevana's walls and her huddled humanity. For a moment there, in the words, he knew he translated the incomparable truth held in starlight.

Devyn's poem forced Talyior to reconsider, for the words conjured images of the country-folk around Talyior's home in the north and the ways they followed. Small shrines to unforgotten gods and spirits still found their place there despite the official status of the King's Theology. Devyn spoke not for himself, but for those folk. He dared to call forth the power and imagery of a simpler, more receptive time. Talyior felt on the edge of understanding the perspective of a world that he had never truly considered: a world outside of himself. Passion that led Talyior to a Pevana of dalliance and seduction led Devyn to reveal another, dreadfully serious side to life. Which was the more worthy? The rally to love or the rally to honor?

"Damn you!" Talyior cursed into his mug. "You wiley bastard!"

Shouts of "Ambrose!" and "Enmbron!" rose above the din, gathering voices with each repetition until the whole place reverberated in an antiphonal chorus. A fight started in a corner, quickly squelched by Saymon and his strong arms. Talyior felt nervous, wondrous, joyful laughter rise up from his gut. Win or lose, the images of this night would follow him forever; if he were lucky enough to live past the dawn.

Sevire's bravos had not returned and yet Talyior had no doubt they awaited him in the dark alleys and shadowed corners between the Cup and Gania's billet. But for the moment, he was safe, ensconced in the cacophony of mob-minded laud and being manhandled to a table near the front of the stage. In three days' time, both he and Devyn would advance to the final Hearing before the Prince and his court.

Two small piles of gold coin lay neatly stacked on the table—the prize they would share. Across from him, flushed and smiling as Talyior himself, Devyn Ambrose glanced up from the glinting gold, to speak words he never got the chance to say, for a hand came down on the table, a clink of coins toppling from their stacks.

"A tie is fine as fiddleheads for the Prince and his Hearing! But who gets bragging rights at the Cup, eh? We want to choose our own winner!"

The crowd took up the cry. "Choose our own! Choose our own!"

"Let them face off and we will choose!"

"A duel of words!"

"Poetry will prevail!"

The Overseer tried to restore order then gave up, shrugging to Saymon who, with a single bellow, brought the house back to order. Shouldering his way through the crowd he plunked down a pitcher of wine and another of beer. Digging in to his pocket, he pulled out a single gold coin and raised it up.

"Let them have the Prince's tainted sums," he said. "But let them duel for pride and the Cup's honest coin! A gold piece to the winner."

"I will write down words and phrases you give him," the Overseer called, warming to the game. "Each man will compose on the spot, using the list in his piece. Agreed?"

Talyior laughed. "Agreed!"

Devyn joined him. "Aye! But who goes first?"

Saymon balanced the single gold piece on his thumb. "Call it in the air. Food or taxes!"

Laughter followed the coin into the air.

"Food!" called Devyn. The coin spun, landing on the side showing vines, fish and grain, leaving the Prince's face in the pitted tabletop. Food it was. Talyior would have to go first.

Audience members shouted out words and phrases that the Overseer wrote down on his pad, waving in consternation for them to stop when he had enough.

"First round!" he announced. "You must both use the following: velvet, celestial dancing patterns, concentric circles, smokey, intangible visions. How much time should they have?"

Saymon sent someone back to the kitchens for a minute glass and added it to the spirits and the coin on the table.

"When the sands run out," Saymon said solemnly. "Let the poet speak."

Talyior and Devyn sat at opposite ends of the table. Someone poured Talyior a fresh mug and he took a long pull, one eye on Devyn, one eye on the glass. When the last grain of sand tumbled through the gap, he put down his ale, belched and said:

"In a surreal dream
Her diaphanous veil touches me,
A *velvet* breath of jasmine and mystery.
She leads, and I follow to grasp her
And together we create *celestial dancing patterns*
Of pleasure and pain,
Moving in *concentric circles*—
A compact universe of skin, taste and hair—
A cosmology of two. . .
And then I awake to desperate emptiness;
Aware of *smokey, intangible visions*
Lingering just beyond the edge of understanding,
Slowly dissipating
And then gone. . ."

"Ooohoo!" cried a woman when he finished. "We know what this one has on his mind, don't we!"

"That's good, uncommon good, eh?"

"Here, youngling." A prostitute wheezed near his ear. "Never you mind. I'll not disappear."

Talyior laughed along with the others even as he leaned away from the stink of her breath. And then it was Devyn's turn. Saymon turned the glass over. Devyn raised his wine in toast to Talyior's effort.

"Very creditable," he said as the sands dribbled down. "I trust this won't offend." And with that he offered up his response:

"We move in *concentric circles*
Speaking lies in *velvet* tones
That hide the truth.
We prattle on about the reasons the ways we are—
Odd partners in *celestial dancing patterns*
That produce *intangible visions* the wise
Would call prophecy.
But the common man knows it's all just *smokey*
Murmurings sent up the chimney
And in the end amount to nothing."

There was perhaps a second of silence from the crowd, and then everyone talked and shouted at once.

"The first! Enmbron's!"

"Don't be daft! The second! Young Devyn has it best!"

"Let's have it again!"

"Yes! One pass is not enough!"

"Again! Again, Masters!"

"I have a word, use *storerooms*."

"How about *silent thoughts*?" gasped the bad-breathed prostitute. "Sounds pretty, eh?"

"*Falling leaves.*"

"*Private longing!*"

"Here, here! Keep yer privates in your pants you drunken doxy-boy!"

"Quiet, all of you," Saymon bellowed, "or I'll cut you off!" He turned the glass over, but before time was up, Talyior, caught in the moment, tossed out his offering:

"*Silent thoughts* parade before me
Like muted scenes from a play,
Falling leaves of memory
Collect in the corners of my soul
Like the dust in the *empty storeroom*
Wherein I have placed my *private longing*
For you. . .

Devyn joined in with the others as they cheered Talyior's lines. Before Saymon could call for it, Ambrose called out his riposte:

"*Private longing* and sweet reverie
Play in my mind like memories from my youth
While tears of joy and pain mingle together
In a bittersweet rain of truth.
And yet secret desires remain *silent thoughts*
Refusing to reveal the depths of my emotion.
And so hopes fade like *falling leaves.*
The shattered, abandoned dream—it grieves,
Becoming part of the dust
In the corner of an *empty storeroom.*

The pattern thus begun went on and on through the late hours of the morning, back and forth, the both of them weaving the drunken spewing of their listeners into verse until it ceased to matter who was the victor; they would not let them stop. Talyior half-noticed the crowd had grown since the end of the hearing. Word must have spread about the unusual happenings at the Golden Cup, and patrons from the other establishments came to witness the duel. Devyn and Talyior did not disappoint. They spun out their words like witches casting glamours, leading them in a merry chase through a maze of rhyme and cadence. In the end, only Saymon and the snoring Overseer were left. All the others were passed out or gone home, exhausted but satiated by the night's entertainment.

Talyior's lips were a little numb. He lost track of how many pints he consumed. Across from him, Devyn looked in similar condition. The power of the experience would come with a price.

"Well, lads," Saymon croaked, bleary-eyed. "Is it enough?"

Talyior took one last swallow. "Enough?" he asked Devyn, who paused, looking carefully at the dregs in his wine glass before deciding.

"It is enough," he answered. "But who wins?"

"We all do." Saymon chuckled, placing another coin next to the original. "The Cup has never seen a night like this. Pevana herself has never seen the like. You'll be heroes when you wake up, I suspect sometime this afternoon, eh?"

The duelists pocketed their coins, retrieved their swords and made their way out into the early dawn light. The sun, just poking over the horizon outside the harbor, cast the entire square in lurid tones of black shadow and red light. Talyior noticed the hulking shape of the young saddlemaker making his sleepy way to his labors. He turned to face Devyn, thinking *What are you? Opponent? Friend? What has happened*? But instead pointed to the saddlemaker, saying, "At least that one got a few hours sleep, yes? His wife makes my shirts."

"She makes more than your shirts, if I heard correctly yestereve."

"What's that?" Talyior asked, and Devyn told him what he had overheard between the pair.

"Then you think she wrote the piece he spoke last night?" Talyior asked.

"I don't know, but I suspect so, if what I overheard before her husband spoke is true," Devyn answered. "In truth, I think she is the poet, and what is more, I thought her verse better than both of ours."

"If you are right, the poem takes on greater meaning. Yes, she is good. Better."

"But alas for her, she's a woman in these times."

"Alas for us all, I think." Devyn settled his sword belt and scabbard on his shoulders.

"More truth, there."

Both men paused, suddenly awkward and slightly embarrassed, as if minutes ago they had not mixed words and images together like a painter mixes his hues.

"In two days, then?" Talyior asked.

"Two days," Devyn answered, nodding his head and hurrying off.

Talyior kept to the shadows as much as he could, retracing his steps through the back alleys swiftly until he reached Gania's. Ignoring the kitchen door—doubtless locked anyway—he climbed up the drain spout, used his sword point to lever the latch of his window. He did not even bother to undress. Placing his sword on the table, tossing his hat at the peg and missing, he flung himself down on the mattress and fell asleep, his mind awhirl with a kaleidoscope of images: Demona, the Cup, the crowd, the saddlemaker and his wife, Ambrose and words, words.

Words.

Chapter 6: Plans within Plans

Plans within Plans, within a vortex spinning,
Evil, like Tolimon's cat, sitting there grinning
Waiting for the first mistake...

THE OUTLINE OF A PLAN PRESENTED ITSELF by the time Donari and Senden walked side by side through the gates of the palace, much to the consternation of the guards. He felt small remorse for the unease he caused by being out and about during festival with only Senden to watch over him, without even their knowledge. Donari waved off the apologies from the Captain on duty, too embroiled in his own thoughts to stop. Senden slowed to share a quick, quiet word; thereafter, the apologies stopped.

Full night still reigned; dawn saw some hours off. Behind and below them the city rolled on through its celebration. Two days later would see the populace exhausted and wrung out. Donari smiled, pausing, with one foot on the lowest level of the marble steps running up to the ornate palace doorways. He did not want to go in. Tonight felt like a portal back to his younger days when he still felt part of the city's life. Now the sounds of merrymaking in the city were cut off by thick walls and shuttered windows, by etiquette and intrigue, by the roles he had to play when he wore the diadem of power.

He had enjoyed himself immensely. He missed those reckless, intemperate days. He cocked an ear once more to capture a sense of the life he had been forced by station to give up. Then he turned and paced swiftly up the stairs and through the huge double doors that swung open as he approached.

Donari shook his head, chuckling softly to himself. *Have I become this predictable? This watched?* The answer was as clear as those doors swinging wide. In younger days, he kept folk off balance to make use of the leverage it gave him. Such unbalancing foiled all his mother's marriage plots. It used to confound his grandfather. Life had been something of a game to Donari, despite his princely state. Pevana went on about its business despite the absence of any real seriousness in his rule. He had thought his methods irreverent and daring. But now he realized his quest to keep all others unbalanced had cost him his *own*. Complacency was the bed-fellow to self-absorption; a dangerous pairing for those in power. He had thought himself subtle, but he had just been stupid, but no more. Not after tonight. His grandfather had been a hammer. Donari would be the rapier point, insinuating himself between the ribs and stirring up the vitals of his adversary's plans.

He passed into the wide entry hall. Cryso appeared to take his cloak and hat. He made no mention of his Prince's appearance, reeking of the Maze and two hours after midnight. Cryso simply took the garments and motioned forward a sleepy page holding a tray with two goblets. Donari took one and sipped the dust of the city away. *Position does have its perks,* he grudgingly admitted. Motioning to Senden to take the other and follow, he headed for his library instead of his bed.

"My thanks, Cryso!" the Prince tossed over his shoulder. "See that I am not disturbed until true morning."

The library, his comfort and solace in a palace so grand there were rooms he had not seen since taking the circlet, waited for him as if an old friend. A lamp turned low on the desk, the remainder of the bottle of the wine in his goblet, his comfortable chair pulled up to the window, Donari might have sighed if Senden were not present. Taking a pen and inkhorn from a drawer in his desk, he pushed them over to his chief spy and friend.

"How is your penmanship?"

"Sufficient, my lord."

"Excellent! I'll talk, you write. And then I suggest you grab an hour's rest or so. I'll want you to deliver this yourself. I want to *know* it has reached the right hands, not hope."

"I understand, my lord."

"Right, let us see now. Standard salutation, that sort of thing, then how does this sound? 'Sevire, my dear fellow! It has come to my attention that we should do our utmost to make this festival memorable for our honored Prelate. Most of the major houses are in the city as well. What better way to honor the victors from the first reading, as well as impress the Prelate, than a banquet attended by the most noble Pevanese houses?

"'With preparations for the finals already underway here at the palace, I can think of no better place than your beautiful home. Tonight. There should be plenty of time to send messengers about the city. I will gladly supply a troop of pages. Anything you need from the palace kitchens, please do not hesitate to send word. Yours, etc, etc.' Well?"

Senden scribbled out a copy, his smile deepening with each word. "It should send him into apoplexy."

"Good! Then it is perfect."

"He will seek to use this command to his advantage."

"Let him try. The fat fool."

"He's fat, my lord, but he's no fool."

The Prince looked over the rim of his goblet. "Neither am I," he said, draining the wine and placing the empty cup down on the desk. "Sevire needs to learn that."

"And the Prelate?" asked Senden, moving to refill their glasses with the bottle he had purloined from Cryso's tray.

"Aye, there's a double bonus, eh?" Donari paused to take a drink. "He needs to know it too. It is a small cry of rebellion, perhaps, but a cry nonetheless." He gave a tired, rueful chuckle that ended in a sigh and stared at the raised decoration of his goblet. "Ah, me," he said quietly. "Is it too little, too late? Have I lost my city before ever realizing it was being stolen?"

Senden did not answer at first. He put down the pen and took up his goblet, draining it in one long draught before placing it on the desk next to Donari's. "I think, my lord, my friend," he said with finality, "that perhaps it has taken a while longer than wisdom might have allowed, but it is not too late. Pevana and its people are yours to rule, not Sevire's or Casan's to use. It is time they understood that. Your grandfather would be proud of you."

"Truth?"

"Always, my lord." Senden stood, took the copy of the note and turned to go but paused at the door. "I'll find some of the ceremonial gold ink for this. As well as the men I will send to watch over our poets, I would like to place a few on the grounds of House Anargi tonight in case it gets ugly. I suspect he will be hiring extra help. I want that help to be ours if possible. With your leave—"

"You have it. Of course you do, Senden. Make your arrangements, but get some rest, too."

"Yes, my lord."

Senden bowed and left, closing the door behind him, leaving Donari alone with his thoughts. Pouring a small measure of wine, he sat in his comfortable chair set by the window, and swirled it in his goblet. He gazed out over the city, *his* city, letting the pride wash through him.

He thought of those poets in the Cup that night, of young Ambrose who had packed more passion in his one poem than Donari had in a lifetime in the public eye. He had dabbled in verse once, and the contrasts between himself and Devyn could not be more striking. Ambrose threw his intent like a gauntlet at the feet of polity. Donari tucked his among the library books as a game, a series of questions for posterity.

He still remembered one of the last poems he composed. No doubt it still lay stuck amongst its fellows in a bound volume of Pevanese verse:

As the young man in hope of change,
All of my prior doubts remain:
How to be different and yet the same.

And what if I live out all my days
In pursuit of lofty aims
Only to find that wisdom never came?

Donari once thought he knew his city and the Old Ways the way Ambrose did, but he didn't, or he had forgotten. The Prince had played at blurring the lines between the classes, pretended to be one of the people before going back to his palace and the comfort of plenty.

Like you did tonight.

The Prince hung his head, shame overwhelming the pride. He had fobbed off King Roderran's politics, played the petty games of the merchant houses in Pevana off each other, all along missing the finer point: the Old Ways of Devyn Ambrose's deep passion were being destroyed not as reform to greater things, but were being made a sacrificial offering to a game of political power. Those moving the pieces cared nothing for gods, old or new.

The stakes were far, far higher than Donari had assumed. Power was indeed being gathered in the city, and the trail led north, to Perspa and King Roderran—callous, vengeful, pragmatic Roderran. And his agents were the Prelate Byrnard Casan and Sevire Anargi, zeal and avarice, present and well placed to do his bidding. And but for a trio of poets, they might have continued unimpeded.

Donari rose from his chair, set his goblet down carefully lest his anger send it sailing. Change was inevitable. Between Sevire's foolish greed and Casan's false fervor, something was sure to pass away forever. But the Prince would strive to keep the memories of the Old Ways Gods and the Pevanese identity intact.

Donari questioned the depth of his own faith on the best of days, but he sent a silent prayer to Renia, Boriman and the others as he climbed the sweeping staircase to his apartments, in the name of Devyn Ambrose, a true believer if ever there was one. Exhaustion swarmed him like shadows between hall-tapers. He threw himself on the down-turned bed, such pert servants he had, and willed his mind to stillness. He needed rest, for that evening he would have to perform like never before—for Pevana, his city.

PRELATE BYRNARD CASAN LISTENED as Jaryd Corvale presented his observations from his evening at the Cup. The Prelate had given him enough men to spread about the city to search for their disruptive quarry, but folk were bent more on celebration than answering questions. The fool's inability to persuade without force did not help. In the end, on orders, Corvale insinuated his men in the taverns selected for the competition readings. He was either competent or lucky, for he had chosen the Golden Cup for his evening's watch.

"Tell me." Byrnard breathed from behind fingers steepled at his lips. "You say you saw him?"

"Yes, my Lord Prelate," Corvale answered. "I got there just as it started. Stood in the back behind a one-legged beggar. He stank. The wine stank. Poetry, bah!" He spat the word like a curse. "But he was there."

Unsophisticated as well as unimaginative, excellent. "Do go on." Byrnard poured each of them a measure of wine. Corvale accepted the glass gladly and took a long pull.

"I listened through all the silly, sorry business," he said. "No wonder this place seems so soft. Too much energy spent on idle pursuits."

"I do not want your opinion, Jaryd; I want your report. What did you discover?"

Corvale put down the glass unfinished, chastened. "Ambrose, he spoke after the one tupping Anargi's wife. The mob went mad for his lusty drivel. Thought Ambrose might beg out, but he stepped up and spoke his piece. Mob went wild again."

"Did they now?" Byrnard thumbed his lip. "Interesting. And you are certain Ambrose is the same one who upset Aemile in the square?"

"I recognized him right away. I had Asina scratch out what he could of the poem he squawked."

Byrnard snatched the scrap of paper from Jaryd's hand. At least the man had the fortitude not to wince. It took only a scan to know

131

the lines scrawled there matched those in the copy he had burned that afternoon.

"And then?" he asked, setting the scrap aside.

"And then what, sir?"

"Did you congratulate Ambrose on his success? What did you *do,* Corvale?"

Jaryd's jaw twitched. His face darkened slightly. Prelate Byrnard suppressed the urge to smile.

"They were still going on with that poetry nonsense when I left," Jaryd said. "I couldn't stand any more, so I set one of my men outside to follow him, see where he lives."

"Good thinking," Byrnard said, surprised by Corvale's caution. "He must be silenced, of course, but we must take care with this one. He'll be a hero to the mob after tonight. King Roderran would not abide a bungle now."

"Accidents happen." Jaryd's eyes narrowed, his clenched jaw loosened in a grin. "This *is* festival."

"Yes it is, so choose your moment with some care."

"With the utmost care, my Lord Prelate. Devyn Ambrose will be dead by this time tomorrow."

Devyn Ambrose; a nondescript sort of name to be sure. Byrnard found the young man's courage and effrontery strangely curious. Up to the present, few in the city had openly questioned anything about the particulars of his campaign of reform and removal. The effort lingered in the last stages of a year long process. There had been whispers, most of them inconsequential; the loudest and most insistent easily rendered impotent. The city had seen more than a few corpses floating in the tidal scum since the spring.

Ambrose's demise was a little more complicated, considering recent events. A poem? Foolery, like the Old Ways themselves. Too much superstition and myth; not enough pragmatism and acceptance. Not enough order. It tweaked Byrnard's latent curiosity, why a young, vital man might waste his time, even risk his life, in such a way.

"Of course he must be dealt with," he said. He rose to his feet. "But if you could contrive to find and corner him, I would like to spend a few moments with our hero before you slit his throat."

"Yes, sir."

"Yes, who? I didn't quite hear you."

Again the clenched, twitching jaw. "Yes, my Lord Prelate."

Prelate Byrnard Casan watched Jaryd leave and judged him a grumbling bully who would take out his frustrations on someone unwary and likely smaller. As long as Corvale accomplished his tasks, the Prelate did not care.

DEMONA ANARGI LAY IN HER SILKEN SHEETS, hot, awake and restless. Sevire's snores rumbled on in the next room. Her devoted husband had retired to his rest after an excess of wine and food without even trying to cajole her into his bed. She had not dared sneak out to the readings, but word of Talyior's poem reached her nonetheless.

Appalled that he should be so bold, she confessed herself excited at the same time. She turned over in bed, the movement of her skin over the sheets hardened her nipples. She moaned, arching her back and spreading her legs so that the sheets touched her.

Oh, Talyior, Talyior! How I want you—to come climbing over the garden wall, to whisper his lines into her ear as he entered her, his chest pressing up against her breasts as he thrust away at the despair of her days.

Sweat began to form her cleavage. It beaded, coalesced and ran down her stomach to pool in her navel. Her fingers found a nipple, just as his had done through the summer. She felt herself grow moist, wanton—lust incarnate. She stretched and lost herself in a delicious moment, mind awhirl with images of Talyior—his face, his lips, his hands, his phallus, a shadowy figure poised above her; his voice out of the darkness, professing passion and conviction, caressing her with sound, taking her to places Sevire never could.

A ridiculously loud snort, shattered the moment, scattered her conjuring. She opened her eyes and sat up. In the moonlight opulence of her bedchamber, Demona pouted.

Being alone was a horror, but being without all her fine things was worse. She cursed herself a coward. Talyior risked everything for her love, but even contemplating leaving Sevire made her quake in fear. He would crush her before he let her go. He would kill her if she tried.

Unfairly as she treated him, Talyior always came back. Men always did, even Sevire. Until Talyior, her poet, she had come to accept the disappointment of bedding her husband. He liked to have her touch him, to tease and wheedle him to attention, pleasuring him orally or with her hand. In truth, she preferred that to the weight of his corpulent flesh pressing her into the bedding. Talyior made her sweat. Sevire merely exhausted her.

She looked around the room, the pale moonlight illuminating the scope of her life: a collection of unguents, gilt mirrors, beaded combs and baubles that spilled out from several small, trayed boxes. Demona satisfied herself by never being satisfied. The dress she had ordered for festival would never wear out from over-use. It hung on its stand waiting for its next, and likely last, exposure. She tried to recall a time when she would have been happy with less, a time, perhaps, when love would have sufficed. But she had been too long in a loveless match to discern. She loved her things instead. Sevire surrounded her with beautiful tools; their only purpose to help her retain her beauty and soften her cage. She needed them. She led a tactile life, and what emptiness she perceived, she let Talyior fill.

She rose from the bed, naked and glowing in the moonlight, and moved to the open window where an offshore breeze tickled across her skin, drying the space between her breasts. Turning, she saw herself reflected in the full-length mirror next to her clothes chest. She smiled at the fullness of her figure, the curve of her thigh. She ran both hands down the small of her back to cup each smooth buttock the way Talyior did when he took her from behind.

The memory made her smile deepen, and she forgot, for a moment, about despair.

Chapter 7: The Day after Dicing with Destiny

DEVYN WOKE UP RATHER QUICKLY to a full bucket of water tossed in his face and Malom's iron fist trapping Devyn's hand inches short of his sword hilts.

"Now, now, none of that sauce!" A knee on his chest kept him down. "You are lucky I didn't use the blade to stick you myself, and you thinking of sticking me? Me, who's given you plenty of good work these last years?"

Devyn struggled half-heartedly. "And who lets me sleep in a stable."

Malom's face, unlovely and framed by dark hair and straggly beard, broke into a genuine smile that softened the features—a little.

"It's a good stable, when you keep it clean anyway." He sniffed loudly, let Devyn up and tossed him a towel. "And by the smell I'd say you've a deal of cleaning to do. So, up and about it, boy! Sanya tells me you made quite a stir at the Cup last night. Stupid move. Stupid."

"Maybe." Devyn rubbed his hair. "But I won."

"True, so I've heard. But what did you win, I ask? What could you possibly gain from putting yourself out like that?"

"Attention."

"Ha! Attention! For the likes of you and me that can be a bad thing. If I get noted for the quality of my tack, the polish I train into horses. That's all to the good. But there's other attention that would be better avoided."

"What if that's the attention I wanted to attract?"

"Then I'd say you're more the fool than I feared."

Devyn dried his face, hiding it in the towel. Malom had been good to him, a friend. What was done was done, and he was still alive. For the moment. He tossed the towel back and said, "It was a competition, Malom. I won. Fifteen golds! And I'm in the finals. That's good, right?"

A mixture of pride and fear softened Malom's scowl.

"A competition?" Malom grimaced. "Rolling dice with drunks more likely. You've slept way past time. See to the feed and water and then take the Tilloti pairs through their paces. That's the only competition you need worry about, boy. Get it done or feel my boot up your arse!"

"Such compassion for the weary," Devyn sighed as he shrugged on a work shirt.

"Compassion is for them as can afford it. You've a job to do, festival or no; competition or no."

"I wanted to find Kembril, to ask him about last night. He was there but left just after I finished my piece. I wanted to tell him about what happened afterwards."

Malom twisted the towel in his hands. He looked at it instead of Devy, saying, "If half of what Sanya spewed this morning—sorry boy, but I kept her out of here—if half of what she said was true, then doubtless Kembril peg-leg already knows. Your name and that of the rug-merchant's brat are all over the city and every crack in the Maze. You've stirred up something lad, and I don' want to see you skewered for it. Now, eat a bite and get to the horses. Best you stick to your work today and lay low back here. If you got to see Kembril, do it later. You got me?"

Devyn noted the flat bread and some fruit on a plate on his camp desk. He picked up an apple and bit into it. Malom liked to grump, but he cared. "Got it, Mal," he said. "Horses first, Kembril afterwards."

Devyn moved through his chores by habit, not thought. Memories of last night's experiences inflamed his mind all over again. He had never felt so connected with words and their power before. The way the crowd responded to his piece thrilled and frightened him. He felt weary, emptied from the effort. And Talyior, with whom he had composed, had been a stranger until the magic of rhyme; but now, what? A friend? Collaborator? Competitor?

All, Devyn thought, and in that thought understood: what they had done, the way the crowd responded to their efforts, pointed to something beside chance opponents. He sensed a kinship in the tone and tenure of their feelings. As Devyn shoveled hay into mangers, he smiled at the thought. *A friend would be a good thing.* He wondered if Talyior felt the same.

And yet, not quite buried by his fervor, Malom's warning still rankled. Devyn had gone to the competition knowing he risked his life. In doing so, he found something to live for. He shrugged off the negative thoughts, his movement causing the horse he groomed to shy away. Patting the animal's neck, regaining his own sense of euphoria, he soothed, "I'm not skewered yet, dear heart. If luck is mine, that will hold true long enough for me to speak in the finals."

He finished his tasks by mid afternoon, fully awake and surprisingly eager to test the limits of that luck he hoped for. He wanted to hear some of those rumors bunching Malom's muscles in a knot, and the best person to go to in order to get the real story was Kembril. He washed and dressed himself to go out and find his old mentor, but before he could make the stable door Sanya came bursting in, followed closely by Malom. Sanya held a piece of paper in her hand.

"Look! Look!" she cried, thrusting the paper at him. "You are invited to House Anargi! For a Banquet honoring all of last night's winners!"

He took the note from her, putting up a hand to forestall her embrace while he read it. It was an invitation, in gold ink with flowing script, requesting his presence at House Anargi that evening for *a little entertainment in honor of the skills of Pevana's poets.*

The image of the corpulent Sevire flashed to his mind, followed quickly by the images from Talyior's poem last night. He read the note again. *An honor? Ha! Not by half.*

"Well," he said. "After last night, I expected an arrest warrant or something, not an invitation to a party."

"So you'll not go?"

Devyn glanced her way, noted her pout, and then at Malom scowling.

"Of course I will go," he said. "To turn down such an invitation would be foolish."

"Oh, oh!" Sanya squealed, crushing him to her breast.

"You're a fool!" Malom grumbled.

Devyn gently extricated himself from Sanya. "I'm going. Alone," Devyn said. Sanya stopped trying to impale him with her nipples.

"Alone?"

"Going is the best way to ensure I survive for the finals before the Prince at the palace in two days time," he said, folding the paper and putting it in his pocket. "But I'll not risk your safety, Sanya. I'll tell you all about it when I get back. In great detail, I promise."

"If you get back." Malom spat. "I suppose I might as well start looking for a new trainer."

"Have some faith," Devyn told him.

"If you've not noticed, that's not a wise thing to have these days neither."

Sanya leaned into Devyn, this time tenderly. He put his arm around her, smoothing the gooseflesh prickling her arms. She said, "Of course you will tell me," and pulled away. "And so you do not look like a rag-tag-minion, give me your clothes to set in order for tonight. I'm finished with the day's load. I have time."

"Sanya, my sweet, I am in your debt."

He gave her the clothes he wore last night; they would have to suffice for the banquet as well. She left to find water and a flat iron. Malom stayed while Devyn buckled his sword to his belt and took down his wide brimmed hat from the peg above his pallet. The desire to see Kembril now consumed him. But as he made to pass by Malom to the door, his employer's solid palm on his chest forestalled him.

"You'll end up stuck, boy, mark my words."

Devyn touched his sword hilt. "I'm not defenseless."

"You are still senseless to risk the streets."

Devyn pulled the hat down over his brow, head. "See? None will mark me."

"I'll use your wages for a nice funeral!" Malom called after him.

"But I am alive now," Devyn from the stable door. "And while I am, I want to live, not cower in shadows."

Outside, the sun neared its zenith. Within minutes, Devyn felt the waves of heat beating down the life of the city. Everywhere he looked, people moved as if the totality of Pevana were struggling to recover from the excesses of the festival's first night. He laughed under his breath as he walked, for despite his long night and earlier labors he felt light and connected with all he saw. The veiled threats in the rumors Malom passed on to him, and the knowledge he was *known* about the city, sparked his expectation of adventure awaiting him at day's end.

He passed a group of youths clumped in various attitudes of repose underneath the shade of a tavern awning, victims of too much wine and revels, or perhaps unwilling to waste any time going home. The summer festival turned the peoples' behavior upside down. Logic and reason removed themselves from the domain of sane choices. Life in the extremes of fun took on its own set of rules and priorities; where and with whom one slept frequently became a matter of complete indifference.

He walked down towards the Maze, passing through the main square where he witnessed the beginning of the festival and turned down the side arterial that ran in front of the Cup. On any other day he would stop for words and a mug with Saymon Brimaldi, but he felt the need for talk with Kembril more than the joys of ale.

Devyn noticed a figure detach itself from the shadows of a doorway as he crossed the small square fronting the Cup. The figure, a man, paced him as he moved down the street. The hard lessons learned living in the Maze shoved aside daydreams and visions of poetic glory. He glanced casually at the shape and recognized the same fellow who had stood behind Kembril at last night's reading.

He kept moving, affecting an unhurried gate, even pausing to scan the wares at one of the stalls. As he fingered the fine workmanship of a collections of shawls, he cast quick glances around him and noted his follower had been joined by several others, rather large looking fellows in scruffy clothing, but all of whom bore a red swatch of cloth tied to their belts.

He moved on.

Devyn did not bother trying to convince himself, as he walked slightly faster now, that these men were footpads who wanted his won gold. He had written, and he had spoken, hoping to call attention. Only now, being followed by these red-swatched men, did he truly understand the danger. With each step, Devyn passed further from his old life. He felt Renia's Grace upon him; Minuet's arrows focused on the shadows behind a rickety stall hung with copper and tin pots, pointed to the narrow alleyway beyond.

He paused at the stall. Out of the corner of his eye, he saw his follower raise his hand, and his fellows halted. Fishing a gold coin from his pocket, Devyn tossed it to the old tinker sitting on a stool behind his wares. The man caught if deftly, looking up in question.

"For your troubles," Devyn said. The tinker half rose as Devyn reached up and yanked the crosspiece of the stall. He dodged through before the whole thing came crashing down in a messy, musical heap of tumbling cookery. Devyn dashed off down the shadowy alley, laughing, loudly enough he hoped, for his pursuers to hear him over the sound of all that crashing.

JARYD CORVALE STOOD BREATHING HEAVILY in the heat, frustrated by the ease of his target's escape into what looked like a sea of tents and hardscrabble structures. He turned to his men, all in service to the Prelate, but his to command until Casan said otherwise.

"You," he said, pointing at the nearest to him. "Off with you back to the Prelate and report. And you two," he pointed to the next nearest, "find the other scouting groups and bring them back here. It's time we stirred this cesspool to see what surfaces. You others stay here with me."

He turned back to the opening to the alley. Dust hung thick in the air and combined with the taint sweat and refuse, creating a stifling effect. He sniffed and suppressed the urge to gag.

"We've been burning the wrong places in this city," he coughed. "We should set this latrine to the torch and do Pevana a favor!"

A dog rushed out of a nearby doorway, snarling and barking and lunging at Jaryd's boot. A well-time kick at its head sent the beast into whimpering retreat. Jaryd took a handkerchief from his shirt pocket, wiped the spittle from his boot toe, and tossed the soiled cloth onto the ground.

"I'd give my commission for a torch right now," he muttered. To his gathering men, he said, "Let's flush us out a poet."

Jaryd Corvale and his men passed through the irregular pathway made by the dwellings of the poor, rooting through buildings and pulling down tents and awnings as they went. Voices raised in anger. Children cried. And rumor of the dark, ruthless Temple Guard sped to every corner of the Maze.

DEVYN SPED THROUGH THE TWISTS AND TURNS of the Maze with remembered skill and grace. In moments, all sound of pursuit vanished. He slowed to a walk, hot and blown, laughing softly at the thrill of it all.

He moved on in search of Kembril, although he knew exactly where he would find him at this time of day, and indeed came upon him exactly where he thought he would: in the hollow of the up-thrust roots of the great oak, fast asleep.

Devyn crossed the small open space, mindful of the the faces of the local children staring at him from doorways and tent flaps. Had Kembril just finished telling one of his tales? Or were they still waiting?

Passing quickly underneath the shadows cast by the tree's vibrant canopy, Devyn took his customary seat on the knee of the left hand root. He hesitated suddenly, despite what followed behind him, for Kembril looked deeply asleep. The crease in the old man's cheek looked even deeper than it had the day prior. The rumble in the rise and fall of the aged chest seemed deeper. Kembril had ever been rheumy in Devyn's memory, but he sounded now as though the consumption had finally broken through to strike deep into his vitals. Sorrow at the thought settled around Devyn's heart.

His news of a formal banquet did not seem so important anymore. The humorous tale of his adventures with the Priest in the square and the joys of the first night's competition lay stillborn in his silence as he waited for his friend to awake, if he would awake. Minutes passed. Then Kembril's breathing shallowed and he coughed, and in the cough he cocked open an eye.

"So," he rasped. "You have found me out yet again. I really should find a new napping spot. How am I to get any rest if you keep finding me?" He flashed a sidelong look up at Devyn and shifted himself more upright.

Devyn caught the look in the old man's eyes and his fears eased somewhat. Death might have crept nearer since yesterday, but there was life yet left in that glance.

"You need me to find you, old man, to wake you so you can hobble about telling your tales and thus earn your bread and wine for the day. You'd die of thirst and starvation without me."

Kembril gave a wheezy chuckle and patted Devyn's knee. "'Tis true, doubtless, all true," he said. "And you need me to give you someone to brag to when you set the whole city aflame. That was quite the incendiary piece you performed last night lad. Very creditable."

"Creditable?"

"It was a beginning."

"Only a beginning? Tell that to the bravos who tailed me on the way here. I think they were the Prelate's men."

Kembril suppressed a cough with a sip of the wine skin he produced from his bag of belongings. "And so," he wheezed. "You've come to tell me a tale for once. Tell!"

Devyn obliged, finding it easier than he suspected to regale the old man with the events of the evening after Kembril's departure.

"I WONDERED WHY YOU LEFT," Devyn finished breathlessly. "The fun had only just begun. We had to duel for the prize."

Kembril smiled wanly. Such youthful passion; it was good to see it flush Devyn's cheeks.

"Ah, now, I may look the picture of health, lad, but my missing leg still aches of an eve'n. In truth, I went to see and hear you. I did both and enjoyed the seeing and the hearing and so left to seek the solitude of the dust. Tell me of your duel."

"The poet I tied with and I had a duel of verse to decide a winner for the mob! Kembril, you should have heard it! I've never felt such a power of words and rhyme in all my days."

Kembril silently scratched the end of his stump while Devyn prattled on. And yet he did not listen idly. There were many who could relate a tale, but Kembril had met few he could call true poets. Every year he went to the readings and scoffed at the offerings put forth with such pomp. Invariably he found them tedious and flat; mouthings of skill rather than the real gift. Kembril's wordsmithing always found and held an audience. That he chose for his venue the city streets rather than the halls of the college was his own affair.

He did not care if the upper classes heard him. He never craved their preferment. There had only been one among them who Kembril could acknowledge on a par with his own skills. He entered the lists of the competition as a young man back in the days when Devyn was a dusty, wild savage of the Maze. Kembril remembered that one, for he held the same sort of passion that Devyn held now. He smiled at the memory, even as he listened to Devyn's tale of his trek to meet him here at the tree. They were alike in some ways, Dev and that other poet, he decided. They both were like water damned up by the stones of grief and custom, mortared by mistrust and expectation. Power could change a person, and the dreams that motivated them. A simple coronet of silver could take away the words, and seal the bargain with a signet ring.

He looked up once again at his former pupil. In the glamour gifted to those near death, or simply the afternoon sun framing such a face, Kembril saw not just the face but the young man's future. Devyn spent his life since losing his parents thrusting against his own barriers, angry, afraid, and uncertain. And then in sequence came the temple fires, yesterday's conversation, and last night's apotheosis.

It was time. It was fate. Such passion. A snippet of an old song came to him then:

"And there were none to mark his way
For the passing there was one and the same
As 'hello' or 'goodbye'
'You were my son!' the old man cried. 'But what was I?'"

He returned to himself to realize Devyn's voice had grown silent, his eyes staring worriedly down upon him.

"Where did you go?" Devyn asked simply.

"To the beginning of one story." He paused to sip once more from the wineskin. "And the ending to another."

Devyn's perplexed expression made him laugh, a laugh that ended in a rheumy cough.

"Now, now, don't try and tell me you can't see the signs? I doubt I'll last through the year."

"You would if you would take care of yourself," Devyn responded, emotion making his voice harsh. "But you won't listen."

"Quite right, boy, I won't listen. It has been my calling to get other folk to listen. Besides, it has gone far beyond that."

"What do you mean?"

"Come, come, lad. Don't be so simple. You can surely see Renia's hand in all this? You are her voice. The voice of the Old Ways. Tales that I cannot tell you will now take up. You are involved. You must speak. These years since you were an imp at my knee have led you here, to this moment of action. The time is ripe. You are Renia's poet. You must make them hear."

"It is difficult to believe my words will be enough."

"Ah, they won't be lad. But they're a start. Words and politics have always been bedmates, especially when the words are true. In this time, in this place, I think all you need do is live and be true to your words, to the way you feel about things. It will spark the same in others. You spoke of the joy you felt when you and your opponent went at each other last night. Remember it! Such joy is in danger of passing away. Pevana is at the sword point of change, my young friend. Everything that has happened this past year suggests it. Anyone who has lived through a campaign can see it. I'm sure there are those in Pevana who do. Ask Avarran."

"I doubt Avarran would agree that simple poetry can—"

"Simple poetry!" the old man sputtered, struggling to get his one leg under him so he could stand. "Renia's Grace, you must be joking! The only weapon against the politics of lies is truth! True words about true emotions. Everything counts, then! Even your opponent's romantic descant has a role to play. Being true may cost both of you your lives, but such is the pity of the times."

Kembril settled his crutch under his armpit and jabbed a bony finger into Devyn's chest, spittle flying from his lips as he spoke. "Last night you became what you were meant to be, boy, never doubt. You have known life in the Maze. You've a banquet tonight. See to it you survive to attend. You are not going for the gossip or the meats and wine. You go for truth."

Devyn leaned a hand on the bark of the tree as he bent down to gather Kembril's belongings. His body tensed, and the old man knew the boy was feeling it: the odd thrill of recognition, of awareness as if great power were just beneath the outer layers, coursing through the deep roots, spreading throughout the Maze. Kembril placed his hand beside Devyn's, gently caressed the bark and sensed, ever faint and far away, interest.

DEVYN HANDED KEMBRIL'S WINESKIN over to him, still dazed by the odd tremor that had coursed through his body. The old man took it and squeezed off a long swallow that left him laughing and coughing at the end of it. Rheumy eyes came to his, falling from mirth to caution. He gazed over Devyn's shoulder.

"If I were you," he whispered, "I'd loosen that blade of yours."

Devyn spun, blade drawn, and there, just outside the shadows of the tree, stood the man who had tried to intercept him in the square and behind him, several men, all with swords drawn.

"There's someone who wants a word with you, boy." The man inched closer. "Come along without a fuss and you might not get hurt."

Kembril hopped out of the way, barking, "Who are you? What need for this? This is festival, fool!"

The man glanced briefly at Kembril. "Who I am is none of your concern, old man. Hop off, and leave well enough alone."

So this is it, the battle begun with my words. Devyn moved to put himself between Kembril and the stranger. He tossed over his shoulder, "Go, Kembril. Take your skin and find a bed somewhere."

"Dev—?"

"Best take his advice, old man," the man said, "lest you gain the Prelate's interest as well."

"Ah," cackled Kembril, backing away towards the door of one of the tenement buildings that lined the open space around the tree. "So our General Priest has come south has he? I thought I heard that gossip ruffle about. Then would you be his guard dog, Jaryd Corvale?"

"What's it to you? Now move along or—"

"Or what? Think you he'd want a murder in broad daylight with his name attached? Look around you, fool. There will be witnesses."

Jaryd paused. Devyn moved slightly to the right gauging his chances. Behind Kembril, he spied a row of little faces in windows and doorways just as the old man put fingers in his mouth and gave a shrill whistle. "A tale!" he called. "Time for a tale!"

The children of the Maze swarmed out of their hovels, surrounding Kembril and blocking the path between Jaryd Corvale and the old man as effectively as a dam. Devyn let his sword dip. Not even the Prelate's men would kill children; and not even this Corvale could do so in broad daylight.

"Accidents happen, friend," Jaryd smiled. "Your verses have landed you in the shit. This cesspool of a place might hide you for a time, but it won't hide you forever."

"It's best you and yours leave now," Kembril said. The square began to fill with people, men, women, and children young and older. Some held staves in their hands; a few had knives. "This cesspool is home to many souls, souls willing to defend it."

"Assault the Prelate's representatives and the city will burn." Jaryd started backing away, addressing the crowd. "This is the Lord Prelate's business. The King's Theology charges us to investigate all lapsed thinking and reform when needed. Will you protect those who will be your downfall? Haven't enough temples already burned?"

Fury rose like bile from Devyn's gut. His sword hand ached. He said, "Leave now and you won't suffer an *accident* on your way back to your master."

Corvale's men fidgeted from foot to foot, waiting for his order. The denizens of the Maze seemed to fill every available space under the Tree as if it gave them the courage to do so. Devyn's heart raced; it was true! The Old Ways were still alive, and thrumming like a heartbeat in the Tree, its roots, into the Maze itself.

Corvale sheathed his weapon. Glancing up into the Tree's branches, he waved a flippant hand skyward. "You'd think there was something to all the false words and superstition the Lord Prelate works to evict from this place." He sketched a mock bow to Devyn. "Enjoy your banquet, friend. Afterwards, perhaps we will have that word?"

Devyn returned the mocking bow. "I'll tell you a tale in sword points and blood, gladly."

Jaryd laughed, waved to his men, and pushed his way through the crowd. Devyn glanced at Kembril, surrounded by the children, beneath the Tree. Fury rising up overwhelmed. He shouted after Corvale, "And may Renia's Grace protect you!"

Jaryd Corvale stopped in his tracks. He turned slowly back to Devyn, looked again to the Tree, to the crowd, to the children surrounding Kembril. And then he tilted his head back and laughed, the sound lingering long after he and his men vanished into the Maze.

TALYIOR DID NOT RISE UNTIL THE SUN began its slow decent through the afternoon. He lay abed some few hours, undisturbed by either Gania or Lyssa, trying to sort out what he accomplished, and cost himself, last night. He knew he had a chance at winning going in, his vision had seemed too sure to feel otherwise, but all the rest . . . that was magic. The faces, the words, the thrill of matching wits against Devyn, it all threatened to be too much and yet not enough. It would never be enough; at least until he met his destiny at the palace in two days time.

"Two days," he mused aloud to a spider busily reconstructing the web Lyssa destroyed every time she noticed it. Talyior smiled a little. He and the spider shared a world made tenuous by outside forces difficult to manage save by determination and stealth.

"Work hard, mistress," he continued, "for you play with fate. Best you weave while you may, but beware Lyssa's broom!"

He arose finally, slightly disturbed by the thought the spider actually stood a better chance than he did of surviving the next two days.

"Well," he said to his face in the mirror. "At least Gania won't kill me. I've the coin to pay her now. And yet. . ."

A smile spread across his face. It was folly to even think about attempting to see Demona. Such tragedy it would be if Sevire killed him before the finals. The whole city would be up in arms. To try would prove Gania's low opinions of him true and make his father's sarcastic judgments fact.

He determined to try that very night.

He dressed in cavalier good humor, words running through his head like wind through the willows down by the riverbank, teasing rhythms and patterns, moving leaves like ideas back and forth, tantalizing and close. After tasting their power last night, he knew his life would never be the same. Words and Demona had changed him. Before going downstairs to test the temper of his world, he dipped his quill in ink to try to catch that wind. The words fairly flew onto the page:

One word begets two
Two words collide and create
Worlds anew
And enough for me.
For in the patterns so conceived
Lay a Man's destiny perceived;
First as just sense—
Effort without recompense,
And then later as a hope, a dream
To be more than he might seem.
And in the windings of the words
Hide Truths unheard
Of a Man's life
Of a Man's loves
Spinning out the days in rhyme
Waiting for their moments in time
To be known. . .

"What is happening to me," he said to himself, staring down at the paper. "What am I becoming?" But he had no answer, for in that moment his stomach remembered he had missed breakfast, and there was a delicious smell sneaking underneath his door-jamb from the kitchens below. Hunger overruled introspection. He tucked his shirt into his breeches and went downstairs.

He fingered a gold piece, easily worth twice what he owed Gania, from his purse as he entered the kitchen. Seeing Gania bent over her accounts at the table, he stepped quickly up next to her, slammed his hand down with the coin beneath his palm, and thrust his face into hers.

"Never doubt me!" he cried. And as she turned her astonished, angry face, he grabbed her enormous cheeks with both hands and kissed her right on the lips. He released her before she could hit him and sat back in a chair laughing as she nearly over-balanced backwards. She had to grab the table to keep from tipping over.

"You, you, miscreant!" she sputtered, trying to find breath to dress him down. "Who do you think you are? You, you. . ." And then she noticed the coin. "You darling boy! Who'd you have to tumble to get this? A proper gold piece no less! You must be a stallion to claim such a price!"

Talyior continued laughing. "Come, come, Gania. You know where. Although I am truly a stallion of impressive stamina, this I earned with other sweat."

"Oh, I know, I know," she said, laughing in her turn. "I know I'm about to feed lunch to a dead man. That's a new experience."

"And there you go, doubting me again, Gania"

"No, no yourself, young corpse. I have all the faith in you I need. I'm certain I'll have to use this coin to buy mourning garments before the week is out. And then to tie for your efforts! I almost couldn't believe my ears. And I wouldn't have, either, if it weren't Ana the butcher's wife who told me. She and her Tamor were at the Cup last night and saw the whole thing. The story's been running up and down the streets like bad news."

"So, am I still a fool?"

"Of course you are, didn't you hear me? *Like bad news.* There's some who've seen types not usually seen in this quarter wandering about, asking questions, marveling at the story like and wondering where they might find the young poet with a rich married woman's dugs in his eyes and sheep dung for brains."

"You flatter me."

"I'd just as soon flatten you. I'd never thought you'd go through with it. Points to you for that, I suppose, but you'll just wind up dead. Sevire Anargi made his fortune by being tenacious and ruthless. You've left a rather broad scent trail, lad. Couldn't you have used a different one of your scribblings for the task?"

"No, dear Gania," Talyior feigned affront. "It had to be that *scribbling* and no other. If I had used the one I wrote about you, all Pevana would have fallen in riot and ruin."

She paused, anger still in the set of her jaw, but laughter dancing in her eyes. She ran a fat hand through her thick, greying, greasy hair; a hint of affection tinged her words. "Well, best you lie low for now."

"Perhaps," he told her.

Pushing her bulk away from the table, she made her way over to the stew pot bubbling on the hearth. "Men don't have minds," she grumbled over her shoulder. "They have something else that thinks for them. Get you over to the bucket and wash up a little. This is near ready to eat. If you've a mind to get yourself killed tonight, you might as well have a decent last meal."

She served him a bowl and tossed him a fresh baked roll before she left him to eat in peace. As he ate, Lyssa burst into the kitchen.

"Gania! Oh, Tal, you're up! Excellent! Missy Sanra's husband just told her that messages have been sent out to all the Readings locations. It's all over the city! I cannot believe it!"

"What are you going on about, girl?" Gania groused. "Out with it!"

Lyssa caught her breath, smiling so that her eyes lit with mischief. "There is to be a ball and banquet honoring the winning poets tonight, given by none other than Sevire Anargi!"

Talyior choked on his mouthful, nearly fulfilling Gania's promise of it being his last meal. Lyssa patted his back, chattering on and on, while Gania only stirred her pot, refusing to look his way at all.

Darkness just missed catching Talyior before he slipped surreptitiously into the Golden Cup to collect his official invitation to Sevire's web. The trek from Gania's to the Cup had proven uneventful. Never once did his hackles signal pursuit. Even the square fronting the place seemed unwatched. Perhaps Sevire had called in his minions. Perhaps he chose to let his fly buzz around the sweetness of his wife so as to better snare him.

But I am such a fly as has a sting. I just hope they don't all come at me at once. I'd like to at least eat first.

The idea of eating Sevire's food, drinking his wine all while lusting after Demona appealed to Talyior's sense of the poetic, for he intended to steal a kiss ere the night was over. Then let Sevire rant as he would to his sell-swords and bravos. They would have to catch him to kill him. The old fool might think his house a trap for a foolish poet with grand designs, but Talyior had already had the run of the place in Sevire's absence. Besides, he only intended to enter by the front gates, not leave by them; and not alone. The kiss would assure it!

Saymon waved Talyior behind the bar as he entered the Cup, to the little office room where he kept his papers and strongbox. He handed over the letter addressed to Talyior Enmbron, care of the Golden Cup, and sealed with the Prince's own sigil in wax. Talyior broke the seal and read the contents, all very formal and congratulatory, requesting his presence at the fete, drawing attention to the gracious host Sevire Anargi and the Merchants' Guild. The festivities were to commence promptly at the second hour after sunset. Lyssa's rumors proved accurate, a useful thing to know; especially considering another bit of the woman's gossip had Saymon running markers on various kinds of wagers.

Talyior ran his fingers over the lettering. "What do you think my chances are?" he asked, looking up at Saymon, smiling. "Of coming out alive, not winning."

Saymon's answering grin showed a surprisingly good set of teeth. "At the moment, about one in three you go in but don't come out. There's one fool who wants to wager his horse that even if you do come out, you leave your stones and spike behind."

"Oh? What's the wager on that?"

"You can't be serious."

"What better way to top off the night's tale than to wager on myself? Of course I am serious! When have you known me to be anything but?"

"Ha! Never, and you never will. That's a wager I'll take any day in a thousand."

Talyior clapped his burly shoulder. "What covers the bet?"

"The horse is a nag. The other line? Two gold pieces minimum. For what it's worth to you, I put five on your nose to make it back here by morning."

"I'll prove your faith in my prowess, my friend."

"It's your luck, I'm betting on, boy!"

Talyior fished out two of the coins he won at the Hearing and waited while Saymon shuffled around looking for materials to write him out a receipt. *After tonight, I'll have enough for a new set of clothes for the final hearing at the palace!*

"What?" he asked.

"You were thinking. Care to share?"

Talyior quirked an eyebrow. "Looking to hedge a bet?"

"Always." Saymon smiled, reached over and grabbed two glasses from a shelf above the table and poured each of them a measure from a half empty bottle. "So?"

Talyior sipped his wine, the tartness after being left out all night puckering his lips. Gania called him a fool, but were men not fools for love? His poem had proven his audacity; the kiss would, before Sevire and all his ilk, prove his righteous courage. Once spoken, Talyior's course was set. He set his wine glass down.

"How much do the odds rise if I tell you I mean to steal a kiss from Demona on the dance floor?"

Saymon chuckled and raised his glass in toast. "Those tits have addled your better sense. I am just glad you have paid your bar bill! I am going to miss your business."

"I am serious, Saymon!"

"You are insane! No woman is worth your life, especially if you have to risk it to win her."

The wine turned bitter in Talyior's gut. "You do not understand her," he told Saymon. "She is trapped in a marriage she hasn't the courage yet to leave, but she will. Trust me. And it will be worth every chance I take."

"Bah! Now I wish I'd not wagered on you."

Talyior winked. "I'll cover your odds. We will both be rich men!"

Lifting the glass of bitter wine, Talyior drank it down in a single gulp. He was locked in a tale written by someone else; his fate changing with every page, his life a spool of multi-hued thread spun out on the loom of some fantastic giant. The white thread of innocence long pulled free of the tapestry of his life, he wondered what would come next: blood's red? Death's black? Or, like the glow of last night's winnings now resting on Saymon's counting table, would he still run gold?

Saymon brought him out of his reverie with a quiet cough and his receipt. "Shall I send one of my strong arms with you?"

"Hedging again, Saymon?" Talyior laughed. "No, no, I don't think so. There will be no trouble in arriving. Webs never have tricky entrances; it is the leaving that gets dicey. Have my money ready for me tomorrow."

"You are that certain?"

"I am."

Saymon walked Talyior out to the square and left him with a slap on the back and a wish for luck. It was now near full dark. The lamps were being lit. Talyior took a deep breath and set off on his way.

He walked beneath the summer-night sky, his steps tapping out a counterpoint rhythm to the beating of his heart. Even now, at this crossroads in his life, he found words his constant companions. They hung about him like a swarm of sense impressions, not distracting or perplexing, but running to lines and images. By the time he had paced the length of the street running by the Cup and crossed over to the main avenue that coursed into the better parts of the city, he found himself singing quietly under his breath:

Staring at the world with the eyes of a child
On the low side of manhood, young and wild
Fingers pressed against the window glass
Leaving greasy prints that speak of the past
When you were still innocent
Of your fate and ignorant

Of the perils you would come to face
On your own in a far off place.
And your friends told you not to worry
They said you'd come out all right,
But you recall your mother's tears
And her farewell kiss that night.
And your friends may not have understood you
As they kept on handing you the dice
For you began to see life as a wager
And you despaired of paying the price.
But you would never lose
For Youth could never choose
To bury Hope under a cairn of stones.
And you would have your day
Whatever come what may
It's time to break the glass and roll the bones.

He sang the whole way up to the gates of the Anargi Estate. Several carriages passed through ahead of him. Jogging in a crouch alongside the last of them, Talyior hitched a ride on the runningboard. Better than walking, or having to give up his sword at the gate. He hopped off once inside the grounds, but not before doffing his hat to the outraged occupants of the carriage.

Talyior made his way to the marble steps leading up to the portico of the most opulent home in Pevana, a gaudy, if impressive, cairn of stones. Presenting his invitation to the doorman, he enjoyed watching the man stiffen in alarm.

That's right, he thought as the bewildered man handed back the invitation. *I'm here and in through the front door!*

Instead, he nodded politely, bending slightly at the waist, and passed into his destiny, chuckling softly to himself.

"Time to roll the bones."

Chapter 8: Afternoon Moves

DEVYN'S WALK HOME TURNED INTO A JOG, then a sprint. His mind ran faster than his feet as he dodged and twisted through the denser portions of the Maze. The smell brought back memories of his former life, when he was one of those children gathered at Kembril's legs. He remembered feeling protected, but those little ones, an army of innocents, had done the protecting.

The memory shamed him. Why should men like Jaryd Corvale hold any power at all? Those children, those people of the Maze were worth a thousand of his ilk, and yet led the fetid existence demanded within the Maze. Who was to blame for the inequity? The Avedun scepter, certainly, but could it possibly be Renia's will? Punishment for turning their backs while her Old Ways Temples burned?

Did life turn on the whims of higher powers?

Was it Renia who took his parents from him? His grandfather? Could it have been her divine will that cast him adrift in the Maze?

He ran faster, his breath bursting from his lungs, his side stitching like a tailor's needle. *It's true,* he thought. *Renia tasked Minuet to shoot into the future, to skewer a champion for a cause not yet in existence. She took all, and in place left anger that she could use to do her bidding!*

Fury rose with his heartbeat—against Corvale, against the gods themselves. Devyn had wanted words, and he got them, and those words had led him to the Cup, and to Kembril beneath his Tree where that bastard Corvale threatened him, threatened them all.

Devyn stuttered to a halt, bending over his knees and gasping for air. He stood in a small open space, stunned, like the soldier who suddenly finds himself in the dusty breach of a wall he had been beating against. Around him the late afternoon sun cast shadows stretching. Time slowed. Devyn blinked once. Twice. A third time.

Straightening, hands on his hips, Devyn shook his head free of those thoughts anger and shame poured into his head. *Anger blinds you, Devyn,* he could almost hear Avarran tell him, *you can never fight effectively in rage.*

Devyn looked down at his boots, scratched and dusted by his race, letting sense catch him. Beneath the filth and dust of the Maze, the roots of the Tree spread themselves, patiently wending their way through rock and soil, there, simply there, doing what needed to be done. No higher power swayed it; the Tree was a higher power itself. No temple could be more sacred.

"No wonder Kembril chooses the hollow of those great roots to rest and tell his stories from," Devyn muttered softly. Sitting in the dust, leaning against the solid trunk, the old, dying man drew his strength from the Tree. The Maze itself sketched a path of its roots, twisting through Pevana like veins.

Did anyone else realize? Having grown enamored of the ornate, the lofty, people made temples of stone, peaked roofs, golden statuary and silver, and so missed the primal truth. But the poor folk of the Maze stayed, never straying from the Tree even if they strayed from the Old Ways, and kept silent if they did so. There exists in poverty an unspoken loyalty.

Devyn turned around slowly, sensing, orienting. Jaryd Corvale and the incident at the Tree brought full circle to the understanding that his misadventure with the temple fire and the priestly escapade yesternoon had been immature protests of youth. His poem announced a man's defiance. Devyn had spoken the words, tied his life to them. The incident at the Tree proved that words were not enough. They needed action to give them life. Devyn would not simply be Renia's poet, he would be her warrior, and that meant surviving the competition. *And is that, too, a part of the pattern? Do I really have a choice?*

Devyn froze at the thought. *The people choose to stay. The Tree. Roots.* He took a deep breath and let it out slowly, raising his head to scan the area around. To the untutored eye the shabby decay would be indistinguishable from the rest of the Maze, but Devyn now saw otherwise. *There is pattern here. Life. Love. Need.* He had run away out of necessity before, urged to flight by Kembril's wisdom and the odds. Now he stood amidst the settling dust, taking in shame with each breath, tasking himself for fleeing even though better sense knew he made the right choice. *But I have been running away my whole life.*

"Kembril," he muttered, turning to go back.

"Not advisable, under the present circumstances," a calm voice said.

Devyn drew his blade and wheeled around at the sound as a man followed the voice out from behind a crumbling wall, one hand held up in a calming fashion, the other well away from a sword slung at the hip.

"Now, is that really necessary?" he asked, smiling. "You wouldn't draw on Jaryd Corvale, but you'll draw on me?"

Devyn took another step back, but again, the sound of the man's voice sparked memory. Images flashed to him of darkness, coughing, flames, a terse set of words in an alley. His arm tingled. He looked at the man's eyes and saw recognition there. They had met once before.

"I see you remember," the man said carefully. "Not a pleasant night, that, as I recall."

"Yes, I remember," Devyn responded, but he kept his sword up just the same. "And I decide whether or not my blade is necessary. Who are you? And why this second meeting? Quickly, for I have affairs to see to."

"Yes, Jaryd Corvale. Again, not advisable, friend. He's rather dangerous."

"I'm not afraid."

"Then why did you run?"

"What is it to you?"

158

"Let's say you have become part of my job, but now that I think about it, maybe you have been part of my job for some time now. That was a hot fire back in the spring. Corvale knows his work too well."

Devyn let the sword tip sink to the ground. The memory of their shared escape from the temple fire clinched it.

"I never thanked you properly," he said, sheathing his blade. "I owe you my life. I am Devyn Ambrose, and you still have not told me who you are."

The man gave a smirk and a curt bow.

"Senden Arolli, eyes and ears to Prince Donari Avedun," he said. "And I think you had best keep to ground until the evening. Corvale means business."

"I sensed that. But how did you find me?"

"I was on my way to see you, actually, Devyn Ambrose, erstwhile poet, and public rabble-rouser. I missed my time. Jaryd and his crew got in front of me as they trailed you down the street. That was a neat move at the tinker's cart, however, but they found you just the same."

"So you saw?"

Senden nodded. "Part of my job. Preventing accidents. That was a near thing. Don't worry about Kembril. The people faced Corvale down, and he left the old man unmolested. Rushing back with sword swinging won't accomplish anything. Confronting Corvale might get you killed, and that would displease my master."

"Why should the Prince care?"

"Why? You present *that* poem last night, and you have to ask? You know the answer to that. That scar on your arm is part of it. Open your eyes, boy. I do not have time to coddle fools who take unnecessary risks. The Prince contends with things beyond your ken. Corvale and his ilk are just appendages attached to more sinister designs. You knew your words would bring a reaction. Don't tell me you are surprised. I can see it in your eyes, so don't deny it."

Devyn's ire wilted as Senden spoke.

"Why should I trust you?" he asked. "You speak of threats. What part do I play in them?"

"Stay alive until the finals and see. Trust? Trust has nothing to do with it. Act the fool, and you will die."

"For words?"

"For the ideas behind them."

The truth of Senden's words mimicked Kembril's. Devyn fell silent.

"So, I see it. What would you have me do?"

"Lay low for now, then get yourself home and ready for the banquet. Yes, of course I know. I helped set it up. Your piece at the Cup last night may have bought you some nasty enemies, but it also brought you into Prince Donari's thoughts. His interest is not an insignificant thing, but it only has value if you live. Avoid Corvale. Find yourself a hole. You know the Maze."

"So do you, since you managed to trail me."

Senden smiled. "Now you are talking sense. I'll take that as a complement. That's twice I have saved your life. I think that means you owe me something."

"Payment?"

"Get yourself cleaned up and safe to Anargi's. Keep your eyes open and your tongue attached because I want to be there when you spout that poem in front of the Prelate and gentry at the Finals."

Devyn let himself smile at that, his fears for Kembril and the Tree receded as the idea of even more mayhem blossomed for him. *Stay alive. Party. Finals. Perfect.*

"Done," he said. "Will I see you there?"

"Not if I see you first. Remember: no risks. You and your fellow competitor, what was his name? Talyior? Yes? The two of you have spiced things nicely. Let them run their course. Have you a place in mind?"

The image of a shady corner on the roof of a storage building near the Cup came to Devyn, along with the pleasant prospect of a nap to while away the rest of the afternoon.

"As a matter of fact, I do."

"Good. Off with you then." Senden turned to go.

"Senden?" Devyn asked. "My thanks, for before and today."

Senden smiled. "Like I said. Part of my job. The least I could do for one of Pevana's poets." He gave a last, curt bow, ducked behind the crumbling wall and vanished, leaving Devyn awhirl with threat, promise, and deepening purpose.

AN HOUR BEFORE SUNSET the Lord Prelate Byrnard paced along the long hallway that branched off from the main entrance to the palace. It led down the northern wing of the place and ended in the apartments set aside for visiting dignitaries. Two steps behind him followed his secretary, the hapless Brother Aemile, newly assigned to keep him off the streets in the wake of his dismal performance yesterday afternoon. Byrnard walked slowly to give his racing mind time to digest the information he now possessed and to decide best what to do with it.

The announcement of the banquet to take place that evening at the Anargi estate precipitated a request for a meeting from the corpulent merchant and a visit outside the city to compare notes and prepare. The man's obsequious greed made him most amenable to suggestion, and Byrnard took care to suggest subtle additions to his plans. Despite Sevire's unpleasant demeanor, Byrnard found the whole episode interesting.

Still, he did not like Sevire Anargi. He did not care about his culkolded honor, for sex had lost its allure long ago for the Prelate. He made a show of dismay for appearances only. Sevire did not comprehend how grotesque he was; breathing made him sweat. His thunder and fume were pathetic and embarrassing to observe, but at least the carriage had been covered, minimizing Byrnard's exposure to curious eyes and gossiping tongues.

Sevire served his purpose as an unedged tool, the promise of money and ships. Involving him meant Donari had to spread his watch to other doors. Donari watched the Prelate's every move, and yet had done nothing to stop him from seeing whom he wished or hatching his plots. Byrnard found the lack of challenge a bit disappointing.

The campaign in Pevana was proving almost too easy, he decided as he passed within to drop his hat, cloak and gloves in Aemile's outstretched arms. Peoples' temples burned and hardly anyone raised questions. Foreigners harangued them from every street corner and no one openly disputed. Byrnard had faced sterner campaigns in the past when subduing the north. King Roderran was right. If one took Pevana as a sign, then the South was weak and ready for the taking. His letter, already a full day into its journey to the King's Court at Perspa, would bring decisive action. The King would move.

Byrnard poured himself a glass of water from the pitcher on his desk, promising himself wine later at the banquet. He held it to his lips, glimpsing the ghost of his own smile in the rippling surface. *It will be good,* he thought, *to put an end to this piety nonsense. Curse Roderran, that brilliant fool.*

He passed through the double doors beyond his desk to lean against the railing of the balcony. By winter the army could be there, training and preparing winter quarters. And when the season warmed in spring—war.

Lord Prelate Byrnard Casan, formerly Lord of Collum smiled, a thin, calculating smile, as he contemplated the variables he held within reach that would achieve those goals. He had a city lost in its own pleasures, too distracted by the festival to question an entire season's worth of destruction. He had a dilettante of a Prince, too busy playing at politics to see the traps laid before him. He had the most powerful merchant, leader of the entire class running to him with news and anger and greed. Much still hung in the balance, but whatever the outcome, Donari's power would be compromised.

He sighed in expectation of the evening. If the afternoon's intrigue was any indication of what was to come, then ware Donari.

Or not and even better.

THE COUGH THAT BROUGHT THE COPPERY TAINT of blood shook Kembril wake. He looked up, figuring the hour of the day by the way shadows played among the limbs of the Oak's canopy. Looking down he locked eyes with one of the Maze children, a little blond slip, and felt a moment's panic when he could not recall her name. And that bothered him; to not remember names. *Unthinkable.* Another cough took him, worse, and while he struggled for breath his mind struggled to recall. Suddenly, that became as vital as finding a way to fill his lungs with air. For an awkward second he floundered.

And then she smiled at him, and both air and memory returned at the same time.

"Ah, Tasia," he whispered, tilting his head to the side and returning her grin. What can I do for you child?"

"It's too hot for a nap," she said. "I tried because mama said I should, but I just couldn't. All I saw when I closed my eyes was Tolimon, and he scares me."

Kembril allowed a soft smile to crease his wrinkled face, for he well understood young Tasia's unease. His own afternoon dreams had been filled with similar images of the god Tolimon's influence, but his took the form of the man who had come to the Tree in pursuit of Devyn and echoed with his cruel, sneering threats. Tasia seemed to feel something akin to his own fears.

In all the years of his sojourn beneath and around the Tree, he had kept a close relationship to the folk who came to listen to him. His tales had helped, in part, to save Devyn. As he gazed down at Tasia's serious seven-year-old face, another consumptive rush swept over him; and he knew, with an intensity rivaling the humors that daily filled his lungs, that Tasia was yet another urchin on his list to save.

"He scares me, too," he said, shifting into a more comfortable position. "He is a trickster and mischief-maker. I can see why you would run away from such a sleep. I envy you that you have two stout little legs and the happy recovery of youth. I can run away neither here nor in the dream world."

"Because of your leg and your cough?"

Kembril wheezed out a little laugh. "Yes," he answered, "because of my leg and my cough." Yes, squeaky, cheeky little street urchin Tasia, should she survive her youth and the coming days, would become something special. She would need every word, every tale he could give her. "So, come now, sleepless one," he finished. "What will you have of me?"

She raised her head. "I want a story," she said. "Please? Before my mother finds me out and calls me home?"

"Well, a story I can give," he chortled. "A story it is then. Sit."

Tasia settled herself at his feet and looked up expectantly. In the late afternoon light, she looked half-like a creature from one of his stories. As if privy to some silent signal, other Maze-children collected around the dusty space between the Tree's great roots to listen. Taking strength from their youth, Kembril began.

"Well met my friends," he said. "Tasia here wanted a story, and what better time for one than on the mid-point eve of the festival, an in-between time—neither beginning nor ending but just so. This is a tale of how Minuet missed her target for the first and only time in her existence."

Tasia's voice rose above the swell of surprise from the other children. "But Minuet never misses!"

"That is true," said another. "How could Renia ever allow such a thing?"

"My mama says Minuet was the perfect one, who never upset her bowl or left a mess or ever did anything wrong!" said yet another.

Disbelief rose like a wave to the towering clouds just visible through the leaves. The mass loomed above the coast off the headland and pushed down the air over Pevana into a heavy, still, oppression. Kembril could not shake the feeling that he spoke into a moment of time grown suddenly like an hour glass whose sands were quickly running out. Eventually, there would be no one there to turn the glass over and so keep time going. *Time! Time! I have so little.*

He fought a battle with despair and nearly won, but he did not let that stop him from putting everything he had left in to this one last effort. He stilled the tickle in his lungs, gathered his voice like a magic spell, and cast.

"Minuet soared," he began, "above the land intent on her mistress's bidding, loosing shafts at times to prick the dreams of men to work for the betterment of their lot, for that was Renia's main charge: she has always been the Goddess of Plenty, which is why our fields above the river are heavy with vintage and the grasslands to the south succor our horses and kine so that they are the finest in the kingdom."

"My mama says we could use a little more of that plenty," a disheveled child in the back announced.

Tasia leapt to her feet, "You shut up, Ernil!" she shouted. "Stop pouting. Let the storyteller speak!"

Kembril raised a palm to quiet the budding argument. "Na, na, Tasia, my friends, young Ernil is not wrong, and it is true that we all have felt the lack from time to time. In fact, my story tells a part of why that is so for some and not for others. Hush you now and let me finish before we lose the light. This is Festival! A time for tales, not arguments. Listen."

All grew settled and quiet; he continued.

"Now, Minuet was diligent about her business and roamed the land and the air above keeping watch and ware on the lives of Renia's people. She never missed her aim; that is true! Young Tasia was right, and all the legends agree: Minuet was Renia's familiar and privy to her grand designs. All she did set threads in motion on the great loom, for are we all not part of a fine and mystical cloth? Our young Ernil may protest a lack, but that too might be part of the pattern. Life is a messy prospect, and the gods deal in wide gestures in the lives of men. So it is that there are the rich and the poor, the happy and the sad, light and dark, good and evil. All of you have had enough life to know these things."

There were nods too solemn for their ages. *Too sage by far*, Kemdril thought, but these were children of the Maze; such knowledge often came young. It defined their lives. Some would never grasp it completely. For many, life's ritual and dogma provided the panacea for painful truth. But others would understand. Tasia would. She would need to know that even the gods were fallible, and ultimate happiness remained a personal responsibility. Always, the seeds of joy or tragedy lay in the choices.

"So it came to pass," he continued, an undercurrent of sorrow adding timbre to the words, "that man spread his seed over the land, pricked and guided to do so by Minuet's barbs and the flow of Renia's tears. Man built, man sowed, man harvested, man grew. And all this was well-intentioned and monitored by Minuet. And yet even Minuet, ever mindful of her mistress' wishes though she was, still had a sprite's demeanor. She craved for something new and different to distract her from her more wearisome tasks.

"Now Tolimon had watched through the ages as Renia set her ordered pattern over the land and ever sought to ply his mischievous bent on her designs, but she foiled him at every attempt for she had Minuet's aide. And Tolimon watched Minuet and learned how she aimed her barbs to weave the dreams of Man into Renia's intent and saw thereby a way, possibly, to affect the merest upset.

"He set stars in the night sky, a vast, twinkling canopy of lights, and sent them careening through the vault in unusual collections and patterns. But he did not stop there, for he knew stars alone were not enough to affect Minuet's aim. He next fashioned the moon and set it racing above the land but gave it the added mischief of changing its shape and light through the days, now waxing full and bright, now waning small and slight.

"At first his efforts bore no fruit. Minuet noted the stars in the heavens, took ease in their gentle light, noted the changes in the moon, but she did not let that deflect her aim or her attention to her tasks. And Tolimon grew wroth and sought for yet another way to inject his will. For an age he sat and pondered, perched on the mountaintop that borders our valley to the west, and thought and thought and thought while Renia's pattern waxed and grew and all was ordered on the earth.

"And then he set the moon to run for a time *between* the sun and the earth." The children gasped in unison and Kembril suppressed a smile. "Yes, children, that is correct. Tolimon set the moon to block the sun's light for a brief space in time, and it was then, at the point where the moon paused directly in front of the sun, that light changed. And the first time this happened, Minuet, busily engaged in loosing shafts, wavered, and by the briefest margin, *she missed!*"

"How can that be?"

"Tolimon is bad."

"He should get a whipping!"

"What happened when Minuet missed?" Tasia's question brought instant silence.

Kembril suppressed no smile this time but reveled in the warmth it spread from his wizened cheeks to his tattered lungs.

"Minuet's barb left her bow and flew out into the supernatural dark followed by Tolimon's wild laugh, which we have all heard in our dreams, yes?" More sage nods. "And that laughter influenced the wayward shaft, and Minuet's momentary distraction added more so that the arrow, intended to prick a maid to fall in love with her heart's desire, struck instead the dreams of the one she was to love. And he, awakening grew in time to love himself above all others and so *pride* and *arrogance* entered the land and were added, unfortunately, to the great weave.

"And Minuet grew wroth in her turn at her failure, for she could see what effect this one failed loosing would have in the life of Man, and she was correct, of course, for pride and arrogance has ever been at the root of Man's conflicts. Not all Renia's tears, flowing for eternity as they do, can serve to remove the taint.

"How Tolimon rejoiced! His laughter rolled through eternity. We can still hear its echoes today in the rumble of thunder that precedes our storms and lightning flares. Poor Minuet; it was the smallest of misses, really, but like the pebble one tosses into the pond the ripples so begun have grown through the ages such that kingdoms have fallen, love has ended and Man has made a practice of defining the nature of evil. So it is even now that when the moon is full, we watch and ware ourselves. And when there is an eclipse, we refrain from making contracts in business, marriage bonds in love and all clannish feuds pause, so as to minimize if possible the taint of Tolimon's one success. And that, my friends, is the tale of how Minuet missed her mark."

His voice faded to silence; he felt weary beyond reason. For a moment the spell lingered and then faded away in the face of youth's natural swell.

"Great story, Kembril!"

"Is the moon full tonight?"

"I can't wait to tell my mama this one!"

By ones and threes they bled away into the shadows. Kembril had talked the last daylight hours away. Devyn would be at the banquet rumor said was going on up at House Anargi. He slumped back against the tree and closed his eyes, waving a weak hand at the whispered thank you's and farewells. He sighed and then opened his eyes once again at a gentle touch on his forearm.

Tasia looked at him with eyes as round as the full moon in his tale. One of Renia's tears hung quivering on the lid of her left eye. And the motion of that suspended liquid fixed Kembril's attention and he thought he now understood why he chose to tell a story of failure. Everything pointed to chaos—Devyn, the times themselves, the man at the Tree—and all of it mirrored in that one tear hanging like suspended fate from Tasia's eye. *If that tear should fall,* he thought, *would all else also fall? Did I miss something, something important? I am too old for this.*

Kembril smiled to reassure himself and his young listener. But Tasia blinked and the track of that one tear coursing down her dusty cheek whispered to him of hope falling to the dark. Mortality's clench seized upon the small of his back.

"Thank you, Kembril," she said. "I have to go now."

"Thank you, Tasia," he replied woodenly. "It is a sad story, perhaps, but a good one for these days, I think."

Tasia patted his arm again in farewell and left; a little figure flitting away like the memory of a daydream. Kembril shifted back against the bole of the oak, searching for that one spot where use and the tree's slow growth provided the most support for his old bones. But his world had shifted, and he searched in vain for comfort as slumber took him. The distant sounds of revelry came to him as a rumor whispered into his doze as the Tree sucked up the last of the light and expelled shadow from its leaves.

THE SETTING SUN GLEAMED RED-ORANGE through the arched windows of the banquet hall of House Anargi, illuminating a scene of semi-controlled chaos.

"No!" boomed Sevire, surveying the row of tables arranged along one side of his ballroom. "No, no, no! Not there, you fools! I want them off to the side, along the columns near the far wall. We must have room for the dances!"

The servants scurried to move the offending tables even though Sevire's orders countermanded those he had given before he left for his meeting with the Prelate. He pushed his wheezing, bulbous body into the kitchens to bark orders at the cooks, waddled out to the grounds to urge the gardeners to finish trimming the shrubbery, gasped out directions to all and sundry to the point that House Anargi resembled an anthill disturbed by a wicked child's stick. The servants avoided eye contact with him as they rushed to follow the contradicting orders. He showered them with sweat and spittle, savaging them into desparate action.

He could feel his heart beating, laboriously trying to keep up with the unfair demands he made of it as he went about arranging his banquet. Inwardly he seethed with wrath at the idea of Donari's *suggestion* that he throw a fete to honor the finalists in the competition.

A fete! So that I can honor my wife's lover? Preposterous! The man goes too far!

He grabbed a glass of cooled white wine from a waiting servant and gulped it down. The letter from the palace had caught him off guard completely, putting him at a loss for an hour or so. Word of the events at the Golden Cup, a scrofulous pit of an alehouse, reached his ears through the whispers of his bedchamber servants when he awoke that morning; the note handed to him while he was in mid-tirade at his wife. He nearly took a letter opener and plunged it between her beautiful breasts to make an end of it all. Even now the memory caused his loins to stir, somewhere down there hidden by his fat rolls of power and pride. He had thrown her back on the bed from which she had half-arisen in fear and confusion and held the point of the letter opener at her throat.

"No, no, please Sevire!" she wailed, tears springing to her eyes. She lay naked and quivering, legs spread wide as he loomed above her. He tossed the blade away, grabbed her breasts and squeezed cruelly.

"These," he said, bringing his face close to hers. "These are mine, and I can cut them off like I would trim my nails. Truth, slut, who is he?"

"Ta, Ta, Talyior Enmbron," she had stuttered. "We have several of his father's rugs in your study. We met once or twice. I had no idea! We shared a dance or two. Nothing more, I swear. Sevire, please, you're hurting me!"

Sevire had seen the lie in her eyes as she spoke.

"Sevire, Sevire, how could you even think such a thing were true," she had said in a weeping whisper. "It's just a poem. He's nothing more than an infatuated youth. All we did was dance."

"That's not what the whole of the city thinks," he snarled through teeth clenched in anger.

"What care we for what the mob assumes?" She pushed one hand through wispy, disheveled tresses, the other held up in supplication. "You know how this place is, how much rumor magnifies half-truth." She ran her tongue over her lips, just so, in a way that left their fullness moist and supple.

"I'll not be laughed at, Demona! You are lying to me, don't deny it," He raised a hand to slap her but then paused, taking in all of her: the red welts on her breasts, her flat stomach, the mysterious triangle between her spread legs. Always, her beauty caught him. He hated her for it.

"Sevire, Sevire, love, please." Her voice took on a wheedling tone. "How can you believe such a thing?"

He rolled off of her. Demona rose to her knees. He had come into her chambers dressed in nothing but a robe, which fell open around his huge belly as he leaned back on his elbow. Her effect on him was obvious, and her response exactly what he truly wanted.

"You risk much, wife," he had said quietly. "Wayward eye, even at dalliance, may cost you."

Demona had smiled then. She ran her finger over the grey down of his chest, continuing on passed his belly to fondle his stiffening manhood. Sevire let go a musky sigh. He relaxed and allowed her to prove her love and loyalty to him.

Slowly his pulse regulated itself as memory and wine soothed. His breathing slowed. He waved for the servant to refill his glass. Sipping at the vintage—a fine mixing from several years ago—he surveyed the chaos he had made of the preparations. *Donari seeks to rub my nose it in, but no one gets the better of Sevire Angari, not even Prince Fop at his most wicked.*

He finished the glass, gave it to a passing servant and turned to mount the steps to the upstairs gallery where he could look down on the whole scene. Despite the frenzy, Sevire had everything under control: Demona, the banquet, the delicious plans he had earlier made with the dour, but useful, Prelate Byrnard. The one variable he did not control would do his bidding eagerly, desperately, most foolishly, and he smiled to know Donari would not be the only one to wish he had not underestimated Sevire Angari.

Chapter 9: Stitches

BY NOON THE DAY AFTER THE READING, the wives and daughters of Pevana's elite crowded Eleni Caralon's shop. All of them clamored for last minute alterations and creations for the surprise banquet being thrown by Sevire Anargi in honor of the finalists in the Competition of Poets. Rumor ran from a slew of mouths about the scandalous pieces presented by two of the participants at the Golden Cup. The idea of a party at House Anargi and the possibilities for further scandal ran through the streets like bad news.

Eleni was too busy with the sudden bonanza of patrons who flocked to her door to fuss over the fact that her own poem had not warranted more attention. She sewed through her day a whirlwind of needle and thread, lace and sashes, taxing the limits of her creativity. She finished the lot of them by workday's end and collapsed on her stool to catch her breath only to rise again at a knock on her front door.

A footman from House Anargi stood there with a handwritten note from Demona Anargi, herself:

Mistress Caralon,
Forgive this note, but I need *you to help save me! I'm sure you must have heard about the banquet for tonight. I love the changes you made on the one I will wear for the Finals, but I need something for tonight! Please, I am desperate! I have several choices, but they need your touch. Save me, I beg of you. The footman will bring you by coach.*
Please, please, please?
~Demona

Eleni sighed, exasperated. Demona well knew she could not refuse such a summons without risking all future work from House Angari and its cronies. Picque tempted her to, but the chance to be in House Anargi with all its imminent drama intrigued. Demona would make it worth her while, certainly; the woman was haphazardly generous. Eleni stretched her back, grabbed up her sewing kit, wrote Tomais a hasty note and dashed out the door and into the waiting carriage.

She arrived at the Anargi Estate, showed the signed note to a servant who hustled her through the chaos up to Demona's chambers. The opulence and bustled preparations for that evening's banquet made Eleni uneasy. She was a successful artisan, respected in her way, and yet in those surroundings she felt a rustic, clutching her basket of sewing materials and trying to make herself as small as possible.

Demona whirled around at the sound of her entrance, a gown in one hand. "Oh, there you are!" she squealed. Gowns lay everywhere, strewn about the floor, half-draped over dressing dummies and on the bed. Near the pillows lay one Eleni remembered making earlier that year. "I was afraid you'd not get the note! Eleni, dearest, most clever of seamstresses, you simply must save me! I cannot decide what to wear or what to do to make any of these suitable for this evening. Sevire insists I look ravishing, but right now I feel ordinary and swollen."

Eleni fumbled for words, unsure of what shocked her more. Demona actually remembering her name, or talking to her as though they were intimates of long standing. She hid her surprise, her eye drawn again to the gowns tossed about the room, her mind already assessing the possibilities.

She set her basket on the edge of the bed. They were all lovely garments, any one of which would be more than sufficient for the evening. She lightly touched a blue satin dress; the fabric crackled beneath her fingertips. Eleni made beautiful gowns, but these were something beyond her ken. Trembled intimidation fluttered in her stomach, but she stilled them with an effort of will that surprised her. She looked from the gown to Demona. The elite of Pevana would be there. Her dresses, her handiwork would adorn more than a few of the notables of the city. And she had been asked by the wife of the most powerful man in the merchant set to make her somehow more beautiful and noteworthy than she already was. This was risk and opportunity all threaded into one stitch.

Renia save me, she thought to herself as she held up the red satin gown to the light, *what price failure?*

Demona gave a perplexed sigh. "Well, my dear? Do you see any hope in any of these?"

Eleni cocked an eyebrow. "My lady, any of these would cause all eyes to stare as you entered the room."

Demona tossed her hair, stomped a foot. "But that's not good enough! I need to cause a sensation. Everyone will be here tonight. Everyone! And, after what happened last night, I need to be worthy of the moment."

So the rumors were true. The young fool of a poet Talyior, who owed her money for the shirt he wore last night, even though he had not recognized her in the crowd, was the real reason for Demona's upset.

"I see, my lady," she said, setting the gown back down on the bed. "Worthy of the moment. I understand."

Demona turned to her, her eyes a mixture of puzzlement and fear. "You do? Really?"

"I was at the Cup last night with my husband. We witnessed quite a performance from a rather handsome young poet. Your name was on the mob's lips last night."

Demona plumped herself down on the chair in front of her dressing table. "I know, I know," she sobbed into her hands. "I can't believe it. What was he thinking?" She paused, peeking out between her fingers. "On everyone's lips?" she asked.

"Everyone's," Eleni replied. "One would assume the boy is positively smitten."

Back over the face went the hands, but Demona recovered herself quickly. "Let the mob assume what they like," she said tritely. "It doesn't matter to me. Talyior is a fool for taking such chances."

"Oh, was that his name?"

The look Demona shot her would have frozen one of the city fountains, but Eleni judged it a fair trade. She smiled innocently to take away the sting of her words and reached for her basket. Demona turned and began brushing her hair in quick, exasperated strokes.

"Don't forget your place, seamstress," she said.

Forget my *place? The woman forgot her place entirely, letting a flirtation go too far and risking Sevire's wrath and the city's scorn.*

And yet Eleni could see the hint of a plea in Demona's eyes finding hers in the mirror. For help. For an ally. Somewhere behind the perfume and the exotic eyeshadow lurked true emotions; or as near to true as Demona would likely get. Eleni took pity on her. If the moment was troublesome for her, it was desperately so for Demona.

"Of course, my lady," she said meekly, picking up her fabric shears. "I would not presume to be other than I am. So," and she smiled at the face in the mirror, "Let us see if we can make you *worthy of the moment.*"

Demona cooed relief. Her frown disappeared and she clapped her hands like a child given a present rather than the expected punishment.

"How long do we have?" Eleni asked.

"The guests will begin arriving just after sundown."

Eleni looked out the window to check the position of the sun. They would have three hours, no more. Perhaps less.

"Well, then we mustn't waste time," she said. "Please, could word be sent to my husband at our home, telling him I shall be late?"

"Of course, and thank you!" Demona rang a bell. Instantly, the white-haired servant who had shown Eleni up to Demona's chambers entered, received his instructions silently and then bowed himself back out again.

Eleni smiled around the pins in her mouth, and attacked the stitching on the blue satin gown. Each stitch she undid separated her a little more from her past life, a life wherein she had sewn herself into a pattern that precluded words. All that changed at the hearing at the Cup. Now, he worked with poetic rhythm as though undoing someone else's words and restitching them into a new pattern, one tied together by her own hand. In transforming Demona's gown, Eleni transformed herself.

Eleni spent the rest of the daylight hours adjusting Demona's clothes for the evening. She even allowed Demona to press her into serving as her hairdresser for the night's festivities. Three hours of work . . . and talk. Demona chattered as Eleni cut and stitched away the minutes. Nothing seemed too delicate to bring up. Eleni learned three of the eldest daughters of the Edari family were actually bastards sired by a footman in the employ of the house. Demona delighted in such stories oblivious to the hypocrisy of her behavior and her own roll as grist for the gossip mill.

Tonight would see the whispers rise to hissing crescendo. Eleni watched Demona model the adjusted gown in the tri-mirror. Every move seemed more intense than it needed to be. *Perhaps Demona was just lonely,* she thought. She was the wife of Sevire Anargi, living in *his* house, served by *his* servants. She might have an ally among them, but most of them would be his folk, obviously set to serve and watch over her. Who could she talk to without fear of the conversation being repeated to her dreaded husband?

"You must stay and watch for me," Demona urged while Eleni applied the brush to draw sparks from Demona's hair. "I'll be too busy to stand back and take it all in, you know."

"Yes, my lady, but I have a husband I must attend to."

Demona pouted into the mirror. "But you must! Please? I'll triple your fees. I need you."

I know you do, thought Eleni. *But I don't need you or Sevire's gold.* And yet the thought of seeing her handiwork on display pleased her. "I will stay," she said. "But you need not trouble about my fees. The watching alone will be worth it."

"Nonsense!" Demona reached into her jewelry box and took out a string of pearls and bright stones. "You must at least allow me to give you a gift. Take this, with my thanks. And stay."

Eleni took the bauble worth a year's wages at least. "My lady, I'm, I'm. . ."

Demona laughed. "Yes, yes, of course you are," she chided. "Now, help me decide which color for my eyes. Time! Time! They will expect me downstairs!"

Chapter 10: The Banquet of Fate: Talyior

TALYIOR MADE HIS WAY DOWN AN ORNATE HALLWAY and entered the ballroom of House Anargi, the announcement of his name drowned out by music's hum and chatter. He checked his cloak and blade at a side table. Rules were rules, no matter the personal threats he faced by being there. Besides, for what he intended, he would not need a blade, only Demona's lips and Sevire's rage.

He moved into the room and surveyed the glittering sea of piled hair, jewel-adorned throats and pearl-bedecked lobes moving in currents of money and influence before him. Faces a little too bright from swilling Sevire's fine wines, gowns a little too expensive and ill fitting for having been purchased in a rush and altered swam before his vision like a school of gaudy, shallow-dwelling fish. The image gave him a moment's queasiness. This was the world he had desired entrance to; that had lured him with its society and power? He envisioned a gathering of crows plumed in peacock feathers, the chief rook overseeing it all.

Sevire stood near a fluted column, an obelisk of wrath surrounded by a cackle of over-dressed fellow merchants, glaring at Talyior as he moved into the room. Jowls bulged over a stiff, golden collar and belly-extended tunic, making him look for all the world like a festering boil on the top of the sun. Talyior would not look away first. He offered a small, mocking bow. *So much for deception and pretense,* he thought. *Glare all you wish, you fat old man. I've had worse from my father.*

Talyior felt a slight tug on his elbow and turned to find the white-haired servant who often looked after Demona. He held a small slip of paper with a number written on it.

"For your blade, sir," the man said, smiling slightly, "to reclaim it when you leave."

Talyior returned the smile. "Thank you," he said. There were secrets they shared; not all of Sevire's servants answered only to him. "Please keep it close for me, eh? On such a night as this, one never knows when one will need a prop."

"As you wish. A fine blade, indeed. See, I will place it there on the corner of the table. There you may reclaim it, even in haste, should you suddenly find you have need."

Talyior bowed slightly, mouthing another, silent thank you, and turned away to meander through the crowd, putting some distance between himself and Sevire.

A rank of pillars ran along one side of the ostentatious ballroom. An enormous chandelier loomed over the dance floor, and flowers festooned a phalanx of tables clustered to one side. Women and their well-heeled escorts tried to out-duel the blossoms; scents both natural and unnatural filled the air. Talyior nibbled from a tray of sweetmeats, glancing sidelong about the room, searching for and finding Demona. Her luminescence drew his eye across the room where she stood laughing with a covey of less distinctive beauties. If she saw him, she remained coy, looking away and laughing gaily. Talyior made an effort to take his time filling a glass of chilled wine punch.

"Well met." The voice suddenly beside him made Talyior's pour sloppy. Devyn Ambrose slipped a cup deftly underneath Talyior's to catch the spill. Talyior finished pouring his measure and scooped another ladleful for Ambrose's cup, stopping at a half glass in response to Devyn's small wave.

"My thanks," Devyn said. "Small wine for me tonight, I think. Too much refinement here for my tastes. I want a clear head."

"Have you been by the Cup, then?" Talyior asked.

"Yes, I talked the driver into a little detour. It was still three to one on your stones when I left. It was tempting, but I've not the means to gamble as you." He scanned the room meaningfully. "Have a care. There are three bully-boys over there behind the instruments, looking too well groomed, I should think."

Talyior found himself liking his erstwhile dueling partner even more than he did when they parted company that morning. A pity one of them had to lose. "Yes, I have noticed them," he said. "And there's two more over there next to the entrance to the kitchens." He paused, scanning the room before continuing. "So, a carriage ride for you? I wonder about that. This could prove a most entertaining evening."

"Only if you are fool enough to try something . . . extravagant."

Talyior snorted into his cup. "Extravagant is not the word I would choose."

Devyn frowned, then shrugged it away. "As you wish. There's *my* adversary, the pious Prelate. I am told he doesn't much like my choice of subject matter."

Talyior followed Devyn's gaze to the priest Byrnard Casan, Lord Prelate on earth of the King's Theology, and saw an old, wizened man dressed in bright red robes with thinning white hair falling from beneath a red felt cap. He looked, in Talyior's estimation, the perfect representation of calculated indifference.

He glanced at Devyn. *Poor fools us,* he thought. *We both run risks, but whose are worse?*

"'*Odd things fall when one shakes the tree of Faith*' my old tutor used to say," Talyior said lightly. "Something like that, anyway. Or could it be progress?"

"Progress? Or power?" Devyn responded. "Look at him! Those eyes! He's a carrion bird feeding on Calamides' liver, the bastard. Progress? Quite the opposite, I'd say."

"Then have a care yourself, my friend," Talyior murmured, raising his glass in salute.

Devyn shrugged as he sipped his wine. "Oh, I think I am less a threat to that priest than you are to our fat, red-faced host over there. Saymon told me about a kiss you mean to steal."

"Hedging his bets, no doubt."

"Is it true, then?"

"True as my heart for Demona."

"You are a fool. I wish now I had made that bet. He won't let you live. Even with the Prince here, he'll howl up something."

"He'll have to catch me."

"But do you know where to run?" Devyn replied. "I might stand a chance, but you? Luck to you in that, friend." Devyn refreshed his half-glass. "I'm off to test the wills of that covey of bosoms near the orchestra. I see your Demona is, for the moment, alone."

A disturbance swelled through the room, taking both Devyn and Demona from view. The Prince rushed in and swept away all those in his path, like the tide tumbling and taking seashells from the sand. Talyior observed this social dance before the physical one: the Prince entered, flamboyant in blue and green to be greeted first by Sevire. Banter followed bows. The Prince laughed at some jest. Sevire forced himself, unconvincingly, to respond in kind. Eyes swept the room, assessed it. More bows. And then the women. Curtsey's dangerously deep for such low-cut gowns. Demona a shinning, tittering, blue draped vision. More laughter. Sevire's smile even more forced to mask flaming eyes. Donari signaled the musicians and music swelled. Folk partnered and moved off, a receding tide, to take places on the dance floor. The Prince led Demona to the center, led her smoothly into the first steps.

Talyior sipped at his chilled wine punch, the taste slightly less sweet than it had been. He watched his Demona dance with the Prince of Pevana as of course she must. They came floating by; Talyior tried to catch Demona's eye but instead found Prince Donari's. A wayward grin, a wink, and the man, and Demona, floated away again.

Talyior passed the first hour in a miasma of whirling forms, music, and voices, punctuated by brief glimpses of Demona, Devyn, Sevire and the Prince as they passed each other in the patterns and movements of the dances. He exchanged pleasantries with a host of the curious, eager for a look and a word with the most daring young man in Pevana. He received a fair number of open propositions. He even had one old gentleman sidle up to him at the punch bowl and ask if he had any spare verses to mind that one could buy or borrow? At no time, however, did he chance upon any unguarded moments where he might speak with Demona alone.

And always there was Sevire.

His age and girth soon put him out of the lists; he kept watch over the festivities from a raised table set off to one side of the dance floor. Once and again, Talyior felt Sevire's eyes on him as he danced with one of Demona's friends or some matron giggling girlishly, but Talyior only caught that baleful glance as it turned away to whisper something to one of those overly-dressed bully-boys Devyn pointed out earlier. Summer heat and Pevanese intrigue, Talyior imagined himself dancing around the edge of a whirlpool, its vortex sweeping him inexorably down into dark waters.

Partners changed, as the dance called for. Talyior took his new partner into his arms and found himself face to face with Demona. He startled. She blushed. He kept his posture scrupulously formal, head erect, as he led her through first positions; and yet his fingertips against the small of her back flamed. Talyior heard her breathe in quick, little rushes and in one pass turned too sharply. Her breast brushed across his ribs. A cutlass blow could not have scored him more deeply.

"Tonight?" he whispered.

"Impossible," she responded, and stepping away once again she let her finger linger, the barest touch, against his right cheek. "He suspects me."

"The garden."

"No, love. I'll not be the death of you."

"I'm wounded to the death, just now."

Her smile deepened. Talyior noticed a bead of sweat running down between her breasts. He fought the urge to lick it away.

"Of course you are, love. I can heal that, but I cannot stop Sevire's sell-swords."

"Demona."

"Your words are on the lips of the whole city, my sweet. Foolish."

"I..."

"Patience." And then she was gone, spun off to another partner and away, lost in the whirl and lights, replaced by the wife of a rival rug merchant, a well-dressed slattern who grabbed his crotch.

"Be careful where you shoot your arrow, dearie," she said breathing into his ear. Her beath smelled of too much mint and wine. She gave a gentle squeeze. "Or you might lose it."

At the first opportunity, Talyior bowed himself out of the pattern and made his retreat. His earlier bravado somewhat shaken, he lurked off to the side as the final notes of the last song spun themselves out. The timing had been wrong. She had caught him by surprise. He would not squander another chance at his stolen kiss, by Toliman's beard he would not!

The music ended and the Prince appeared in the center of the ballroom, a glass raised.

"Friends!" he spoke loudly. "Let us thank our host, Sevire Anargi and his lovely Demona for this wonderful entertainment!"

He raised his glass higher in Sevire's direction. Sevire nodded a bow, calling back over the applause, "Tonight, as in all nights, what I have is at your service, my Prince."

"You enrich us and our city, good sir." The Prince laughed. "You are an ornament to Pevana in these times. This Festival will be long remembered because of this night. Yes?" He turned back to the crowd now howling like any mob at a tavern on a restday night. "But this Festival will be remembered for another and perhaps even better reason! For we are met in this hall to honor the finalists in the Competition of Poets! On the morrow's eve these seven shall present themselves and their poems for judgement by the committee in the Civic Hall in the Palace. Honored guests, take note and welcome the Poets of Pevana!"

One by one he named the seven winners of the first round. Talyior was caught a little off guard; other than Devyn, he had never even thought about who the other finalists might be. Two of them were students from the college, both looking a little worse for wear from spending too much time at the punchbowl. One was the court harpist, Ellaran Benydict, a former winner of the prize. The fourth was the son of the largest shipping magnate in Pevana, Bertole Fumari, an ascetic looking, pale-faced, lank-haired youth just passed adolescence. The fifth was a young priest who lurked next to and just behind the Prelate. Talyior noted the man's eyes as they darted, cat-like, about the room as though calculating the effect of his name on the hearers.

"And finally," the Prince announced, pausing until the applause died away. "In the annals of the competition, such a thing as took place at the ale house known as the Golden Cup has never happened before. A tie! And so I give you your last two finalists: Devyn Ambrose and Talyior Enmbron!"

Applause greeted the Talyior as he stepped forward, which grew loud and sustained when Devyn joined him from the opposite side of the crowd. They met to stand side by side in the open space around the Prince with the others. Talyior experienced a curious blend of pride, fear and excitement. He caught Demona's eye as she clapped with the others and saw there, he was certain, a promise waiting to be kept. He dipped his most dramatic, cavalier bow, and came up caught squarely in Sevire's dark, furious eyes, his left eye-lid twitching like an irregular heartbeat.

Talyior fought the duelist's instinct to step back. He took a calm breath. But before he could summon words, Sevire spoke.

"Congratulations, young man. I take honor by your choice of topic," he said, quietly, stiff smile carved into his stoney face. Leaning forward, he added, "But, I will take even more by your death."

Talyior felt the color drain from his cheeks, but he kept his shoulders square. Sevire leaned back again, chuckling darkly.

"I'll send your prick home to your father in brine," he said, still smiling. "I'll feed your heart to my cats. You've stepped in too deep, boy, and you will pay."

Talyior did step back but not away. The man's sweaty wrath repelled him. His threats infuriated him. Demona looked on, fear darkening her expression. Over her shoulder, Talyior saw the Prince, eyebrows raised as if to say, *Have you nothing to say for yourself?*

"I doubt my father would take delivery," Talyior said. "He already has one, but if rumors are true, you could use some help."

Sevire's grin faltered. Sweat beaded his brow. "Toss off what words you will, cur, your fame will be less than fleeting, and then they'll find your prickless, gutless corpse on the midden heap behind a house of prostitution."

"Thank you, Sir! My only intent was to extol the virtues of House Anargi!" he said loudly, and then, more quietly. "Better a short life, then, with the taste of your wife on my lips. Besides, you've guts enough for the two of us, old man."

Sevire stood motionless long moments. Talyior felt sweat now on his own brow. The man smiled that feral, dangerous smile again and backed away into the crowd, looking like a fat tomcat with a secret.

Talyior forced himself to return the smile, which turned genuine as a group of ladies swept him up with their good cheer.

"I was at the Cup, dearie," cackled a plump matron. "And I *loved* your poem! And so cheeky, too!" She pinched his arm. "Shameful but bold! A woman loves a bold one."

Talyior gave her a perplexed look before turning aside in response to a light touch on his ear. He found himself face to face with another, middle-aged maven with a pair of bold eyes undressing him from beneath a mass of hair piled ridiculously high. The woman pulled him close, crushing his arm with her enormous cleavage.

"I wasn't there," the lady husked. "But I wish I had been. If you grow tired of your Demona, my husband is often away." She sketched a kiss and floated away, leaving her scent behind, a disturbing, distracting promise. There were a handful of others who all wished him luck or hinted propositions. Talyior felt a little hemmed in by lace and sudden interest. He mouthed what pleasantries as came to mind and edged away until the crowd thinned. Folk headed for the food and wine tables to refresh themselves before the next round of music.

He found himself next to Devyn as the crowd began to thin, folks heading toward the food and wine tables for a bite before the next round of dances. Before they, too, could make their way off the

185

floor, the Prince appeared in front of them looking as if he were enjoying a joke at someone else's expense.

"Ah! There are you are gentlemen! No, not necessary!" he said stopping them when they made shift to bow. "Not tonight. It is I, who should bow to you. I swear, I've never seen Sevire so angry—unless I get him talking about taxes." He smiled at Talyior. "If the whispers are true, I admire your aim."

"My lord, I am not sure I understand you."

"What, false modesty? After *those* lines? *None of those fools can ever understand...*"

"My lord?"

"So, it is true!" the Prince laughed. "Of course, it must be difficult to contemplate seduction when you've stirred up such a hornet's nest."

Talyior's senses whirled even worse than they had with Sevire. Suddenly, he felt exposed and vulnerable. The Prince chuckled companionably.

"Easy now. I happen to like love and all its trials. Sevire may be a wealthy old bastard, but he's a fool. And that is where the danger to you becomes real, for he is just fool enough to try something." His voice dropped lower. "I'd rather you not die before having a chance to present to the committee tomorrow evening, so take care."

"And you, farrier," he continued, turning to Devyn. "Bold words! Well! Two hornets' nests disturbed in one pass. The good Byrnard, bless his pious, balding head, is not pleased, as I'm sure you've guessed."

Devyn managed to retain his equanimity better than Talyior, for he had a reply ready.

"I felt inspiration's sparks early and often, my lord."

"I see. And you meant no offense?"

"The Muses led me, my lord. Perhaps those offended gave offense?"

"I'm sure Brother Byrnard and his ilk would rather they led you to orthodoxy! And I am not offended, not in the least, but the good

Prelate is frowning, and his frowns are the frowns of the Church of the Realm."

"Church of frauds and manipulators," Devyn scoffed. "Begging your pardon, my Prince. You have done much to help me and the King is your cousin, but why did they have to burn the temples? Why did no one stop them?"

The Prince's expression grew serious. "Yes," the Prince continued somberly. "There have been . . . regrettable events, and not all of them foreseen by the players involved. I don't expect you to understand. I am Prince, not King."

"Try me," Devyn said. "I'm smarter than I look."

Prince Donari's laughed softly. He said, "Tell me how one defines *unity*?"

"My lord?"

The Prince looked from Devyn to Talyior, and in that glance Talyior saw something spark. Donari put a hand on each of their shoulders.

"Unity is one of those things that the powerful use to cover their abuse. They grant themselves a mandate, and so temples get closed, suffer combustible accidents and clerics get to strut their dogma in the colleges and councils. And so Piety, whether true or false, becomes one with Politics. What role for Poetry, then?" And he looked squarely into Devyn's eyes.

"Poetry, must always serve Truth, or so I have been taught, my lord."

"I'll grant you a touch there, my friend," the Prince replied laughing. "I remember that lesson, too." His expression turned knowing. "Yes, I remember. But even you must agree that Truth is a term that gets defined by those in power. And so there you are." He held up a hand, halting Devyn's words before they left his mouth. "You are a man of admirable passion, I can see. Be passionate! As I said, the good Prelate is sensitive to *imagery*. Have a care. Luck to you both tomorrow. I look forward to listening. Ah! It appears we are to have another round of music. Gentlemen, I'll leave you to secure your partners."

Donari moved off, the press parting for him like water flowing around a rock. Talyior frowned, concentrating, aware that he parsed maybe half of what just took place. He turned to Devyn with the question on his lips, but his fellow poet stood transfixed, staring at where the Avedun Prince had been swallowed by the crowd. Talyior suspected his new friend knew the answer to his question, but he refrained from asking.

STAYING TRUE TO DEMONA'S WISHES, Eleni positioned herself on the balustrade overlooking the ballroom as the guests began arriving. Folk entered and collected in well-dressed groups of fools driven by curiosity and the lure of entertainment to talk, watch and be watched. Demona commanded all eyes, standing like a goddess in her blue satin dress, hair piled in a glittering pillar of bejeweled hairpins and combs. She looked larger than life, a shining counterpoint to the looming hugeness of her overdressed, rotund husband. Where she glowed, gracing her guests with a beguiling smile, his grin seemed pasted on his face, an affectation at odds with his eyes darting about the throng, watching, calculating, plotting and scheming. Eleni watched them, wondering which of them was the more false, and decided they were, in this at least, equal.

She saw Talyior enter and move over to one of the tables that held cups and a punch bowl. If Demona saw him enter, she gave no notice. Sevire's face had fallen into a genuine scowl as his gaze followed his quarry about the room. He whispered quickly to a waiting footman. A moment later Devyn Ambrose entered and quietly moved to stand next to Talyior. The Prince and the Lord Prelate entered together, greeting those they came upon. Eleni stared, fascinated and repelled, by the multiplicity of threads and patterns running through the fabric of humanity assembled below her.

She felt a presence at her elbow, turned her head and looked up at a seamed, quiet countenance with a shrewd pair of blue eyes sparkling on the edge of open amusement. She stepped back a pace to observe a man, who looked on the nether side of middle age, dressed completely in well-cut black clothing that seemed to suit him like a second skin. The effect was set off by a silver dolphin pendant, the sigil of house Avedun in Pevana, pinned to the breast of his doublet. Strangely enough, the man's look made sense even on a night so filled with light and color. Before she could muster up words for a greeting, he spoke, his voice soft and sinuous.

"Well met. Allow me to introduce myself: Senden Arolli, assistant to Prince Donari. See the footman over there by the cloak room?" He gestured to the far end of the room where the white-haired servant who had escorted her to Demona's chambers took the hats and decorative coverings of the guests. "He tells me you are Eleni the Seamstress, daughter of the famous Streni Larosi. Good even' to you, mistress."

Eleni felt her guard go up, despite his cordial tone. She thought she had come to the estate unnoticed in the chaos of the afternoon's preparations.

"Good even' to you, Senden Arolli, assistant to the Prince. Forgive my rudeness, but do I know you?"

Senden breathed a chuckle and turned to observe the tableau below them.

"Admirable caution. Actually, I knew your father passingly. And I have heard of you and your—" He waved a hand, his amusement turning inward. "—skills. But enough of that. I see you've chosen a prime spot to observe Pevana's finest in their finest. Tell me, mistress, what do you see?"

Eleni frowned yet followed his eyes and scanned the room once again. She noted the dresses she had worked on, took in the ostentatious display and matching behavior, and found the whole scene hollow.

"I see clothes upon perfumed bodies without souls," she whispered, surprised by the rancor behind her words. "I'm sorry, I..."

"No, don't apologize," he murmured. "Look there, and there, and there." And he pointed to several places on the floor. "The Prelate, Sevire, and Donari. Pillars around whom swirl the seekers of power and favor. Can you see?"

Eleni looked again and saw it clearly. Nearly everyone in the ballroom was moving in a cycle of greeting and interaction, moving from one group to the other like school children looking for acceptance on the play yard. The only ones not coasting about in the swim were anchored to the pillars along one side, looking on in envy and curiosity at the goings on.

"Yes, I do see." Eleni's vision blurred. Below, color and chatter and intrigue melted together into a soup she wanted no taste of, despite her curiosity, and her promise to Demona. Neither, she felt quite certain, did the man standing beside her. She turned her eyes to Senden.

"Forgive me, sir, but what have you to do with me? I don't imagine a man in service to the Avedun Prince makes it a habit of chatting idly with a seamstress he has only heard tales of."

"Dust hangs in a sunbeam/ That misses me/ And covers the torn pieces/ Of all the promises you made."

Eleni looked away, her cheeks suddenly burning.

"I *listened*, last night at the Cup," Senden told her. "The young man who presented it had a beautiful voice, but he did not write that poem, did he?"

"I . . . he. . ." Eleni bit her lip, fell silent.

"It must be difficult," Senden said gently, "to be a spirit that longs to fly but who is held to the earth by custom and tradition."

Exposed, as if every eye on the floor were suddenly, knowingly, scornfully turned up at her, Eleni grasped for words to counter Senden's comment. How he had known did not matter; what did matter was why he sought her out to tell her so.

"The piece did not win. There was no harm done."

Senden raised his hands in surrender. "Please, mistress. I did not intend to frighten or offend you. I wish to help, as does Prince Donari."

"Help me?" Eleni frowned. "Help me to what?"

"You have applied several times for entrance into the college."

"How did—" she shook her head. Her frown deepened. "I did not know my efforts were public knowledge."

"They aren't," he replied. "But I am the Prince's man. It is my job to know and listen. When I hear odd things, I remember them. Such things tend to come in handy, I've found."

"Handy?" she scoffed. "So, do you play with people's lives, Prince's Man? Are hopes and dreams the pieces on your board? Will you squash my impudence with exposure? All I am guilty of is having talent and passion. How am I lesser than the fops cavorting down below us?"

She spun away from him but he grasped her elbow, his expression so pained her scream died in her throat. Eleni expelled a breath, her body relaxing. Senden let her go to lean against the railing.

"You misunderstand, though I do not blame you. To be a woman like you in a Pevana such as this, in these times—" He broke off, shaking his head. "These are days of change and reform. Surely you have seen it this past year. But it is not *our* change, not *our* reform. Change is being thrust upon us. Please, mistress, hear me. Pevana has need of all those with talent and passion to put things right. Sometimes old ways must make way for the new, but that should come from within, at the volition of the people, don't you think?"

Eleni's mind nibbled around the edges of understanding. All she ever wanted was to pursue her dreams unhindered by rules that made no sense. She knew about the temple fires, one could not live in Pevana oblivious to them; she had seen the red clad priests spreading throughout the city. But what has this to do with her and her poems that this man—this important man—would seek her out? Eleni sensed the edge of a drop off into deep waters, and her foot hovering just one step away.

"I am a tailor," she said. "I am a poet; yes, a poet. It was my work last night; I admit it. But that is all."

"Yes, a tailor," he said. "You make patterns. You create order. Don't you ever think about changing those patterns?"

"All the time. See most of the gowns down there? I remade many of them today."

"Did you do only what they requested of you?"

191

Eleni paused, mouth open, but found her lips clamping shut as thought became conscious thought. She *did* please her patrons. She listened to what they wanted and all their suggestions, but she was the seamstress, not they. None of them could know that a bodice could not be boned to cinch a matronly body back to youth, or that too many pearls sewn into a hem would be impossible to walk in. In the end, Eleni realized, it was always *her* design they went home with, believing it was their idea all along.

Just like the competition at the Cup, she thought. *My work given over to another.*

"No more," she whispered, turning to look down at the crowd below. Music started up anew and folk looked to find their partners. The Prelate, Sevire, temple fires, rumors. They slipped into place in her mind with surprising ease. "Change must come from within," she said, finally looking up at him, "or it never truly comes at all."

"Exactly." Again that gentle smile. "Pevana has need of all those with passion and talent, yes, but she will also have need of all those who can embrace change. Change *will* happen, Donari will see to it, *is* seeing to it even as we stand here talking to one another. There are too many like the opportunists below us right now. Pevana must keep her heart, her core. She needs Pevana's warriors *and* her poets."

Eleni laughed. "What good are poets in battle?"

"Laugh if you wish," Senden told her. "But remember this, Eleni Seamstress: not all battles are fought with swords and shields. Some are fought with ideas and courage. You have both. Your city, your Prince, will have need of you in time to come. I hope you rise to the call."

Eleni remained on the balcony long after Senden Arolli returned to the dance floor. His words, and all the words behind them, whispered through her mind. Her will. The will of a people. The will of Pevana. The will of the Avedun King and his Theology. And poetry. All threads wended and weft through the tapestry of her present, unbalanced her, because somehow, it all meant something to her.

The whirls of turned heads and voiceless whispers as Demona was paired with Talyior, as off at the table Sevire seethed only touched the edges of her awareness. She watched in growing disaffection as the colors, hair and lace spun themselves into patterns of insulated deceit. *We bend our knees, temper our thoughts and actions for such as these?* A desire for Tomais' sturdy, dependable love filled her, and yet she stayed rooted at the balcony railing, poised on the edge of something indefinite. *Home? The security of Tomais' embrace?* She wondered where *security* and *contentment* existed in this new world Senden Arolli had forced her to see.

She pushed herself away from the balcony as Prince Donari introduced the poets contending in the finals. She headed back to Demona's rooms to collect her things, escorted by a maid. She put her gear back in her basket and noticed how disordered it felt, haphazard, jumbled, much like her life *felt* at that moment. She took a last look at Demona's excessive dresses, took up her light wrap and left.

The maid took her down a back stair to the kitchens and through the tumult of action quite different from the drama unfolding above. Here there was purpose; behind her affectation. She snagged a bun from a tray. *Final payment.* She took a reflective bite of the rich, buttery roll. *No wonder Sevire is so fat.* She smiled her thanks to the cook as she slipped out the door.

She made her way through the kitchen yard, through a gate and down a walkway that skirted the house. She walked underneath windows bright with light that bled music. *More dancing. More pointless patterns.* She hurried by the line of carriages and their attendant drivers and footmen, only slowing when she neared the gates. She stood there for a moment underneath the wrought iron arch, her attention drawn by a swell in the noise from the house, and then she was off, walking slowly, contemplatively down the main way to the citadel gate.

She felt as heavy as the air she breathed, weighed down by new knowledge and questions. She glanced up at the night sky as she neared the gate. A star winked at her momentarily before the clouds obscured it, and then she noticed the tint that gave those clouds definition. She sniffed and did not hear the footsteps pounding the cobblestones behind her.

TALYIOR DANCED SEVERAL OF THE EARLY NUMBERS, but eventually found himself unpartnered. The throng had broken up somewhat. The Prince and some of his entourage left the floor to take places at Sevire's table. Groups of people collected in the shadows of the pillars to sip wine, steal glances, and gossip. Such a group collected Devyn, who seemed to be enjoying himself as he regaled his listeners with his rendition of the duel he and Talyior fought at the Golden Cup. But Talyior resisted all attempts to engage him in conversation. The surreal quality of his encounter with Sevire, the scent of Demona's perfume that still lingered on his sleeve and the odd interaction with the Prince combined to quench some of his youthful fires. He lusted for Demona, and yet, despite the absurdity of the evening, he had to consider himself in serious danger.

Devyn had seen it right from the start: House Anargi was full of too many eyes connected to too little brains. He thought back to Gania's words to him before he left and chuckled a little to himself, for she, too, had been right. He was a fool captivated by Demona's charms; adrift in a sea of emotion created by his own youthful exuberance. Where before all he could see had been Demona, the look, the feel of her, now he began to see some of the other threads that ran through the web he had landed in.

Beyond Demona's luxuriant, auburn hair there lurked a world of politics and deceit; just as did the words and passion that marked his time in Pevana. Blind before, he now began to sense some of the other rhythms of the place. Everything pointed toward the need for wisdom and care.

And stealing a kiss from Demona under Sevire's red nose would indeed be foolish. It would be a step even more tragic than bedding her in Sevire's own chambers, something he done twice already. It would be unforgivable, for it would be known. Talyior began to piece together how the wealthy of Pevana operated: adultery could perhaps be condoned within the class, but once things went public. . .

A hand working around his waste to grab his crotch broke into his thoughts, spun him to face the lady with the puffed up tresses looming before him.

"My husband is in his cups," she whispered. "I think it is time for a kiss."

Talyior leaned away in disgust and, looking past the woman's listing pile of hair, for someone, anyone to come to his rescue—and noticed Sevire. Laughing. Leering. Nudging companions to either side of his corpulent self to point at him. Ringed fingers pressed to painted lips, barely suppressing their laughter at his expense. Talyior firmly moved the woman aside.

"Quite right, my lady," he told her, brushed by her upturned lips, and headed for the dance floor.

He tossed off the last of his wine and walked over to the middle of the dance floor where Demona conversed with the Prelate Byrnard. There, beneath the shimmering lights of the main chandelier, before the aged priest could intervene, before Demona could even think of resisting, he took her forcefully in his arms and kissed her, once, deeply on the mouth. His tongue deftly teased her teeth before briefly meeting the tip of hers. For a moment, a deliciously eternal moment, Talyior felt her hand reach up to his neck, and then she pulled away, her face a mask of passion and perplexity.

"You fool," she breathed, backing away. "What have you done? Sevire. . ."

"Step back, away!" screeched the Prelate, reaching a claw-like hand to paw at Talyior's arm.

The entire room fell silent, collectively stunned and left breathless. Then chaos erupted. Sevire howled. Someone grabbed Talyior by his shirt collar and hauled him backwards. Other hands clutched at him, pulling and pushing him out of Sevire's reach.

"I'll come for you, tomorrow night!" Talyior shouted. "Be in the garden at midnight!"

Demona sputtered, pulled away by a handful of her outraged friends. From the shadows behind the orchestra, several of Sevire's servants moved to thrust themselves through the crowd. Out of the corner of his eye, Talyior caught a glimpse of Sevire shouting and gesticulating madly in righteous fury. A hand grabbed Talyior's shoulder and spun him around.

"Enough of that, pup." Sevire's bully-boy growled. Before he could grip Talyior in earnest, someone cracked the man on the head with a silver serving platter. Devyn loomed beside and hauled Talyior away before the man fell.

"Devyn!" Talyior hooted, stumbling behind. "Just in the nick. My thanks."

Devyn waved the dented plate in Talyior's face. "Boriman and Renia!" he shouted over the din. "Strange design for an orthodox house. Time for you to leave, don't you think?"

"A good time, yes."

"This way." Devyn tossed the platter away, ducking low and gesturing Talyior to do the same. They made their way through the chaos of gowns and hose to the shadow of one of the pillars near the door where he had first entered.

"It is you Sevire wants," Devyn said. "I will go back and point them in the wrong direction. Once you are out of here, keep going. A good night to you, friend. I hope you survive until tomorrow's hearing. I'd hate to win by default."

The taste of Demona's lips still on his tongue, Sevire's raging in his ears, mad laughter welled up from Talyior's gut. He choked it down.

"Tomorrow, then," he said to Devyn, who smiled, smoothed back his hair, and moved out from the shadow of the pillar into the melee. Talyior darted to the table where he had checked in his things. The servant had been true to his word, for there they were, placed well within reach. The old man gave him a wry smile.

"Your hat and blade, sir."

"Over there by the entrance!"

The cry went up, followed by more shouts and pointed fingers. Talyior grabbed at his rapier blade, nodded thanks to the old man and made to move past. The old man fell forward as though dragged, over-turning the table right in the middle of the hallway.

"Run, my boy," the old servant commanded. "And don't look back!"

Those in pursuit could not get past the old man still crying, "Oh, oh! My arm is broken! And my leg! I think a rib!" or the overturned table of belongings. Talyior dashed down the hall, out of the house and into the Pevanese night, pursued by half a dozen of Sevire's finest.

Talyior ran headlong down the main street of the citadel, his feet seeming to barely touch the paving stones. Perhaps the wine lent him speed, perhaps the memory of Demona's tongue sliding against his own when he kissed her, transformed him; it didn't matter. He left death behind him in the lighted hallways of House Anargi, followed by bully-boys with a mandate to kill.

He slowed as he neared the citadel gates, fearing they might be closed, and on any other night they would be. But this was festival week and all areas of the city were open for revelers and the watch. Talyior risked a look back at his pursuers. They were still after him but some way behind. He did not see the slim form of a woman, pausing in the shadows between street lamps. Talyior's foot caught an uneven cobblestone, and he tumbled into her, sending both of them head over heels in a clatter of sword sheath, shoes, and the contents of her basket. He picked himself up, assisted her to her feet, and recognized the girl from the Cup.

"You!" he gasped.

"You!" she returned in breathless whisper. Then her eyes widened as a shout went up behind and she saw those pursuing. Pushing him away, she too commanded, "Run!" and then screamed before slumping to the ground in front of the onrushing group.

Chapter 11: Flames, Fear, and Faith

KEMBRIL HALF-DOZED AS THE TWILIGHT SETTLED AROUND THE TREE. Into that gathering darkness he watched, without surprise, the approach of a group of figures moving furtively, exiting from the passage through the Maze that led to the Golden Cup. Some spread out to surround the tree and ward the approaches. Others clustered about a central figure. There was a spark as though from a tinder, and then flames caught on torches. Soon a score of them were burning brightly, and in their flickering light Kembril saw the gleam of drawn steel.

The sight made him feel tired beyond physical exhaustion. He patted the great root that supported his left side and, using his crutch-stick, struggled to rise, to face what was coming upright at the least. A figure, taller than the others, detached itself from the group and came forward. Kembril recognized him in the half-light as the same fellow from that afternoon, the Prelate's guard dog: Jaryd Corvale.

Death is loose in the Maze.

"Flames are never the final answer, son," he said at last, drawing himself up as best he could. "You do not know what you do."

"I know exactly what I *do*, old man," Corvale sneered. He stepped back a pace, turned and shouted out an order. Instantly, shadow archers ignited arrows wrapped in oily rags and launched them deep into the Maze. Kembril watched their progress as flickering trails of despair glimpsed through the boughs and leaves of the Oak's canopy.

"You cannot do this," Kembril cried. "There are people, innocent children..."

"Shut up."

Corvale motioned to the right and left and torches quickly spread around the tree.

"Right," he called out. "Get on with it, but leave our way clear until I finish here. We will see to this 'Tree' last. Should be quite the show, eh, old man? Did you think I wouldn't return? Silly of you, but then this whole place reeks of foolishness."

"None more than your own," Kembril said, and he tried to sound defiant, but such was his infirmity that his voice cracked and his words came out as a rheumy wheeze. Corvale laughed. Torches were set to bone dry canvass and wood beams. Shouts of alarm were met by the armed men ready for those who sought to fight the flames. The shouts turned to fear and despair. The flames spread quickly. The heat grew. Folk fled.

Thunder rolled off to the east. Kembril watched, as if in a dream, the flames grow higher, higher, licking the lowest, branches of the Tree. The Oak. Pevana's last and truest temple. For a moment, a last, organically brave moment, the moisture retaining leaves withstood the assault before the edges curled, withered and floated skyward.

Corvale's men cavorted in a dance-macabre, lurid shadows against the blaze. They tossed torches high up into the Tree, shot flaming arrows higher still. Within moments the whole thing was a sizzling, snapping conflagration. Hovels about the open space collapsed in fiery ruin, a terror of sparks and flames. Corvale leaned back, smiled beatifically, horrifically into Kembril's face.

"That, my friend, is a *fire*!"

THE CHAOS OF TALYIOR'S DEATH-WISH KISS, his flight and ensuing pursuit, created a morass of bodies in the ballroom and hallway in House Anargi. It took a few minutes to sort things out, then the place emptied like water through a burst dam. Devyn found himself momentarily forgotten, a reality he found somewhat disappointing.

He followed the rest of the guests as they crowded down the hallway and out the doors. The grounds were a muddle of carriages, shouts for order, torn dresses and stubbed toes as folk attempted to

Mark Nelson

either leave the scene or follow the action. Over it all, Sevire bellowed for blood.

The Prince, now joined by Senden Arolli, pushed through the crowd to the edge of the steps. The area about roiled in a confusion of carriages, footmen and anxious gentry. Talyior's departure had infected the rest with the same notion.

Donari sniffed the air, and felt the need to follow as well, his reasons far different than following a miscreant busker.

"Senden," he said quietly. "This is no good. We'll never get the carriage clear." He tested the air again. "Do you smell something?"

"I do, my lord, and I do not like it."

"Nor I. We need horses. Now. Choose, I'll follow."

Senden descended the entry stairs and worked his way around the edge of the mob to where a matched pair waited stoically in their traces despite the chaos. Donari followed, only mildly amused when Senden produced a knife and cut the bindings. Ignoring shouts of outrage, he and Donari mounted bareback. Donari kicked his horse into motion, Senden following as they pushed through the crowd that choked the way. Senden felt a grab at his foot and looked down to see the poet, Devyn Ambrose, jogging alongside.

"You, too?" he asked. "Your friend has kissed the hornet's nest this time. But I fear there is more afoot than Sevire's ire."

"He might need help," Devyn responded.

"We all might, before this night is ended."

Senden reigned back his mount, reached down, and helped the poet scramble up behind him.

"What do you mean?" Devyn asked.

"Is your nose too full of perfume? Smell the air, fool. That is not dalliance or whimsy. Hold on," he finished grimly and urged their mount to more speed. Within moments they had drew even with Donari and together they clattered out through the gates of the Anargi estate to the cobblestone street beyond. Down the slope they raced, ironshod hooves drawing sparks from the cobblestones. They reached the citadel gates, reigning in to a sliding, skittering halt among a group of guards clustered about a young woman. Devyn looked over

Senden's shoulder and saw for himself the tell-tale glow of the rising flames.

"By Tolimon's Wrath," Senden whispered. "What have the fools done?"

For a moment the group at the citadel gate stood awed to silence by the scene revealed to them. Devyn slid from the back of Senden's horse. He looked up at the Prince, who had ceased staring at the glow of the fire below. Donari looked down at Devyn, anguish spreading over his face.

"The Maze," he said. "What?" He left the question unfinished. Devyn glanced skyward and nodded mutely. Up there in the darkness the great thunderheads forming all afternoon from the summer's heat held the promise of rain. Devyn sniffed the air, sensed the heavy humidity, the smoke, felt the faint beginning of a landward breeze and measured the chance. *Perhaps, but we will need more than rain.* He caught the Prince's eye. *We will need Renia's Grace.*

"My lord," he said, gesturing vaguely back through the gates. "You said you *remembered*. About poetry, and people, I mean. Do you?"

Donari started at the comment, as though slapped, and then comprehension dawned on him. He looked south once again.

"The Tree. And. . ." He seemed to choke on the words.

"The old man, Kembril." Devyn finished.

Then one of the gate guards shouted, pointing south toward the Maze district. "My Lord! There, see?"

All looked south and saw, as though expelled out from the center of the rising glow, an arc of flaming missiles searing through the night to descend in sparks and fire. Within seconds attendant blazes started up, splashes of red and orange leaching outward, reaching to join with others and spread the destruction. Another flight followed the first, and then another. The flames arching outward galvanized Devyn into action. He touched Donari's foot to draw his attention. "Lord, I must go."

He did not linger for permission but dashed off into the night, urged on by fear, chasing his heart.

"SPEED, AND RENIA'S GRACE GO WITH YOU."

The Prince watched the young poet race off, his pulse keeping time with Devyn's retreating footfalls. Shaking it off, he grabbed the nearest soldier. "Send a man to the guard at the Landward gate, and another to the watch at Harbor Gate. By my order, they are to proceed to the area of the fire and help as best they can. All of you! Go!"

An open carriage clattered near; in it Donari could see the Prelate and Sevire. Behind it clustered other carriages full of chattering banquet guests.

"What goes here?" Byrnard's pinched face leaned low to ask. "Is that fire I smell?"

"A scent you should know well," Donari answered. "The Maze is burning."

Anxious murmuring whiffled through the gathered party guests. Byrnard sniffed, dabbing his nose with the corner of his red sleeve.

Sevire snorted a burbling chuckle. "Fire in the city and you send your soldiers off to fight it when there are dignitaries to escort home?"

Donari sidled his horse over to the carriage. The dull light of the gate torches, mixed with the lurid glow from the burning Maze, gave his face a pale, stone-like quality.

"Sevire Anargi," he said coldly. "There is nothing humorous about this. Enough!"

"So, flames in the slums!" Sevire sneered. "That's a nest that should have been cleaned out long ago. Fire's as good a method as any."

A murmured chorus of agreement came from the clustered carriages. Prelate Byrnard looked down his beak of a nose, a grin not quite twitching at his thin lips. Donari danced his horse in a circle.

"The poor?" He growled. "Fire is as good a method? Is this the extent of the King's Theology, then, Casan? To burn what it cannot control? What will Roderran do with a Pevana that is a burnt out shell of itself?"

The Prelate rose in the carriage so that he stood over Donari. "The King weighs loyalty to his policies and his faith. Even for those of the blood. Are you wanting, Lord Prince?"

"Loyalty?" Donari asked in return. "I question yours, Prelate, and your motives. Have you eyes? Do you see the flaming arrows? This is no accident! You speak of loyalty. I suspect treachery, Priest. You question me? Would you have answers were I to question you? You claim I am wanting. Yes, I am wanting both rain and assistance. Is your belief strong enough to provide both?" He turned to Sevire. "And you, you fat fool! Have you no sense for anything other than your profits? Those are people's homes, man! Their lives are threatened."

Sevire shrunk back but Byrnard, sputtering in indignation, thrust a quivering, boney finger under Donari's nose.

"How dare you!" he shrieked. "I am the Vicar of the King's Theology! I am Lord of Collum! I . . ."

"You are a cleric without compassion for the poor!" Donari shouted over him. "How is that, pray tell? Do your joints ache so that you need fire my entire city to warm your cockles? Remember this, old man. Pevana is *my* city, and the lives of all her people are my concern. These are my folk." He lifted his eyes to those party guests still cowering behind the Prelate and Sevire. "Yes, those of the Maze as well as all of you! And if Roderran wants them entire," he glared again at Byrnard, "he might find a more gentle method than fire and murder. Put that in your next missive to my cousin the King."

Nudging his horse into a walk, Donari left Sevire and Prelate Byrnard still sputtering venom he had no stomach or patience to listen to. His guardsmen fell in, as did Senden and, to his pride, several young men from those clustered carriages. They rode as one down the avenue, heading toward the Maze, and the center of the flames.

ELENI STOOD FOR A MOMENT INDETERMINATE, watching Devyn race off while others dispersed back towards their homes and still others collected around the Prince. The image of Talyior's shocked face swam before her mind's eye, and she read there fear, amazement and concern. His visage faded to redrimmed real time darkness as the night and its flames claimed her attention. She looked once more down the way Devyn had gone and followed the Prince.

Their group descended the slope, Donari's presence causing folk to collect in his wake. Tradesmen, city guards, folk well and ill dressed followed him down towards the Maze, breaking up into separate clumps as he motioned people down side streets. Red light bathed everything with drama. The heat grew apace with the flames that had now begun to spread. They reached the outskirts of the slum. Donari reached up and tore a length of canvas from a dilapidated awning and plunged it in a horse trough. Others followed his lead and advanced, damp and dripping towards the glow.

Donari paused and turned to Senden. "This is not good enough," he said. "We will need to beat these flames back from all sides or risk losing everything. Gather what you can. Work around to the west. Yes? Go!"

Senden nodded wordlessly and turned to go and nearly ran over Eleni. "Mistress Caralon! You'd be safer at home."

"While other folks' homes burn? What safety in that? I can help."

"But..."

"*Pevana needs all her poets,* yes? Well, *this* poet intends to douse some flames. We will pass by my house, actually. I have a store of unused cloth that might be useful."

Senden smiled. "Come, then, we must be quick." He turned and sped back up the street, grabbing several sturdy looking fellows in passing. Within minutes, Eleni found herself at the back of a jostling, hurrying mass that ran against time and hope to an uncertain destiny.

DEVYN SPRINTED DOWN THE MAIN STREET, looking for the alleyway that opened off the corner of the square fronting the Cup. Concern for Kembril dominated his thoughts as he pounded along, the old man's name reverberating, matching the frenzied rhythm of his steps and breathing. *Kem . . . Bril . . . Kem . . . Bril. Please Renia, let him have gone to the Cup. Kem . . . Bril . . . Kem . . .*

An arm shot out of nowhere, grabbing him, spinning him to a stumbling halt. Devyn tensed to throw off his assailant.

"Whoa, hold, Devyn! Where are you going at such a pace?"

"Avarran!" Devyn gasped. "The Maze—"

"—is burning," Avarran finished, letting go of Devyn's arm. He gestured to the men behind him. "We know. We saw the flames from the Gate towers. Where is the Prince?"

"I just left him. Back at the citadel gate. He and help are on the way."

"Then we should get to him quickly and—"

Devyn stepped back. "You go, Av. I can't. Those flames are meant for the Tree . . . and Kembril."

Avarran glanced south to where the inferno blazed the hottest.

"You'll be too late," he said. "You'll burn along with the old poet."

"No! Don't say that! I have to try!"

Avarran growled curses under his breath. He fuddled with the straps of his breastplate, turning as he did to motion one of his men forward.

"Taril," he said forcefully. "Take the others and find Prince Donari. Do what you can. Samsar, Oder—leave your shields. Now, off with you!"

"What are you doing?" asked Devyn as the squad trotted off into the night's growing chaos.

Avarran kept working at the laces of his armor-bindings. "I know you too well to try and dissuade you, and I haven't time to arrest you or the men to waste in keeping you safe." He loosed the last tie of his armor, bent to pick up one of the heavy infantry shields. "So I am coming with you. Now grab that shield. We may need them to keep the flames off of us."

Devyn hesitated. "Av, your men, they'll need you to—"

"He is my friend, too." He thrust the other shield into Devyn's hands. "Do you think you survived the streets totally by chance? Who do you think got me into the Prince's service? Come, lead, Maze-rat, and let us see if we can save him."

Devyn slid his arm through the shield straps, nodded to his friend and set off on a wild course towards the fire-glow in the distance. The twists and turns slowed them, but there was no other way; the fire had already spread too far. Devyn cursed the excruciating heat, led Avarran through a tunnel of flames, shields raised above their heads. Falling matter struck them and bounced off. Devyn's nose hair singed with each breath. He stumbled over a burning beam, righted himself, felt Avarran give him a sturdy push forward and continued on, gathering what pace he could. Running near blind towards the heart of the Maze and Kembril, he burst through a skein of burning canvas and rolled, tumbling to his knees in the open space before the Tree.

KEMBRIL BLINKED THE DREAM AWAY—a nightmare of all he had sensed coming but did not want to believe. Had he two knees to drop to, he might have. He raised his fist instead.

"Why do this?" he cried. "Were the temples not enough?"

Corvale moved closer, put a fiendishly casual arm about Kembril's shoulders.

"Temples, trees, slums. What the Prelate orders, I do. Call it what you like: reform, cleaning. It's all the same to me, friend."

"You are a fool!" Kembril shook him off. "The King's Theology will not win followers this way!"

Corvale shrugged. "It has nothing to do with *winning*; it is about taking. The King sees what he wants, and he takes. With some help, of course."

"But these people! The Maze!"

"No more *buts*," Corvale said coldly. "It is time this place got cleaned up. I have had enough from you, old man. Stay and burn with your tree for all I care."

Corvale started away. Kembril stumbled forward, nearly fell over root and cane and sorrow. Wheezing himself upright, the smoke gathering in his damaged lungs made him cough so that his vision blurred. He stumbled after Corvale, for what he would never know, and spied Devyn kneeling at the opening to the way that led east and north, another man at his side. The old storyteller's heart clenched. *What is he doing here?*

Kembril shook his head. Pride and sorrow mixed to form a bitter pigment as he realized he was left with but one choice. Death seared the region around the Tree, and he had not saved Devyn for such a fate. He shuffled closer and shifted his grip on his crutch just as Corvale, too, noted Devyn's presence. The villain pointed with his sword, called out to his men. Kembril tried to shout a warning, but his feeble voice would not pierce the roar of the flames. With his last strength he swung his crutch wildly at Corvale's back, fell forward with the effort, and onto the sword that came up to deflect Kembril's last, feeble call to arms.

The blade plunged deep into Kembril's bowels. He felt it like heat. Corvale grabbed the tattered remains of his shirt and dragged him up the blade, twisting it. Heat turned to ice. Kembril shuddered. Blood erupted from his mouth. Corvale leaned in close, an intimacy belonging to lovers, and there the old storyteller saw the end of his tale in a madman's eyes.

"You talk too much." Corvale growled and shoved Kembril off his blade.

He slumped against the trunk of the Tree, his Tree, slid down bark warmed by the flames claiming the canopy until he lay in a crude caricature of his wonted position. He felt his blood pool about the Tree's roots beneath him, the surreal light of the rising flames turning the liquid, a deep, deep crimson. Kembril's head tipped back, lolling on his neck as if no longer quite attached. He gazed up at the dearly remembered tracery of limbs and smiled. Even now, engulfed in fiery leaf that ran from red to white hot, there was beauty. Colors blended, trickled down the trunk like rain, and life departed even as the flames' scorch reached him.

No more need for words. They no longer exist.

The constriction of his lungs relaxed. Kembril Edri, Pegleg, Maze-poet, friend, took a last, painless breath. His vision narrowed to a candle point. Then blackness. Then a sound like rain. Then peace.

HOLDING THE SHIELD TO PROTECT HIS EYES, Devyn tried to blink away the nightmare of Jaryd Corvale standing before Kembril. The Tree burned furiously, creating a vortex that sucked up flaming bits of matter, adding fuel to the inferno. Through the heat haze, he saw Kembril slump back against the tree.

Devin lunged forward as a beam from a hovel to his left burned through, showering sparks and cutting him off from Kembril. It struck Avarran's shield.

"Ah, Dev! Help me!"

Devyn quailed, caught in the moment of Kembril dying, Avarran pinned, Corvale calmly sheathing his sword and walking away down the path that led to the Cup. Grief and fury consumed him as fire did the Tree; and Kembril. He was as good as dead. Corvale was too, or would be when Devyn caught him.

Flame-wind wicked away his tears. The moment released Devyn. He jammed his shield under the burning beam, levering it up until Avarran could shimmy out from underneath.

"Go," Avarran coughed. "Corvale! He's getting away! I'll follow!"

Devyn wasted no time on words. The Tree began to drop burning branches that piled up about its base, burying Kembril in so fitting a pyre. Devyn sent a silent prayer for Renia's Grace to see his friend into the next life, and set off through the heat in pursuit of Corvale.

He raced around the edge of the cleared space to that passage his enemy had vanished down, knowing it instantly. This was Devyn's world; and Corvale was only a rat in his Maze. Behind him, a series of pops and the resounding boom of the Tree exploding made Devyn duck, cover his head with his arms and shield, but he did not halt. If Avarran followed, he had not made it.

Devyn raced on through the heat. Within moments he left the burning areas behind.

He tossed the cumbersome shield away. Breathing in short gasps, eyes weeping tears from smoke and sorrow, Devyn neared the end of the passage. Right or left? In his mind's eye, he saw Corvale standing over Kembril, sword in his right hand, his dominant hand. Devyn chose right, and ran headlong into Jaryd Corvale.

The collision knocked both of them off balance. Devyn recovered first and flung himself at the larger man. He reached for the sword he left behind at the banquet, cursing and slamming Corvale in the mouth instead. His lower lower lip burst in a satisfying splash of torn flesh and blood.

First blood to me, you bastard.

Corvale stumbled backwards, recovered, snarled and launched himself at Devyn. He landed a blow to the side of his head that sent Devyn reeling. Jaryd followed with a kick to the stomach and another blow to his head. He was a rat cornered and fighting visciously. Devyn struggled to clear his head and force air into his lungs. He saw Jaryd come at him, dagger drawn. He clamped a fist around Devyn's throat and pressed the blade against his ribs, slamming him back against a wall. The blade pricked. Devyn's eyes opened wide. *Forgive me, Kembril.*

"You are a damned fool, a real simpleton!" Corvale hissed, spraying blood into Devyn's face. He increased the pressure on the dagger. Devyn winced when the tip broke skin. "What, the poet can't find the words to say? About right for a meddling, little sneak like you. Time for the sneak to meet with his accident, so we can finish with his helpless little Prince and this cesspool of a city." He shifted the blade so that its edge lay against Devyn's neck. "Yes, you need a bigger mouth for all those fine words of yours."

The tension in the man's grip built. Devyn closed his eyes, thought of Kembril. Jaryd stiffened. Devyn braced himself for the last bubbling rush of blood, but the pressure on the blade against his throat eased. The dagger clattered to the ground. Devyn opened his eyes to see the tip of a rapier pressed beneath his enemy's bloody chin. He followed the line from blade to hand to face and recognized Senden Arolli. Devyn's knees quivered.

"You are welcome," Senden said. Jaryd's eyes burned as he backed away from the pressure of the sword tip. He brought a hand up to swipe the blade away.

"Na, na, none of that, now, Master Corvale," Senden chided, leaning his weight into the blade. "I wouldn't want you to meet with an unfortunate *accident*. I can't imagine what the Prelate would say if his lead dog was found with a rather large hole in his neck."

Arolli prodded Corvale to the end of the alley where a small group clustered around the opening. Saymon Brimaldi balanced his persuader's cudgel on his shoulder. Next to him stood the young woman from the Cup, Tomais's wife, Eleni. She gave him a quivering smile he could not return. Devyn stood blinking in the smoke and torch light. A group of soldiers rushed by them bearing axes and shovels. The fire boomed and roared behind them as more and more of the Maze succumbed to the flames.

Brimaldi lunged forward with his cudgel. "Is this the one? The fire-starter? I say run him through. Just once, and now. No waiting."

"Go ahead," Jaryd rasped. "And once Byrnard learns who did it, how long do you think your Prince will keep his place? Do it, Arolli, be the man! Or are you as useless as your master? Useless, gutless, dandy-boys."

Senden lowered his blade. Jaryd's fanatical leer glowed like the flames in the distance. *Demonic as Tolimon*, Devyn thought. *Life and death mean nothing to him, even his own.*

"Ha! I knew it!" Jaryd scoffed. "Too soft! Too . . . too Pevanese!"

Devyn's blood simmered. One-legged, rheumy Kembril, dearest of friends, beloved teacher, slowly turned to ash while his killer defamed all that he once embodied. *Pevanese.* Yes, Kembril was, and so was Devyn. He lunged for Corvale, sent him stumbling backwards. Senden grabbed his arm, yanked him off and tossed him into Saymon without ever taking his eyes off Corvale.

"Have a care, my friend," Senden told him calmly. "Or perhaps I will let these *soft Pevanese* show you how they deal with murderers like you."

"Murderer like me?" Corvale laughed. "I don't kill *people.* I kill dogs, vermin, maggots. I burn buildings devoted to obsolete deities, slums, hovels. *Under order!* That makes me a soldier, you simpering piece of filth. *King's* order, and not some mimsy Prince!"

Saymon's cudgel slipped from his shoulder. Several of those on-lookers took a step forward. The hair on the back of Devyn's neck rose. Senden never lost his calm.

"I'll be sure to give your compliments to my mimsy Prince," he said. "Come along now. It is time you, and your master, answered some questions for—"

A gut-hollowing boom like the Tree exploding all over again shook the air; lightning flashed before the ground stopped quaking. The heavens opened as the landward breeze finally pushed the great mass of clouds over the shore. Another thunderclap burst another flash of lightning. Someone screamed—Eleni. Devyn reached for her, a chorus of screams rose up, and he stumbled into a cowering Brimaldi instead.

"Hold!" Senden cried, steadying Devyn and reaching down to help Eleni up. As she regained her feet, the rain hit them. Torrents of water obscured Devyn's vision. People scattered. Chaos and rain dousing the fire, sending up thick plumes of black smoke, Devyn clawed through the crowd to where Jaryd Corvale had screamed his mad bravado. He spun, and spun again, slipped and nearly fell.

Corvale was gone.

THE RAINS PELTED DEVYN, extinguishing his wrath even as it beat down the flames that consumed the Maze. He stood there, water dripping into his eyes as he confronted the reality of what had just happened. He, perhaps better than anyone else in Pevana, understood just what the fire of that midsummer night consumed. As the rain soaked him and the others in the group in the square, he added his own tears to the flood.

The awareness he had only just become aware of that afternoon was gone. Like Kembril. Like the Tree. The absence desolated him. Renia's tears, her last gift, washed him. He looked at the rivulets of mud and ash running away down the street and saw the last vestiges of his old life flowing away, replaced by a bleak hardness that had always been there, perhaps, but surfaced now at need.

He shook the water from his hair, offered his hand to Senden and said, "I owe you my life, again." His voice cracked; inhaled smoke or the residue of grief, he could not tell.

"No debts, lad," Senden said kindly. "This was rank luck. Mistress Caralon and I, we came this way to fight flames. You were fortunate this time. Jaryd Corvale is your enemy in earnest now, I'm afraid. Best take your sword with you from now on, eh?"

Devyn looked down the street, almost invisible in the rain that pelted down. *Jaryd Corvale.* All through the spring Devyn had struggled against an unknown, the amorphous results of policy, but Corvale was something flesh and blood, and reachable, that he could hate. He still had tasks: a friend to grieve, a poem to recite in partial payment for the ills done to Pevana's ways, and for Corvale something more complete.

Devyn regarded the woman, Eleni. Despite her bedraggled appearance, he knew her for the same one from the night before, the real poet that evening. He bowed.

"My thanks, madam," he said. "I am in your debt."

"Eleni Caralon," she said, offering her hand. "And no thanks are due to me, either. Pevana has need of her poets, or so I've been told." She looked sidelong at Senden, a ghost of a smile on her lips.

Devyn shook her hand. "Yes, *all* her poets."

They looked at each other in dripping awkwardness. The rain slowed to a drizzle and then faded away. Devyn glanced back toward the Maze. The downpour had drenched the outer edges of the fires, effectively slowing and then stopping their spread, but the hottest spots burned on. The area about the Tree still sent flames shooting skyward, throwing a red yellow glow over the city and dusting the night clouds with color. *They are the colors of grief,* Devyn thought. *Kembril, what will I do without you?*

A shout brought him back to the present. Avarran came limping down the alley. Blood leached away from a nasty gash on his forehead. He still held his shield. He shrugged his arm free of the straps and let it fall with a clatter to the cobble stones. His wet clothes bore the marks of the flames, and his hair was badly singed on one side.

The sight of his friend, even so, eased Devyn's heart. "I am glad you made it."

Avarran shook his head in response, his burned and bloodied face a study in sadness. "The fires blocked your path after you took off. And then the Tree. . ." He glanced over his shoulder as if he could see it. "Renia's Grace, I have never seen the like."

"What happened . . . after?"

He swiped blood from his eye. "I could not follow, so I made a try for Kembril. That's when I got this. Branch almost killed me. And the heat. I couldn't reach him. I'm sorry, Dev," he finished in a strained croak. "All gone, Kembril, there's nothing there but fire, lad."

Devyn put a hand on Avarran's shoulder. Senden approached and offered his arm for support.

"Come," he said. "There are still flames, and we have work to do. We will deal with Corvale later."

AFTER FIFTEEN YEARS AS AN ANOINTED PRINCE OF PEVANA, on that night Donari began to rule. He labored alongside his people combating the fires, clothes sullied and torn, risking himself to save others, shouting out encouragement to those near him, a tireless champion, a dirty, sweaty, blistered hero. People rallied to his call, redoubled their efforts, guardsmen, tradesmen, nobles from the banquet, Maze-dwellers, all working together to salvage what they could. And yet there were many noticeably missing from the fire lines. When dawn finally arrived, wet and smoldering, more than a few eyes turned with dark aspect to observe the untouched great houses on the slopes of the hill.

With the rains and the advent of morning, the danger to other parts of the city passed, and Donari found himself in the square outside the Golden Cup, accepting a cup of water from a grimy, out of sorts Gania, the proprietress of a nearby house. They had worked side by side throughout the night. She left after the rains to see about food and water for the fire parties. Donari graciously accepted the Cup she handed him and drank it down in one draught.

"My thanks, mistress. That tastes better than ten year old Anargi Red." He smiled, leaning in companionably and holding his cup out for more. "See that the others get their fill of this fine water."

Gania's round face beamed. "That I will, my lord. An' it's I an' all the others here as should be thanking your lordship for all your help. Could have been a bad one, that, I grant you."

Donari ran a hand through his wet hair as she refilled his cup and moved on. It could have been worse, he agreed silently, but it was bad enough. He knew about the Tree in the Maze, and what it would mean to these people. To him. As soon as he saw the glow in the distance, he cursed himself a fool for not taking measures earlier. The notion of upsetting Sevire and Byrnard with the banquet had distracted him; and so the Prelate had stolen a march on him.

A reckoning would come, soon enough.

The Festival could not end like this. The Finals *had* to go off as planned, else Byrnard and all his cronies won. Donari could not allow such a victory. He sipped at his water, taking in the damage done and thwarted. It had not been a great fire, but it had been effective; and not all on Byrnard's side of things. Pride swelled in Donari's chest. The fire had kindled a flame in his people. It had pulled them together, driven them to act.

Ah, dear Byrnard. Have you any idea what you have done?

Handing his cup to a young woman gathering them, he called his guard to him. It was time to find Senden and see what preparations he could make that would take the sting of the smoke from the eyes of his city.

Dawn arrived with a glimmer of hopeful light through the steam and smoke. Donari met his eyes and ears at the intersection of the Harbor Street and the Main Way. With him was a young woman who looked vaguely familiar, despite the mud and ash on her clothes and face. He cocked an eye-brow in question.

"Mistress Eleni Caralon, my lord," Senden said. "Seamstress and tailor. She . . . her husband spoke at the hearing two nights ago at the Cup."

"Ah, yes," Donari said. She was indeed the young blond woman who looked with such insistent eyes on her husband as he had run through his short but powerful piece. Donari remembered the scene with a little self-pity. What had Senden mentioned about her last night? He searched his tired brain for the memory as Eleni dropped him a deep curtsey. He recalled hearing mention of a letter, several letters of application—hers? *Why would a woman do such a thing?* He raised Eleni by the hand, kissed her grimy fingers, and when he looked into her eyes he understood. She bore a different kind of fire there, a talent caged and tempered by her times and manner, but strong and in need of space to grow or risk fading away.

"My thanks, mistress, for your efforts tonight," he murmured quietly. "You appear unharmed. A mercy. Allow me to assign a guard to escort you home. The rain and the fire may have dampened somewhat the activities of the city, but it is still an unsafe place for a woman alone."

"My lord, it is not necessary. I live close by."

"Nonsense," he said. "I won't hear of it." He signaled to one of his men. "See to it that Mistress Caralon arrives at her door unmolested, and report to Senden when the task is done."

"A kind gesture, my lord," Senden murmured as the guard escorted Eleni away. She looked curiously over her shoulder once. Donari waved and she turned back, quickening her pace. "A king's guard for a local seamstress in the broad light of day."

"I can't keep Byrnard from torching my city," he responded, "but I can at least ensure a young lady gets back safe to her husband. Walk with me, Senden." He eschewed the mount offered him; the need to linger among his people, to let them *see* him among them, held him fast. He kept his voice low. "How came she to be with you?"

"She was at Sevire's; apparently a house call to save Demona's pride. Poor lass missed the kiss that put paid to her efforts, though. She was in the group at the gate when you began giving orders. She followed us, and when you sent me off she went with me. I arrived just in time."

"Hmm?"

"To keep Ambrose alive. Corvale had him cornered."

The Prince hissed. "And then you cornered Corvale, I take it."

"Momentarily, my lord."

"Did you kill him?"

"No. There were too many witnesses, and he's too closely connected to Byrnard. I worried what his sudden absence might bring."

Donari looked over his shoulder at the smoldering ruin of the Maze. "Perhaps you are right," he grunted. "But after last night, I fear we may be running out of time. Where are you holding him?"

"Nowhere, my lord." Senden cleared his throat. "He got away during the storm."

"Got away?" Donari composed himself. "You should have killed him."

"Perhaps, my lord, but I think Corvale will get his in the end."

"How so?"

"Young Ambrose. The fire took only a few lives, but one of them was the one-legged poet Edri, who folk called Kembril Peg-leg. He was Ambrose's friend and teacher. His death will be avenged, mark my words."

The news smote Donari like a blow to the face. Memories swam in his mind's eye. Youth and freedom. Wine and poetry. *Such a loss.* Donari bowed his head, felt the sting of tears.

"What is it, my lord?"

Donari looked up. "I knew him, Senden. The old storyteller."

"Everyone knows of him. He was as much a fixture as the Tree that died with him."

"No, Senden, I *knew* him, when I was a boy, back before you came to work for my grandfather. I used to sneak out to the city to annoy my tutors. The freedom, the disguise, the dirt, it was bliss. I met Edri, he was old even then. We shared wine purloined from the palace storerooms. He told wonderful tales. He listened to my awkward verse and pronounced me a poet, and he never once let on that he knew who I was." Donari laughed softly, glancing sidelong at Senden. "Of course he did know. I gave myself away far too many times. But he pretended, and I have always appreciated that."

He let the thought fall to silence, then, "So, Corvale escaped. Can you find him?"

"The Lord Prelate will have him long gone or hidden by now, but I can try. I will set watch on the roads."

"And if he has gone to ground in the city?"

"Then I would have to beat young Ambrose to him."

Donari grimaced. "Can the boy take him?"

"He deserves the chance to try, my lord."

Donari considered the notion briefly. Donari could do nothing himself, not now, with things coming so swiftly to a head. That very evening could see decisions made, and all beneath the guise of a poetry reading.

"Fine," he said decisively. "Watch him, though. Nothing untoward must happen to keep him from speaking tonight. I want the moneyed fools and that serpent Byrnard to hear it first hand. Rot them all."

"He has his own escort home, my lord, and he will be watched and safe-guarded. Corvale hates him, but I don't think he will try anything. Byrnard doesn't want anything to upset *his* plans, either. And, as for our own, my lord, there is no sign yet of Enmbron. He disappeared in the chaos that resulted from that kiss. Sevire's bully-boys were after him."

Donari cast a worried glance, but found himself chuckling at the absurdity of it all. "Ah, my friend, ways change and lives are lost over words, over kisses to strumpets masquerading as rich men's wives. Policies are enacted and changes made in the name of faith, but truly for power. And, as usual, the innocent suffer most." He stopped walking, put a hand on Senden's shoulder. "But no longer. Not if I can help it. Come. We have much to accomplish before the Finals."

He let his hands fall and started off again into the growing morning. The idea of a bath and a glass, no, several glasses of Anargi Red appealed in ways both calming and devious. He laughed in spite of his exhaustion, and because of it, as does a man whose plans were snicking neatly into place. He had not slept, but day was just beginning, and so was Donari.

ELENI TRUDGED HOME, followed a step behind by her unneeded escort, dazed by just how far she had come since she first put ink to parchment. How had her letters ever come to the attention of Prince Donari? He was a person removed from her sphere, a distant figure of wealth and privilege, ignorant of her personal struggles and set far above the weave of life in the city.

Festival changes all.

The Prince had known her; he had kissed her hand! She looked at it, kissed twice by men not her husband in the same night. And in both of them she had sensed tension of power and rage barely suppressed. She turned her hand over to gaze at her wedding band; and there was a third man whose hand and soul had touched her. Tomais' was a different sort of touch—a more lasting impression. She had sensed those fires within both Devyn and Donari, but they were beyond her ken. She could only observe and try to parse her thoughts out with words. She knew, eventually, words would come. She would write the history of that night. But right then she knew what she needed most in the world was her husband, and as if in answer to her prayer, he was there, opening the door even as she reached for the latch. His face bore a twisted look of despair and fear, turned to joy when he saw her on the doorstep. *Two worlds*, she thought to herself as she let him crush her against his chest. *Changed, and yet. . .* She returned his embrace with the intensity of one hanging on to at least some of the familiar in the face of the new.

Chapter 12: Day Three

TALYIOR GREETED THE DAWN WET, TIRED AND HAPPY TO BE ALIVE. He thought back to his ordeal of the night before and confessed himself lucky to have survived his own foolishness. After fleeing through the citadel gate, he raced for his life down darkened streets pursued by a squad of Sevire's men. At first he led them on a winding course, trying to lose them in the twists and turns of the lanes that criss-crossed the slopes below the citadel.

But he soon ran out of such streets and in desperation cut down an alley, leapt for a low-hanging beam from a warehouse, swung himself up from the ground and quickly climbed to the roof. The adjoining structures either abutted seamlessly, or were lined by small alleys, easily leaped. Talyior raced down this surreal pathway, eluding all but one of Sevire's men.

Talyior led his pursuer on his rooftop chase, winding far quicker than he ever thought he would. Each pushed stride, each gathered leap became less sure, more clumsy. A narrow alley nearly did Talyior in. Sevire's man failed completely, landing with a rib-crunching thud against the side and clutching desparately at the bricks. Talyior laughed once over his shoulder, kicked a last burst of energy into his flight, and left the man grasping for purchase, to fall or save himself.

He made several more jumps. After the last he listened for further pursuit and, hearing none, settled down to wait out the rest of the night. As his pulse slowed, frenzied thoughts caught up with him. Like a flock of pigeons they flew about in his head, a cacophonic jumble of sense impressions: Sevire's blotched face, Demona's voluptuous form, the Prince, Devyn. He laughed at himself then, painfully aware of the absurdity of his life, so unknowing and foolish.

The flames to the south doused the laughter on his lips. His desperate flight had blinded him to the lurid glow that greeted his ascent to the rooftops. He stood there at the end of his race and watched the city burn, hearing the cries for water and help begin to rise as a wave of sound. The Maze burned in a score of places and one place in particular blossomed ever brighter as though what burned there had ignited some precious store of fuel.

Talyior sat there on his rooftop in awe of the spectacle spread before him. Pevana was not his city; he held no deep connection to it. He was a spectator, nothing more; and yet as the night went on he felt his connection to Pevana and her people grow. He did not dare leave his perch, but to do nothing was—it was unconscionable. And yet nearly everything about that night had been beyond reason. He stayed put, waited out the night, and fretted helplessly over the scenes revealed to him.

Frenzied thoughts took form as he watched the flames, became words, unbidden but welcome:

Out of a chaos of dreams comes the light
Of the consistent day.
And each heart must know, in the morning's glow
That all shadows must fade
To insignificance
With each new experience
That informs the chosen way.
And so on and on and onward
Weighted with knowledge gained in pain and joy,
Each step taken with more surety than the last
Made so by the memories of lessons past—
Goes the life of the young man.
The soul is a sponge that absorbs shadows
And when squeezed brings forth new hope

Witnessed by the sun at dawn.
It is a pathway of many turns
Illuminated by wisdom.

As the lines in his head ran out, there came a great burst of thunder and lightning directly over the city. The instant torrent of rain drenched him in minutes. Talyior stood up to it, the wetness a welcome relief from the heat and stress of his trial. He raised his arms to the rain, letting it wash away his sweat and illusions, and the youth he had clung to so desperately until this night of nights.

Talyior stood and stretched as the light grew, dispelling the memories. Wisdom. His father would say he had no right to the word. *You've let yourself get addled, boy. No proper respect for risk! Get back to your accounts.* Talyior chuckled softly. Yes those would be his words, or close enough.

"I am alive, after last night," he told a pigeon on the ledge above his head. "And I'm *living* these days, not wasting them away sneezing carpet dust in a warehouse. I am one of the Poets of Pevana!" His upthrust arms startled the pigeon off. Talyior watched it flutter away. "For better or for worse. The rest of my days may amount to nothing, but tomorrow night at the Finals I matter. I matter, and that is something."

The bay of Pevana unveiled itself to him as a slowly brightening expanse dotted with the still shadowed forms of the fishing fleet working its way out to work the banks that lay at the bay's mouth. Smoke from the fire hung in a gray fog to the south of the city. Talyior breathed deeply, working tired muscles and exploring the ruin of his clothes. More of the gold from the Cup would find its way to the tailor's today; a regrettable necessity. He turned inland and noticed he was not far from the outer walls. The roof of the Cup was just in view, separated from his rooftop perch by a jumble of dwellings and businesses that made up the hodgepodge of the poorer district. Off to his right lay the stables and corrals of the horse traders, tacksellers and farriers. Gania's house lay somewhere beyond, east, close up to the

Harbor Gate. He sketched for himself a roundabout route that would get him to the alley that ran behind Gania's, thinking it were better to avoid the main streets. Talyior made a half-hearted attempt at straightening his clothes. He kept alert as he descended into the darkness that still held sway in the lane behind the building. The morning was quite still yet, and Talyior saw no one save a handful of cats prowling around a refuse pile. It seemed only the fisher-folk were up and about. The growing light of morning revealed the sodden ruin of the Maze: a blackened spot to the south of the Cup.

ONCE HE RETURNED TO HIS CUBBY HOLE in the stables, Devyn cast himself still damp and filthy on his pallet and fell asleep at once. The same dream perplexed him as in the days before the Festival, flames and falling masonry, but with an even more troubling addition. Before, he would awaken as the flames took the roof of the temple, but this time the flames that shot up heavenward took on the shape of the Oak fully engulfed by fire. He watched, horrified in sleep, as Kembril's face appeared, framed by the tree's burning limbs. He spoke, but the roar of the flames drowned out the sound of his voice. And yet Devyn could make out the words his lips formed: "Fire Poet, fire poet, fire poet" over and over again. And then the dream exploded into shards of meaning, scattering like ash from the inferno. Images presented themselves showing his past with Kembril. They lingered just long enough for Devyn to take them all in before flames burned through their center and sped them away to places where failed hopes and dreams collected on the midden heaps of eternity.

Fire poet, fire poet.

Last one, lost child.

He groaned himself awake, took in the familiar surroundings and judged them desolate of all goodness. His friend, the Tree, both gone. All was ash turned to grey mud by the rain or blown seaward by the land breeze. He felt as lost as he had when his grandfather passed away. And yet this was far worse, for he could see no hope of filling the void Kembril left in his life. Theirs had been the camaraderie of minds: pupil and master. He knew he did not need a master any longer; that, too, had been extinguished in the flames. He was Renia's poet, charged with a final office on her behalf.

He knew he could complete his task. But what after? The things that bound him here lay desecrated, denounced and destroyed. *Hope is ash blown on the wind. Where will it blow me?*

He rose and went through his tasks, dawdling over them, pausing to take a few extra moments with each beast as though attempting to recover the image and the pleasurable sensation such activity had always given him.

By the time he finished his ablutions at the altar and progressed to his sword exercises, Devyn understood there was nothing left to tie him to these well-remembered streets and people. He wrapped the idea around his heart like a blanket of decision and accepted the finality of it. If he survived the Finals, he would leave Pevana.

A sound came from behind him over by the corral fence. He whirled, sword at the ready and saw Talyior Enmbron clapping gently as he leaned over the topmost beam.

Devyn's smile deepened. "You!" he said and walked over, sheathing his blade

"You!" answered Talyior, smiling in turn.

"Well, then," Devyn said. "Now I am doubly glad I didn't take that bet."

"I still have my stones, thank you very much."

"Oh that, ha! Yes, I forgot. I was thinking of the wager I almost made with the Prince's harpist. He was giving four to one that you'd be gutted before morning."

"And morning is come. Never doubt me."

"I shall try not to," he said coming over to the fence. "I told him you'd make it at least until tomorrow night."

Talyior laughed at the jest, and Devyn found himself joining in, despite his dark memories of the evening. He felt something ease; he had not awakened expecting mirth of any kind to find him, and yet there it arrived with Talyior.

His rival motioned to Devyn's altar. "I see not all the Temples to the Old Ways in Pevana have been burned. I knew a shepherd back home who kept just such an altar in the crook of an old oak tree. When I was little he would set me to gathering a supply of wild flowers and grasses. I wonder what the good Prelate would say to that."

Devyn cast a pensive look at his place of prayer and meditation. "He'd claim it blasphemous, spout a prayer, and then sign an order for his arrest. In the end, I suppose, the only ones who would suffer would be your shepherd and the sheep."

"Then he doesn't know our shepherd," Talyior told him. "He's a right demon with his staff. I once saw him lay open the head of a wolf with one back handed blow. I'm sure he'd give his inquisitors some bruises for their curiosity."

"Perhaps," Devyn agreed. "But such are the times that I would not doubt the final outcome: his staff burned, his altar broken and scattered. His gods forgotten and the wolf let loose among the fold. Casan would call it *progress*."

"You are a poet, man! I never picked you for a cynic."

Devyn turned and looked him square in the eyes. "I'm not," he said. "I'm just bitter." He turned and gestured to a small table set near the altar. "I assume you are bound homeward? Perhaps a cup of wine and some bread? It is quite fresh. I have a *friend* who thinks the way to my heart is through my stomach. I was just about to set to, join me?"

Talyior climbed over the fence rails, and the two most notorious poets in Pevana broke their fast together on the morning of the greatest day of their young lives. At first they ate in companionable silence, the need for words forgotten by the taste of bread and lightly watered wine. They ate as only young men who had lived through a night as they could eat; indelicately munching and slurping their way through loaf and flagon, lost in the need to fill the voids they both felt.

As they ate, Devyn sensed a growing connection between them that went beyond wanting the same goal or the magic created during the Duel at the Cup. He considered asking Talyior if he had any such similar thoughts, but the man spoke before he did and Devyn swallowed the words with his wine.

"My compliments to your friend for the quality of her bread," Talyior said.

"Baking is one of her many sterling qualities."

"You say that as though there are other qualities that might apply."

Devyn smirked and tossed off the last of his watered wine. "Yes, she has many talents, as you suggest."

"Special?"

"In her way, but probably not as special to me as is your Demona is to you."

"Ah, how tragic for her."

"Perhaps," Devyn replied laughing. "But I prefer to think of myself as a champion serving as many as I can."

"I see," Talyior scoffed. "A real man of the people."

"I thank the Gods daily for creating women."

Now it was Talyior's turn to laugh. "Ah, yes! A perfect sentiment!"

Both men grew silent, as though each picking his way through a bramble patch of thoughts, half-aware of deeper things but for the moment avoiding the sharp pricks of truth.

Devyn broke the silence. "Why do you pursue Demona?"

Talyior took a deep breath and let it out slowly before responding. "You've seen her," he said simply. "She's amazing."

"Yes, that much I'll give you," returned Devyn. "But I have also seen Sevire."

"A fat, balding bag of impotence."

"Perhaps," countered Devyn. "But he compensates. What do you hope to achieve?"

"She consumes me. She's lonely in that huge house. She wants and needs me."

"Really? Do you trust her?"

"I must. I am compelled."

"I understand. She's a beauty. Matchless. But what of her soul?"

Talyior recoiled. "Don't make light of her! I warn you!"

"I meant no offense. I just ask, as a, friend, I suppose, for I have met and talked with both your lady and her husband, you see, even though they wouldn't remember me."

"When?"

Devyn got up from his stool and walked over to where the first line of stalls began. "See those horses over there? They bear the Anargi crest branded in their hides. I break his raw colts. Once, a few years ago, Sevire brought Demona with him to check on one of his racers. She clung to Sevire's arm like a lampry as they walked about the place. She asked me about the beast. I stammered something, and then she touched my arm and laughed. Sevire actually used his riding crop to move me back away. Demona forgot I was there, instantly. I know I was a young sprig, but I swear she touched me on purpose so Sevire would notice."

He walked over to one of the stalls, Talyior trailing behind. He paused to rub the muzzle of the mare haltered there.

"I mean no disrespect to Demona or your feelings for her," he went on quietly. "It is just that I have had many encounters with the wealthy of Pevana over these last years. Frankly, I find more nobility in their horses than I do in most of them. I begin to think the Prince might be different. Curious." He shook off the thought. "A treasure no one knew about burned in last night's fire. And I lost a friend. I'm not sure which is the greater loss, but something dear is gone now. It feels so vastly different from the grief of losing my parents. I never knew there were this many kinds of sorrow. I just wonder if you feel anything similar in light of all that happened last night."

Talyior moved alongside him and offered his hand to the mare to sniff. "I am truly sorry for your loss. As for Demona, no offense taken. Part of me knows I've quite lost myself with her, but I can't help it, Sevire or no Sevire. I can understand your distaste with Pevana's wealthy. You train their stock, my father's rugs cushion their slippered feet. I've seen them saunter through our warehouse in the harbor, dickering with Espan over prices and quality. Such disdain. Demona is different. At times I felt she found me as much as I found her. I don't know."

The mare whiffled and nuzzled their proffered hands in turn. The morning light brightened further and the sounds of the city awakening filtered into the stable yard. A spell of shared sorrow, of kindred-kind fell over the pair. The sensation was as comforting as it was uncomfortable.

"How did your parents die?" Talyior asked.

Devyn surprised himself, and perhaps Talyior, by launching into a tale of woe he shared with almost no one. He told how he lost his family and wound up on the streets until Malom Banley took him in, taught him about horses and bade him keep them cleaner than Devyn kept himself.

"I've been doing it ever since," he finished. "So you see, I've been dealing with the stink of Pevana for quite some time. There are moments when I feel it is rotten at the core."

"Such bitterness."

"Well earned, I should think. Many folk perished, most of them from the poorest parts of the city. I lived, made it out of my teens, and yet the worst of it only began when Casan set his lot to burning things."

"I remember," Talyior murmured. "Few places escaped the plague. Sad. We were visited by the reformers, also, but the Old Ways were more understated there. It seems there were no great temples to be burned. I remember seeing a great pillar of smoke as my ship neared the harbor back in the spring. I had no idea."

"I nearly lost my life in that blaze," Devyn told him. "The altar you saw is the only thing I was able to save. They kept the people who would have fought the fire away at spear point. That's why my poem uses the images it does, and why I had to ask the Prince that question last night. No one has done anything. I felt I had to."

"But surely, you must see the futility?"

"Just as surely as you must see the outcome of your affair with Demona."

"But. . ."

"But what? But you are different?"

"Exactly."

227

"And how is that? Your better sense has told you what to expect, but you are attracted by the gesture and notion of love. You are a romantic, and I respect you for it."

"And is it the same for you?" Talyior asked. "Notions and gestures?"

Devyn laughed at his own folly. "Yes, I suppose so. I cannot let the Old Ways pass unchampioned. Someone has to ask the questions. Someone has to ask why Sevire Anargi is serving cheese off a platter that used to hold offerings to the Goddess Renia. I have to for my faith, my city, my dead friend."

"A heavy charge, I think."

"Smell the air. These are heavy days." Devyn shook off the dark descending upon him. He bowed as a poet finishing his recitation. "So there you have the whole of me: Devyn Ambrose, orphan-poet, religious-patriot, shoveler of some of the noblest horse shit in Pevana. And what of you? How comes a carpet weaver's son to this sty?"

He brushed the mare as Talyior told him his story, and quirked an eyebrow when Talyior spoke about the fractured relationship with his father.

"I lost my father," he said when Talyior paused. "Yours seems to have lost you. We are both orphans of sorts in the world. I wonder what tonight holds in store for us, eh?"

"Victory, defeat—death?" answered Talyior.

"All three, perhaps. What will you do with the prize money? *If* you win?"

"I'll take Demona and head south. See the world. And you?"

"I'm leaving. After last night, I can see no reason to stay, but I will say my piece before I go. The Prelate has the wind of me now. There's really nothing holding me here."

"Not even friends with sterling qualities?"

Devyn laughed. "That can be found anywhere. I've yet to find my Demona. I don't think she exists in Pevana."

A loud shout startled both men, breaking the spell of kindred-kind and returning them to the present. Devyn pushed past Talyior to grab a pitchfork.

"That's Malom, my employer," he said. "A man with no understanding or time for words, but you won't find a better man with horses in Pevana. I've work to do. And you?"

Talyior fingered a tear in the knee of his breeches. "I've a need to spend some more of the Prince's gold. Tonight, then?"

"Tonight. Luck to you, my friend."

"Luck to us both."

Devyn smirked, hoisting a load of hay into the mare's stall. "A man can buy a lot of luck with two hundred gold coins!"

Talyior smiled as he turned to go. "I'd settle for half!"

"And a glass of Saymon Brimaldi's finest!"

"Two glasses!" Talyior tossed over his shoulder. "Tonight, Ambrose!"

Devyn scooped another forkful of hay but let it slip off the tines as he watched his new friend pass out of sight.

Tonight.

Chapter 13: Visitors and Visitations

BY MIDMORNING ON THE THIRD AND FINAL DAY of the Pevanese Summer Festival, the Prelate Brynard Casan picked at a plate of cheese and fruit with sincere relish. Last night, so offensive at the start with the conflict and chaos at Sevire Anargi's botched banquet, had ended better than he ever could have hoped. True, the miscreant poet Ambrose had not met with a timely end, but Jaryd and his group had succeeded beyond the Prelate's intentions by putting the Maze to light; and in the fire removing the final obstacle to reform and victory. He felt sufficiently secure in his designs, so much so that he composed another missive to Roderran before retiring the night prior, urging the King to begin marshalling his troops and transport. The army could winter in Pevana, and in the spring would come the great adventure.

Byrnard took a piece of fruit as sweet in taste as was the image of Roderran at the head of his troops, Byrnard and his brothers by his side, the whole of the Southlands open and ready to enter the Perspan fold.

The hint of smoke still on the cloak tossed on the chair before his desk smelled of promise to him, like the blade to the smith before the final folding that would bring the steel to its strongest, ready for the edge. The only disappointment was Jaryd's failure to eliminate Ambrose. They would have to suffer through another episode with the young firebrand that evening at the Finals. However, he was but a little voice after all. The flames roaring up the Oak tree branches and spreading out to consume the Maze spoke far louder.

What sort of control could such a hapless sop as Donari hope to hold now? The upsets of the season, culminating in last night's chaos, would surely compel the King to come to the aide of his southern dependents, adrift as they were in this time of leaderless confusion.

The Prelate popped a piece of cheese into his mouth and chewed slowly. The texture was glorious. He let the smoothness coat his tongue, savoring it like intrigue. He rather liked the food and wine of the region, but the people left him cold as a northern winter. Sevire would be all but useless once Roderran appropriated his ships and gold as a grateful donation for the war effort. Good food, good spirits, a malleable populace. There was something to like about Pevana, after all.

And yet I think there is too much of the South here; it needs a Northern touch.

Byrnard wished Jaryd were there, an accomplice to gloat with over their shared victory; but the boy had to vanish for a time, of course. Donari's middle-aged snoop would otherwise have him in irons before the day was out. The college library provided a safe place to secret him until such time as Byrnard could figure out how to better use him.

He sat back in his chair, sated on the fruit and cheese and a job as good as completed. With any luck, his second message would reach the King before the first; he had sent his best and fastest to the task, after all. Roderran would assemble and come south. Simple as that. *And then the south.*

The Prelate stretched, a smug smile creasing his beak-like face. A job well and done, indeed.

Prince Donari Avedun reclined in a tub of slowly cooling bathwater, soaking away the smoke from his hair and skin and contemplating the coming evening. The Prelate's most recent missive already winged to Roderran; Donari had it on good authority that a messenger had been sent late the night prior. What it contained, he could guess: a leaderless city, ready for the taking; a cowed populace; a dead faith.

But what will you truly find upon marching south, cousin?

The Prelate and his contingent of reformers had spent a year nibbling away at the fabric of Pevanese life, but last night they stumbled on the taproot to the people's soul. On the surface, life would go on as before, but the fire had resurrected something of the Pevanese awareness—the Old Way's belief in the intrinsic connection between a people and their place.

Change would come now, directed by other currents and fates. He felt it. The bitter knowledge distasteful because he knew he still had to play politics with Byrnard and Roderran in order to save as much as he could from the pending military adventure. His cousin King expected allegiance to the crown; especially from kin. The fire denied Donari the options for large, grand gestures. He was now forced, for good or ill, to rely on small moves, subtle chips at the foundation of Roderran's power and greed. He could not topple it with impunity; he could now only temper its effect, to mitigate the loss of Pevana's spiritual and political independence. But a qualified victory for Roderran might yet seem like a small success for Donari. *Small voices, small moves. That is what is left me, but can I match Casan's penchant for intrigue?*

He slapped the water in frustration, cursing his own apathy for letting things go so far. Roderran was an impatient fool with power in excess and tools, like Casan, set to the purpose. It had taken a loss as great as the Maze fire to effect the change the Prince had only just that day deemed necessary. *Too little, too late. The Tree is gone. Kembril is dead.*

He felt a chill that was more than the bathwater cooling. He had begun last night's adventure in control, or so he had thought, but some of that confidence had burned away. *Kembril was gone.* He sensed an absence that cried out for action. *Action, from a fool who had turned inaction into an art form.*

Donari tucked his remorse deep into his heart. He sighed and dunked his head, rinsing the wretched night from his hair one last time. There would be time to take it out again. For the moment, he needed all his wits to out-fox the old conniver posing as a man of the King's Theology.

Donari strode unattended and with purpose to the Prelate's rooms, rapped a quick staccato on the door and burst in without being given leave. The surprised look on Byrnard's face was worth a year's taxes.

"My Lord Prince. Please, come in, come in, what may I—?"

"Were you anyone else but the King's arm in any of the recent events," Donari spat, backing the old man up against his desk, "I would split your balding head open and feed your brains to pigs."

The Prelate's eyes flared, but his face paled. "What, what?" he stuttered. "How dare you barge in here and—"

"No, how dare *you,* you meddlesome, murderous bag of bones! Last night, you went too far. My patience with your false reforms is done."

"Salvation of the lapsed is not a pretty business," the Prelate retorted. "I work for a higher power, not to be gainsaid by you or your people!"

Ah, all my gold for a sword and silence! Donari breathed deeply, quelling the desire and gathering his calm. "Last night moved us beyond the lies you told and I accepted, Casan. You serve only one higher power: King Roderran. Your actions in the north and here have been nothing but a pretense to fuel his aims. No!" He slammed his palm down on the table. A candlestick clattered to the floor. "I'll not hear your lies! We both know it is true."

Byrnard's eyes flashed. "Lies? You dare much, young man, Prince though you are, to speak to me like this. I always knew you were impetuous and loud. I did not know you were stupid as well. What use your cousin King sees in you eludes me. He should have removed you years ago."

Donari's jaw clenched. He stared at Byrnard's scowling face until his temper cooled. *Oh you old, old fool. How long before Roderran sees no further use for you?*

"Stupid?" Donari said at last. "Perhaps I was to ever believe Roderran's reform had anything to do with faith. I am smart enough to have deduced his true aims for Pevana, and the south, and he, *you,* will use fire and sword to get it, even against our own people."

"Then, oh-wise-Prince, you must know that should the people see the wisdom of the King's Theology, he will spare the sword."

"Take a people's gods from them, you take their souls. If you have their souls, you have them. Is that the gist of it, Lord Prelate?"

"You speak treason, my Lord Prince." All the muscles in Byrnard's pinched face twitched. "You should be embracing Roderran's will as your liege-lord and cousin instead of ruling Pevana as if it were an eternal festival. You allow superstition to survive, just like your grandfather."

"My grandfather?" Donari snorted. "What has he to do with the conversation at hand?"

"Nothing." Byrnard sat behind his desk, began shuffling papers there. "Nothing whatever. It is time for you to leave, my Lord Prince. I have much to do today in light of—"

Donari dropped into a chair, kicking his heels up onto the Prelate's desk. He plucked up a faceted paperweight and held it to the light, admiring the refraction while the old man stewed, likening the effect to that of small pieces of the Prelate's designs chipping and falling away.

"You and my grandfather were contemporaries, isn't that right, my Lord Prelate?"

Byrnard snatched back the crystal. "We served together. Now if you would—"

"Yes, you and my grandfather served the *King* together when you were both young men on your way to power and glory. Have I ever told you how lovely your robes are, my Lord Prelate? Very lovely. So . . . red." Donari thrust his feet from the desk to lean forward in the chair. "Not as lovely as a crown, I'd wager."

Casan slammed his papers down. "It is time for you to *leave,* my lord!"

Donari rose slowly to his feet. He tapped fingernails on the wood desk, leaving fingerprints on the polished surface. "My grandfather," he said calmly, "would have taken your head, Corvale's, and a score of your so called priests for last night's travesty. You know it, and so does my cousin."

"Your grandfather is dead." Casan sneered. "And what I do in the name of the King's Theology is not only Roderran's will, but the One's. I have been given the responsibility of seeing to the reforms. Interfere at your peril."

"Keep trifling with my city at your own."

"Roderran will come."

"And he will find me *properly* loyal, not conveniently."

"If he finds you at all." Byrnard looked him square in the eye, had the audacity to not even blink. Donari leaned over the desk so that their noses nearly touched.

"Threats, my Lord Prelate?"

"Accidents happen, my Lord Prince."

"As I have seen. Have a care, Priest. I still rule in Pevana."

"By the King's Grace."

"By right of blood. My *grandfather's* blood, same as Roderran."

"Your comprehension of events is lacking."

"And yours of me and my rule is misinformed." Donari pushed himself away from the desk, walking backwards as he spoke. "Roderran needs Pevana for his southern plans, fine. But I will see to it my city is not abused. And remember this, Byrnard. You do not know just how much like my grandfather I am."

And until this moment, neither did I.

He turned his back on the Prelate and whatever retort was trying to make its way past his quivering lips. The call to action had been made and answered, the challenge met, the accusations thrown. Donari left the Prelate's chamber a wiser man than when he had entered. He halted at the door, steadying his twitching lips until he could turn without grinning like a fool.

"See you tonight at the Finals, Byrnard. Be sure to wear your lovely robes. I'll be wearing my crown. It will be grand, no?"

Pushing out the door as boldly as he had entered, Prince Donari sent a silent prayer to the departed Renia for grace and courage, and a thanks to Minuet for aiming true.

BYRNARD STARED AT THE CLOSED DOOR after Donari left, a suffusion of rage and contempt. *To be spoken to thus by one such as the Prince? Unacceptable.* He had ordered men executed for less during his campaigning days. Slowly, by degrees minute, he let the anger cool. He could not let any such visitation occur again. He could see the need, now, to absent himself from Donari's roof.

"Aemile!" he barked. Instantly the door to the outer chamber opened and his secretary hustled in.

"My Lord Prelate?"

"It is time we removed ourselves from the Prince's hospitality. Are the rooms prepared in the college?"

"Yes, my lord."

"And Corvale well-ensconced?"

"He awaits your pleasure."

"Good, get us packed up and installed in the college by this afternoon. We will visit before tonight's festivities, and perhaps we will bring a guest back with us. Make sure Jaryd bathes, and find him a suitable robe with a cowl." He considered, nodded. "Yes. Time to go. I will not suffer another day in Donari's debt. See to it. Immediately. Or pay the consequences."

Donari intends to trot out his pair of wordmongers. Fine. I will bring my answer with me.

IT WAS MID-MORNING BY THE TIME TALYIOR made it back to Gania's. Sevire took his chance last night and failed. In the full light of day, he knew nothing would befall him. Talyior walked down the familiar lane to Gania's door, his head an ocean of Demona's image, poetry, and the darker elements of recent events. The competition he had entered to win his heart's desire bore the stench of politics. After last night's dramas it smelled worse than the refuse pile behind the butcher's stalls outside the city walls.

Ambling into the house, Talyior's thoughts slammed out of his head when Gania's fat fist caught him under his right ear. Laid out on the doorstep, only half aware of her immense form standing over him and screaming something about bully-boys and damages, Talyior tried to hear her tirade through the ringing in his ears. Bending to shake her finger in his face, straightening to get her breath before returning to the fray, Gania showered him with her pent up fear and disgust.

"Gania, please!" he managed to croak when she finally lost breath enough to pause. "I was thinking of a bath, but a shower like this is better than rain! Is there more, or are you done?"

"It's you who is done, you swag!" She grunted, grabbing a fistful of his tattered shirt and unceremoniously hauling him upright. Then she all but threw him down the hall. "You done it this time, lad! Look!" And she showed him the ruins of her main parlor: chairs and couches broken, end-stands and vases shattered. There was a large stain on one wall that looked to be the remains of one of Lyssa's stews. Someone had even taken one of the potatoes and mashed an *A* into the carpet.

Talyior turned in a circle, speechless.

"I warned you, didn't I?" She wheezed. "You go sauntering off to the dance like nothing could touch you, behaving the fool and expect to get off clean?"

Talyior dodged the cuff she swiped at his head. "I had no idea this would happen."

"Open your eyes, lover-boy. Pevana is not as soft as she seems. I had to call in a lot of markers to keep those bully-boys from setting fire to the place. This and the flames from last night? It is just too much! Favors, mind you! Long collected and hoarded for need, and I had to use them on you!" She jabbed her thick index finger, rapier-like, into his chest. "You are done, child. I'll have no more of you under my roof. I can't afford it. You go off and moon for Demona's charms if you want to. Pay the price yourself. I'm done. I've other tenants to consider, d'you hear? You're out."

Talyior stopped her leaving with a touch on her arm. She turned her baleful eyes on him, a mixture of raging, sorrowful conflict. He reached for his purse; it was quite full, for he had stopped by the Cup to collect on the previous evening's wagers from Saymon. "Please, take this," he said. "You have been like my own, if vicious, mother since I arrived in Pevana. I need only enough to get cleaned up for tonight. There should be plenty there to set things right. I'll have even more after the Finals."

She took the purse, clutched it in a fist at her hip without looking inside. "Poetry, still? You must be loose in the head, or else I hit you too hard just now. Do you think that fire was an accident? I spent half the night beating sparks out with my good towels and came home to find a group of ruffians at my door. Those bully-boys were out for blood—your blood. Look around you, boy! Look what they done here!" She lifted the hair from her forehead, showing him a bloody scrape. "You'll be dead before tomorrow unless you find some way of leaving today. You could bet on that with Saymon if you're stupid enough. I'll take your money, but you take my advice: leave, now." She looked away. Her jaw worked back and forth. "I—I could arrange it."

"You know I cannot."

"Then die and good riddance!" She growled, throwing up her hands and turning back to her kitchen. "Get up and have a sleep, if there's a bed left in that mess to do so. Your gold bought you that much at least. I'll have Lyssa bring you something to eat later." She turned at the door. "And next time, you might want to keep your papers in a better hiding place."

Talyior bounded up the stairs, threw open the door. His poems were scattered about the room, parchment torn to pieces, his quills broken, ink supply splattered on the wall. Someone had taken most of his clothes and tossed them in a pile. He bent to pick up a favored shirt—a gift from Demona—and smelled the urine soaking it. They left the table upright, and on it lay a single small scrap of parchment. One of the bully-boys had left him a message:

Little fish in big waters
Should stay near shore

And away from other men's wives and daughters.
Else they learn to live a life that's sick
Going thru their days without a prick.

Talyior crumpled up the missive in disgust. He gathered up all the scraps of his work he could find, looking for what he could salvage. Taking his soiled clothes and tossing them out the window, he lit a candle to mask the worst of the smell. He stared at the flame. In his mind's eye, he saw the Maze ablaze. The banquet, Demona, the kiss, the fire, Gania and her bloody forehead—it was all connected, connected to him.

He recalled his rooftop flight, growing breathless as if he ran it now. Taking deep breaths, willing his racing heart to ease, Talyior opened his eyes to that flame. He brought the candlestick to the window ledge, along with a few of the bits and pieces of his ruined poems. Small piece by small piece, he set them afire. Something inside him shriveled, withered away as he watched the words blacken to soot and gently taken by a gust breathing down the alleyway. When the last of the ashes had blown away, he took out his blade to hone its edge and polish its length.

He moved the bed and table off to one side to clear some space in the room. As Devyn had done that morning, Talyior stripped to his under clothing and spent the next hour re-familiarizing himself with the rhythm and cadence of the sword. He flowed from pattern to pattern back and forth across the floor. Talyior Enmbron would not be caught off his guard again.

"Up, up, Tal!" Lyssa roused him from the slumber exhaustion had dropped him into. "Here's some food, a new set of clothes, and a visitor for you. Come on now! Get up!"

Talyior groaned upright, rubbing his eyes. He recalled shooing Lyssa away earlier, and asking her to see to a new set of clothes for him, but had no recollection of falling into bed. Blinking away the blurry remnants of slumber, he found his visitor a most unexpected one.

"Espan!" he said, pulling on the breeches Lyssa left. "Ah, I know why you are here. Save your breath. I'm not leaving."

"Hear me out Tal!" the older man sputtered. "I have to answer to your father!"

"*My father* cut me off, remember? Disappointing degenerate, wasn't it? I'm on my own. He'll not blame you, regardless of the outcome, so stop worrying."

Espan fixed him with a stern glare, the seams and wrinkles on his weathered face deepening. Talyior held his silence. If he did so long enough, the man would surrender to his whims, as he had done so many times in the past. This time it was no whim, however, Talyior would not let Espan sway him no matter how good the intentions.

"Lad, be reasonable," Espan finally burst. "I could have you aboard ship and gone by the even'tide. You've stirred up a wasp's nest of trouble with that poem of yours. We had visitors at the warehouse late last night. Me and the other boys showed them the door quick enough, but, by the looks of things here, your landlady wasn't so lucky."

"I've compensated Gania for her troubles."

"It's not about money, you young fool! I couldn't face your father knowing I'd have to tell him you were dead, and it was death those scoundrels were after. No mistake about it. Go home. Today! It's only a competition. She's a great beauty, but she's only a woman. A *married* woman. She can't be worth it."

Talyior hesitated, and was shamed for it. His course was already plotted and set; and it did not lead homeward just yet. He would have victory in the Finals. He would win Demona, finally and at last, as his own. The south awaited. He could not turn his course, even for Espan's genuine concern.

"I'm sorry to disappoint you, my friend," he said smiling and shaking his head. "But I won't come. I can't. Words lead me a merry chase, Espan. I have to follow them. And Demona? Well, beauty or no, worthy or no, love is *always* worth every risk."

"But, your father—"

"—will have to wait awhile yet to disown me in person."

Espan ran a hand through his graying hair. "Suit yourself, boy. You always have. If you change your mind, the tide turns at an hour after sundown. I will hold the ship until then."

Talyior led him to the door. He took Espan's offered hand in a firm grip at the top of the stairs. "Thank you for trying, and tell my father . . . tell him—"

"—that his son is a fool?"

"He knows that already. No, tell him I am rolling the bones and taking my chances. Tell him that. Perhaps he will understand."

Espan did not respond. He just shook his head, released his grip and stumped down the stairs. Talyior watched him descend the stairway, his poet's mind seeing each step sever the ties that bound him to his old life. All his previous experiences and days were a tide retreating from possibility's shore, leaving the sands smooth and clean. Espan turned at the base of the stairs, disappeared down the hallway, and took with him that last frayed tether flapping behind him like a sail torn free of its guides and dancing in the wild wind.

Talyior sat at his table chasing words in the late afternoon light. They had been eluding him; his head too full of recent images circling round and round to find the words to fix them to the page in some recognizable patter. A small tap at his door sent nib through parchment. He picked up his head, the growl on his lips falling away when he heard, "Talyior, let me in."

He was across the room in a single stride, throwing open the door. Demona slipped into the room, an ocean of loveliness preceded by a wave of perfume; her auburn hair concealed by a netted hat meant to thwart the mosquitoes that swarmed the hot summer days, but instead served on this occasion to hide her identity.

What are you doing here? In all this time, you have never once come to me.

Words would not form out of the thoughts careening through his head. He took in her plain clothing, the risk she had taken, and answers did not matter. Her intent was clear.

And then he was moving towards her.

And then she was in his arms.

And then the world disappeared.

The hat flew off a crumpled ruin to land near the bed. "Oh, Tal," she moaned. Lips found lips and there was no space for words, only the silence between two. Buttons and fastenings came undone, and he lunged to latch the door. Talyior lost himself in her, his mind assailed by images of her hair cascading down, framing her face and breasts as she took him hungrily, desperately, as though she were facing a long fast and he was the final meal. They clashed together like hard syllables in staccato lines of a poem that, rather than whispering romance, rose to howl passion with the fury of nature at war with the world. Her nails raked his chest, drawing flames. His fingers wound themselves in her hair as he pulled her down. They passed the afternoon creating passion's realm bounded by the explorations of tongue, tooth and fingertip.

It was titanic. It was tragic. It was altogether consuming.

Somewhere in it all they slept, spent, Demona draped over Talyior like a coverlet of sex. Their combined sweat, cooling in the fading late-afternoon's heat, brought Talyior back to himself. He stirred, twisting his head to breathe in the scent of her hair, his hand running gently down the small of her back to cup a shapely cheek. His touch roused her, and she kissed his collarbone before rising. She arched above him, her face a confusion of satiation, sorrow and a hint of ferocity.

"Ah, my sweet," she sighed. "You've ruined me forever."

"Ruined?" he answered, idly tracing the fullness of one breast. "How could I ruin perfection?"

She laughed and ground down on him. "Ever the dashing poet. Do you ever tire of words? But I'm serious, really, you've ruined me."

"How?"

"How can I go on with you gone or dead, for Sevire will have you dead if you don't flee the city. And with you gone, well, this place will lose its luster."

"Then come with me after the Finals. Pevana and Sevire be damned. We'll leave together."

She looked at him with all the contained contradictions of their affair; so much half-said, so much more that needed saying. Demona hovered over him, need tempered by fear of both what was, and what might be. If she would not risk the unknown, then this tryst was farewell, and in her own wanton way, with every thrust of her matchless pelvis, she tried to push him out the gates to freedom.

She leaned slowly forward, he thought, to kiss him, to tell him yes, a thousand times yes! But Demona slapped him with a force that made his head spin.

"Fool! This is Pevana. *I* am Pevanese! You were lucky last night. You should be dead now, or at least castrated. Kissing me in front of everybody! How could you? Don't you know what you've done? You've forced Sevire to act! Why could you not let things go on as they were?"

Talyior stared up at her, waiting for the pain from her gold band striking his cheek to subside.

"You were happy with that?"

"What is happiness?" she crossed her arms over her glorious breasts. "We had enough, and you went and spoiled it."

"Don't you see? I had to." He came up on his knees in the bed. "Nothing worth having comes without risk. I don't care about Sevire or his bully-boys. Let all of Pevana talk. I will win tonight, and then we can leave here and never look back."

"Leave? Leave! To where?"

"South. We'll tour the City States."

Demona uncrossed her arms, sat back on her heels. "How would we live?"

"I will have two hundred gold after tonight. And when it is gone, I will compose songs to your beauty and sing them for coins tossed into my hat."

"Oh, Tal," she breathed his name, shook her head sadly. "And what would I do while you sing for our supper and a roof over our heads?"

"You'd love me."

Demona's eyes closed. Tears darkened her lush lashes, trickled down her smooth cheek. Talyior reached up and brushed them away.

"I would," she whispered. "Talyior, I would, if only I could."

"If you will then you can."

She swung her legs over the side of the bed, reaching for her clothes. "You don't understand."

"Then explain it to me." He followed her to the edge of the bed. "If you could come here, today, after last night, take that risk, for me, for *us*, then what is keeping you from the greater thing?"

"I," and she paused, half-dressed and her eyes dull and distant. "You ask too much of me."

"I have never asked a thing from you but this," he said. Cupping her face in his hands, he kissed her, a long, gentle, fear-sucking kiss. She sagged against him, responded in kind, sighed when he released her to whisper, "Is love not worth risking all for?"

"I want to say yes."

"Then do!" He laughed, swallowed down the mad sound before it became a sob. "Come with me, Demona."

Buttoning the last of the buttons on her peasant-like dress, she pushed off the bed, arranged her clothes, retrieved her hat. Talyior reached for her. Demona dodged out of his grasp. She unlatched the door and opened it.

"I'll try," she said. And then she was gone.

Chapter 14: The Finals

LATE AFTERNOON FOUND ELENI CARALON still struggling to make sense of the events of the night previous. To move from surreptitious poet-competitor to observer to direct actor in the drama of the times was too much for her. Escorted home at dawn, drawn into her husband's frantic embrace, she felt herself collapse like the hovels of the poor Maze-dwellers, and so she fell into sleep's emollient spell. Waking, she felt physically solid but deeply perplexed as images of fear, fire and flames assaulted her.

She found a loaf with a cup of juice and a brief note from Tomais waiting for her on her worktable. Smiling at the kindness she sat for a few minutes, sipping and chewing, part of her aware she was on the edge of something deeper. So many nuances to parse. She contemplated yet another attempt at a letter to the college that balked at the salutation. That door was closed. There must be something else. Some other direction. She played with lines, rhythms, but words failed her soon after she began. She stared at the letters on the sheet with a dispassionate eye and found they lacked fire, and at the thought of fire, her third in as many minutes, she felt the first keening of grief.

You the out of breath Talyior had gasped after he slammed his world into her own. And yet she had moved, with more than instinct she felt sure, to help him. Her scream had been more than just sound. And after, she had scrambled around collecting the scattered remains of her sewing basket after he ran off into the night. She managed to reassemble only part as though putting but half her life back into perspective. There had been a choice made, then, and again later when she followed the Prince.

My thanks he had said in the silence after the rain, the one called Devyn. His voice strained but courteous, but how could he have known how his words would affect her?

Pevana needs all her poets, mistress the Prince's man, Senden Arolli had said, earlier, before. And yet what role for her? Anger and frustration had been her muse, fed her words and spiced bitterness with art. And yet now, so suddenly, there was nothing.

She looked out over the city, bathed in the remorseless sunshine of the summer afternoon, and wondered whether it had a soul left after last night. She saw movement; the festival would go on, and the townsfolk would rally their passions to fill the last evening. And yet for Eleni, it was all somehow empty; an expression bereft of any real substance.

Tears came, then, tears of frustration and loss, irreconcilable by reason or pragmatism. She wept for the disruption caused by spiteful men with small minds. She wept for her Prince, so suddenly revealed to her as a man worthy of respect. She felt taken quite out of her element. And she knew she had only herself to blame. Her need for words, to *share* as she so proudly asserted to her husband, had led her to this impasse. She knew too much now to ever accept what she might have been before. She wept, aware she would be driven to know the connection between things. But to what purpose? What value knowledge if she were bound by sex to always exist on the edge of things, unable to act?

Part of her had hoped her poetic adventure at the Cup might quell the restless anger roiling inside of her. There was a part of her that hoped, truly, that Tomais might have made her pregnant in the aftermath.

But then came the banquet and the flames and nothing as it was before could ever be again. She knew it. Innately, she even knew there would not be a babe. Not yet. It was not time. And so tears of sorrow came from different directions, but resulted in the same thing: Loss. She knew a desire for hope, but the moment lacked the strength to lend to actually believe. She felt lost, in limbo, pacing the cage of her confused desires.

Eleni stared down at the half-completed, tear-stained missive, and had to quell the urge to wretch. She crumpled the page up, hung her head in her hands and fought against reliving the images from yesterday, and failed.

AS SUNSET APPROACHED, DEVYN left off from working the matched pair from House Hollaran to prepare himself for the finals. Memories of Kembril flooded his mind as he moved through the motions of his tasks like a wooden puppet. The heat from his earlier exercises and the moment's lightness of the meal shared with Talyior faded, forgotten in the desolation he sketched with each breath. Nothing broke through; even the horses sensed it and sidled away from him in the corrals. Human contact did not suffice, either. Sanya came by twice and attempted to cheer him up, but Devyn shrugged her off both times. Avarran even made an appearance after his watch ended, but even he could not get a rise out of his former pupil. Devyn felt cut off from the life around him as he moved about, a sum of existence similar to the black stain that still smoldered in spots to the south and west.

The Tree was ash commingled with those of its last attendant. Kembril had not even warranted an attempt at burial. The fire's intense heat left nothing recognizable. The fire transformed the old poet and the Tree into heaven's elementals, unacknowledged martyrs to cruel avarice.

Devyn hoped Minuet enjoyed Kembril's tales.

Grief took him. He clung to the edge of the water trough as great, shuddering sobs pushed themselves out of his body. Devyn wept for the pains of his childhood, those dark days on the streets when the only solace he embraced had come in the draperies of Kembril's wonderful words. He wept for the lost wisdom, the quiet asperity and surprising gentleness of a warrior damaged and morphed into something sublime as the dust that had coated his skin like the detritus of stars. He wept, and followed the tears into a darkness perceived only as an afterthought, for memory beset him on all sides and then coalesced into a shadow of Kembril's beloved rasp:

You are Renia's poet, now. You are my voice! Speak!

247

Volition flooded his senses, and he clung to the feeling as though it were a dam set to stop the flow of pain. He gasped and fumbled for his pad and with trembling fingers took up the pen. Words flowed from his soul to its tip almost out of defiance.

And who will speak for the poet?
Who will find the time and the lines
To tell the people the truth?
Who will speak for the poet?
And who will remember for those
Too set in their ways to know
All the gifts the masses disregard?

Who will relate the beauties of a day
Like sun after rain
Joy after pain
Love come at last for the lonely?

Who will speak for the poet when he's gone?

And not all flames are consumption,
Turning hovels to ash and dust,
Flaring an idea into nothingness,
Igniting a funeral pyre for a Goddess. . .
They can be a beacon, whose light reaches up to the heavens,
Calling on the world to take pity.

Let those who will, work their ill
And make up the plan as they go.
The poet still will speak his fill
And let the people know
The Truth.

There is not room on the page to express the rage
When the words fall to ashes in flame.
For the storyteller man has done all he can
And nothing will be the same.
On a night of consequences dire,
High leaped the flames of Kembril's Fire
As the past burned
Leaving a question unanswered:
Who will speak for the poet when he's gone?

He put down the pen and stood up. The mirror nailed to the beam above his camp desk framed his face. He looked at his eyes and wondered why he looked like a stranger.

The stranger asked him, "Who *will* speak for the poet?"

And Devyn answered, "I will."

TALYIOR DOZED UNTIL JUST BEFORE DARK then roused himself to shout down to Lyssa for hot water and towels. While he waited, he took a whetstone to his blade to give his hands something to do while his mind occupied itself with thoughts of his father, Espan's offer, and Demona. Her perfume lingered in the room, clouding his thoughts with desire mixed with a growing despair. Her face had borne such a sad expression when she turned back at him before she left. He clung to the memory of her fingers digging into his chest, her back arched in ecstasy as she shrugged off the oppression of her name, her marriage and her station. In that moment, and asleep afterwards, she had been simply Demona, as Talyior preferred to consider her.

He took particular care as he dressed. He had to fend off Lyssa's over willing hands with the buttons on his shirt. He would miss Lyssa's ministrations after tonight. There was much good in the house; even Gania's penchant for bellowing had its place. Tonight he would get his chance to put the whole of Pevanese society on its ear, to finish off the drama he and Devyn began two nights previous. Once again, venturing out could mean his death, but Talyior had cheated it enough times to confidently judge the odds about even.

He finished tying his neck cloth and scrutinized himself in the fractured mirror that still clung to the wall above the jagged bits of the chamber pot Sevire's bully-boys had thrown against it. His eye skipped from fragment to fragment trying to connect the separate pieces. His heart and mind assured him the parts still composed a whole. He felt the slightest twinge as he considered how like the mirror his life had become: a series of scenes, moments, these last few days a slew of faces, images and intents.

Where is the thread that ties all of it together? he thought as he practiced his bow. Words tumbled into his mind:

And on the epitaph of his youth
They placed a laurel of victory
As a sign
Of one who had passed there in hope
And dared to dream great dreams
And dared to attempt great things.

For, whether
A day
A month,
A year,
In the end it is all just time
And time enough abides.

"And time enough abides," he repeated aloud. "For me. For what comes. Let it come." And he laughed, doffed his plumed hat, and left his room for perhaps the last time.

Talyior made his way down the stairs as the last rays of the sun slipped beneath the level of the city walls, casting Gania's and the surrounding houses quickly into shadow. Entering the parlor now restored to rights, he found Gania pinch-faced and holding a rolled, sealed scroll. Next to her stood a liveried footman dressed in the Prince's colors. Gania handed him the scroll without a word.

Please allow me to offer the use of one of my carriages for your journey to tonight's festivities. I understand it is a much more direct and safer way of getting around than by rooftop.
Luck to you, D.

Talyior looked to the footman after reading, and passed the missive on to Gania, who whistled wetly as she took in the news. She gave him a look worth a season's insults as he made to leave.

"Tell me, fellow," he asked. "Has the Prince made such arrangements for the other finalists?"

The man remained stiffly formal as he replied. "No sir, only one other carriage was ordered out by the Palace."

"Let me guess, Devyn Ambrose?"

"I would not know that, sir. Now, if you are ready, the carriage awaits."

"Gania," Talyior turned to his gaping landlord. "Once again, my thanks and apologies. I will be by to collect my things once Lyssa is finished tidying my room."

He turned to follow the footman out the door, and almost made it to the carriage step before he heard Gania's heavy tread behind him at the doorway. "Look for your rags and bits of scribbling on the trash heap in the alley! You, you, ragamuffin in lace! I hope, I hope. . ."

He settled himself in the luxuriously padded leather seat and closed the door, waiting for the rest. Gania thrust her face through the window, her expression, as always, a blending of rage and tenderness. Talyior wanted to kiss her fleshy, dear cheek in that moment. He would miss her sorely.

"Yes, Gania? What is it you hope?"

"I hope you win," she said quickly, as if the words tasted vile upon her tongue. "Lad, I hope you win and keep your life to live it long and happily." She stepped down off the carriage, pounded the door for the driver to move off, shouting, "Even if it's no great loss to me if you don't!"

Talyior's carriage trundled him up through the city to the citadel, through the gates and up the gently sloping street to the palace much too soon for his piece of mind. This was his first time this close to it, and he had to gather himself to take in its sculpted, lofty grandeur.

House Anargi was a hovel by comparison.

The steps before him flowed up a belled flight of twenty white marble steps to a flat space flanked by stone dolphins that framed two, huge oaken doors banded with gilt-painted steel. Above the doors the great hall reared, four stories high, symmetrically balanced by two multi-windowed wings topped by battlements. The full moon cast an eldritch light on the place that made Talyior's stomach clench. Suddenly, he felt like a child who whined once too often about playing with the bigger kids, only to have his wish granted and thrust into the center of a game too large and complex by half.

Sevire and his house full of bully-boys and sycophants he could handle. This was something quite, quite different. Even with his penchant for words, Talyior had to stretch himself to find the right words.

"It is preposterous. Magnificent, heavy, veiled. . ." The words fluttered above his head like birds startled from their perches. There were too many, and the edifice too grand by far to submit to all but the perfect word.

The carriage neared the entranceway before the doors being pulled open and made fast by doormen, bathing Talyior and others who had arrived with him in light and music. He paused; that perfect word hit him square between the eyes.

Power.

DONARI AVEDUN PACED DOWN THE HALLWAY of the palace with a determined stride, as though by the consistent placing of one foot after the other he could pummel the possibilities implicit in the Finals into something he could control. His interview with the Prelate, while validating and amusing, had still left him feeling insubstantial and out of sorts. He still doubted the strength of his position, and could not escape the notion that the fire, while forging a new bond with the city, had still burned away the carefully nurtured disguise, invented in rebellion and perfected in apathy.

He reviewed the preparations. The poets would have their hearing; he had felt quite convinced of the necessity. The Maze, partially burned, created troubles for the poor, but he had taken what measures he could to allay them. Senden would be a weary ward that night, of that he was certain. Extra guards pulled from the walls now stood watch in the citadel. The Festival would run its course regardless of the Lord Prelate's or Sevire Anargi's efforts. He had angered the Prelate but not cowed him and embarrassed Sevire but not emasculated him. The two carriages dispatched ensured the remaining two catalysts arrival for the evening's tumult. Avarran and a handful of his best men speckled the guest list. With Donari's credibility at risk, he and Senden had taken what measures they could, but uncertainty was a strumpet variable.

He collected Cryso as he entered his chambers to prepare himself for the night's ordeal. While he let his servant take control of his dressing, he reserved his thoughts to search yet again for any lapse in the measures he and Senden had taken. The lark was over. Moves had been made. Corvale had not been found. Sevire had retired to his estate to wait out the fire and the rain, along with the rest of the propertied class. That afternoon word came that the Prelate had removed himself and his entourage to rooms prepared at the college.

It had been the Maze dwellers and the tradesman and shop keepers who had battled the flames alongside their Prince. And that explained some of the hollow feeling Donari experienced as Cryso finished tying his neck cloth and settling the absurdly symbolic silver coronet over his brow. The people had looked to him last night, but not the ones who, in their own minds, mattered most. Those assembled in the main hall to watch the drama conclude. The Finals, suddenly less about words and scandal's titillation, now loomed with darker aspect. The blackened stain to the south that Donari could just make out from his window attested to that truth. He may have begun to rule as he should last night, but if he lost control over events in the hours pending, he might not rule tomorrow.

He looked at his reflection in the mirror. Cryso had extended himself. The man who stared back at him from the glass was the epitome of the station he held. Head to toe in shades of sea-blue green, a pendant of green stones set in silver in the shape of the family dolphin pinned to the left breast below the collar bone. He looked like a ceremonial galley with multiple pennons aflutter. He let a wry smile crease his lips. *Well,* he thought, *one last time to play the fop.*

"My thanks, Cryso," he said, gesturing at the mirror's image. "For this and many other things, my deepest thanks."

Cryso bowed. "My lord is too kind. I judged the night worthy of showing off your best—*our* best. The kitchens have been agog with tales of how things went last night. Quite memorable, my lord."

Donari's smile faded. "You do not know the half of it, my friend, and I fear there is more to come. Has Cook worked her magic for us tonight?"

Cryso beamed confidence. "Oh, indeed, my lord, she has taken the idea of sauce to mythic proportions, but I would have a care of the pastries, for their richness would give Minuet herself pause."

Donari felt his spirits rise. There was so much to love about his city and his people. They were worth any sacrifice, in the end, perhaps even a Prince's diadem. He looked one last time at his reflection. *Or my dignity, at the very least.*

"I will take care to nibble, Cryso, thank you, and thank Cook for me, as well," he said, crossing over to the door, Cryso following his customary two steps behind. "It is time to go meet our *guests*. Renia grant me strength."

"Very good, my lord."

"One hopes, Cryso, one hopes to be very, very good."

TALYIOR'S CARRIAGE RIDE ENDED in a lurching, bouncing rumble over the cobble stones of the citadel courtyard. The disarrangement of his rooms back at Gania's set him on edge. Nothing along the course of this final, perhaps penultimate, journey did anything to persuade him to relax. The image that presented itself to him reinforced that notion. He was in mid-step of his descent when he saw them: Sevire and Demona. Their carriage trundled up to the palace entry steps, and what Talyior observed sent the beginnings of a chill running down his spine despite the lingering summer's heat.

Demona bore jewels festooned in her hair that set off her deeply crimson gown. She was . . . laughing. The hand she placed in Sevire's when he made shift to help her down seemed to Talyior's heightened senses to linger a touch too long, with a firmness that spoke of acceptance rather than tolerance. How? Why? Who was this creature that did not bear the faintest resemblance to the woman who had plunged herself down on him that afternoon?

His knee almost buckled when his foot hit the ground. He made an effort to steady himself before attempting the palace steps. He let Sevire lead Demona ahead of him, screened from their view by a handful of other arrivals, his entire being fixed on Demona's sensuous neck that taunted him from beneath dark tresses piled impossibly high. And then she turned as she reached the topmost step and looked back, half in quest, half in excitement and caught his eye.

And then the height of her hair did not matter, for he felt all of them pierce him in places he once thought protected. She saw him, he was sure of it, and yet the laughter did not die on her lips. Her gaze fixed on him for the eternity of a moment, took him in, assessed his nearness and then swept on as Sevire urged her to enter through the palace's great doors. Sevire half turned himself, and Talyior followed his heavy, jouncing jowls. They made eye contact, Sevire's washed cold loathing, Talyior's tense and befuddled. The fat man opened his pouty lips, laughing silently, turned his bulk in the door and followed after his wife.

Talyior felt his spirit leaching away from punctures beyond metaphor, beyond comprehension. He raised his right hand to his face to sniff once again Demona's scent, dismayed by its absence. He reeled as though drunk on too much of Saymon's cheapest wine. An arm at his elbow steadied him, and he turned to observe a face he could not place but that seemed familiar nonetheless. It smiled at him in pity and understanding, a face just on the other side of middle age, seamed somewhat, but still possessing vestiges of mirth about the eyes.

"Well then, good sir," the man said. "Untoward stumbles at the palace steps, regardless their source, just will not do tonight. If you please, let's pause here for a moment to let the genteel sort themselves out. All those large gowns and trains tend to choke the entry."

Talyior recovered his voice and his balance. "I'm sorry, have we met? You look familiar to me."

"We haven't met, officially, though I know of and have seen you before. I serve Prince Donari in an investigative capacity."

"Investigative capacity?"

The man gave a brief smile that did nothing to soften his hard features. "It is my job to find out things for my lord Prince," he answered. "I am Senden Arolli, the Prince's eyes and ears in Pevana. Ah, the crowd loosens. Please, come this way. The Prince would have a word with you before the program begins. You'll have to secure your blade without. No weapons in the Hall, you understand. You've nothing to fear from Sevire, unless he attempts something outrageous like sitting on you."

He took him by the elbow and, gently but firmly, steered him over to a door on the right just before the entrance to the meeting hall. It opened to reveal a library. Devyn Ambrose stood next to a table, and upon that table, a wine decanter and four glasses. He turned to greet Talyior with raised brows and a smile. They were the only two finalists in the room. Senden moved to the table and poured four glasses from the decanter. As if cued by the last drop splashed into the final cup, the Prince swept into the room.

"Ah, gentlemen! You have arrived, safely. Excellent! I wanted a private moment with you before you are called to the hall. Did you get a look inside yet? I must say, the place looks magnificent for the occasion!" He sipped from his glass, and Talyior noted how his eyes darted back and forth between him and Devyn as though assessing, much the same way a serpent used its tongue.

Talyior glanced over at Devyn, who seemed much less out of sorts with the audience than he felt. Two days ago Talyior had shared idle banter with Donari Avedun at Sevire's banquet, but the man he observed now seemed like a completely different person. And yet again Talyior sensed himself far, far out of his depth. He doubted the certainty of almost everything, going, in the space of three days, from dalliance to desperation. The thought turned his throat into a desert, which he tried to remedy by taking a drink. The resulting, embarrassing slurp, brought a chuckle from Senden and an empathetic smile from the Prince.

"Senden has spoken a little with young Devyn here, but poor Talyior has labored and loved in ignorance. The fire has changed more than the Maze. There are threads spinning, plans progressing, the game of politics on a grand scale, my friends, and you two got caught up in it whether or not you meant to. It is a shame such things should interrupt our festival of words, but so it is. Yours have touched off responses of ill effect, a sad consequence of the times, I'm afraid.

"Faith and Love," he shook his head as if weary. "One would think they might be out of bounds to coercion. And yet in the present the opposite is true. You aimed your words and struck, and well done, I say! About time. But the effects have swept you up and placed you in harm's way, just as they have placed all of Pevana and her people in harm's way." He turned and spoke directly to Devyn. "This should have been a festival of peace and plenty, not of conflict and loss. I am sorry for yours, Devyn Ambrose. I, too, once knew Kembril Edri. We are all much the less for his death. I should have been more aware."

Devyn's jaw clenched, the muscles in his forearm ribboned as the grip on the glass intensified. He bowed stiffly.

"I realize all this must come as something of a shock to you both, or at least to you, Talyior. Devyn here has seen things I should have. In fact, I am in his debt for a well-earned lesson. Things will change from this moment on, for good or ill, and we will see a different fall and winter." He paused, staring down at the lees in his glass. "And what of the spring?" he asked quietly. "I wish I had the foresight to say, but there it is."

"But we will see it through, my lord," Senden said, moving to refill Donari's glass.

"Yes," Donari told them. "We will see it out, Senden and I, but as for you two? I think you have choices to make. Indeed, there are some," he turned to Talyior, "the husband of your lady being the chiefest, who think I have made a rather bad job of my own."

"I am a child of the Maze," Devyn said. "I will survive."

"And I am not without skills, my lord," added Talyior.

Donari took both of them in with a pointed glance and smiled, touched.

"If I am any judge, young man, you and Devyn Ambrose have talents untapped."

Donari turned away again, motioning at the wall and the space beyond as if looking through the panels. "The finery out there has seen challenge made and await the response. You will be the response. They will be out for more blood, I dare say. They have been gleefully consuming each other in the quest for influence and riches for generations, and then here come you two common fellows to set the whole class on its collective ear! With words!" He faced back again. "Was bedding Demona worth it? No, do not start so! I am sorry. That was crass. Do not answer. Love is always worth it."

He looked at Devyn. "So is faith. Do not let those fools out there compromise you. They are here for the show, to see me fail in my rule. Play it out for me, friends, but understand that this is about more than words. I do not know what will happen; my enemies have proven themselves capable of anything. And if that *anything* occurs tonight, then look to Senden and move quickly."

"We have men about the place," Senden offered. "But you should keep your eyes open just the same. I will be near the dais next the Prince and the other judges. Were it not for last night, I would have few concerns." He glanced at Devyn. "But we lost Corvale, and I have not heard from the guards at gate and harbor that he has left the city." He turned back to Talyior. "And Sevire is apt to anything, especially if the Prelate goads him."

Talyior blanched, remembering the mess Sevire's men had made of Gania's. The sound of Donari's glass clicking to rest on the desk brought him back to the present.

"I am needed to lead the procession," Donari said. "Senden here will get you to your places. I am sorry to strike such an ominous note, my friends, but such are the times. Good luck to you both. Again, keep your wits about you." As suddenly as he had swept in, Prince Donari Avedun swept out again.

There remained no more time for thoughts, for the time had come for words. Senden ushered them down the hall, placed them at the rear of the small group of other finalists, and spared a brief look at both of them before leaving to take his position.

As Talyior paced in with the others to a swelling of applause and catcalls, some of them surprisingly ribald given the quality of the audience, he realized with shocking clarity that his first expression of his poem about Demona had served to introduce him to Pevana, but his second would serve as a farewell.

The judges were seated at a table in front of and below the level of the Prince's chair. At their introduction, each contestant advanced to the table and drew a numbered marker from a small bowl. Thus, everyone received an even chance at a fair hearing. By luck or fate, Devyn and Talyior chose the last two markers. This time, Talyior would be last. He had to force his knees to bend so he could sit back down. He struggled to breathe and calm himself.

One of the students from the University spoke first and presented something longwinded and rhythmic about the seasons of the year. Only the length impressed Talyior. The student finished to genteel applause and nothing more. The youngest son of one of the minor houses spoke next. In a voice that seemed to bloom out of his frail shape, he set about raising the stakes of the evening. Talyior listened to the sounds he made more than the words they formed, much of the poem itself nearly unintelligible to him except for the final phrases. They seemed just right, somehow:

. . .for who is to stay the artist from his destined hews,
The composer his quill, the playwright his muse?
To impede the mind in quest of sense
Would be, indeed, pale recompense.

The young man bowed deeply to more appreciative applause, for they were a literate group, and he touched their educated souls. The judges, however, scrupulously refrained from response and made quick notations on their papers before the chairman motioned the fellow to sit.

The young priest who had attended the Prelate at Sevire's banquet rose next, and he lashed the audience with a feral, poetic sermon on the glories of the Most High and the power of the King's Divinely Inspired Theology. He was good, but Talyior felt his piece more political than passionate. It had a caustic cast to the language, almost of scorn. It flashed to him, from that region of the mind that knows all but doles out information like a miser, that there was much more to the young priest than was obvious. Every word, every gesture, spoke of action, of thought directed as though a weapon. The insight might have been influenced by the Prince's earlier speech, but Talyior felt a sudden fear and looked sidelong at Devyn sitting next to him.

Oh, my friend, woe to the Old Ways and their followers if ever this one were to replace his mentor.

The poet finalists had an unusual balance: age and youth, realism and conservatism, power and passion, all were represented. And he and Devyn should have been one man to shake the foundations of everything. And here they were, two men: an Old Ways adherent and a love struck stripling set in place to roil up every political and moral sensibility in Pevana.

He listened to the final stanzas of the young priest's effort. He finished to uproarious applause, almost too loud in Talyior's opinion. The audience seemed to cheer not just the poet, but the religious power behind him as well.

The court poet, Ellaran, a short, grey-haired man with a face that spoke of polish and grace, recited next. Talyior paid close attention, for Ellaran was a professional and known throughout the realm. In a carefully pitched voice, he gave them a simple gem, a small piece of wisdom:

Let all men ask questions of the stars
And while away the hours awaiting answers.
I know stars are silent,
And answers may come from many sources,
Including the heart.

Let all who seek too long and too far
Find a place to pause
And listen to what comes from inside.
Let them thusly understand
That all is not just seasonal dramas
Played out on stages;
Some things are eternal,
But the eye must turn inward
In order to see.

Let all who flail about their lives
Like storm-crossed ships at sea
Lay their hands surely on the tiller ropes
And regain control of their destiny
For that is one of the great gifts of Man:
Chaos and Control
At odds and as one. . .

The applause for Ellaran was genuine and extended. His age and skill warranted nothing less; but it was more than that. Ellaran was their man and they loved him. He had been showering the Pevanese elite with verse since the Prince toddled about in baby-dress. He knew his audience, probably none better, and he knew how to veil his criticisms behind conceit. He bowed deeply as he accepted the accolade. Talyior confessed himself impressed. Where he possessed the brash passion of youth, Ellaran stood out as a competent artist. Doubt of the event's outcome followed hard upon that admition. *How many more illusions must I lose?*

And then Devyn rose to speak.

DEVYN STOOD FOR A MOMENT, milking the time to observe the hall. He swept his gaze around the crowd and perceived them as a myriad of the curious, contemplative and contemptuous. The baubles festooning brows, breasts and wrists created the false impression of a star field, and just as insubstantial. He saw faces carnivorous, patrons at a violent contest more interested in seeing blood spilt than in who might emerge victorious. He kept his face impassive but sneered inwardly.

He strode to the center of the hall, eyes darting right and left and saw Avarran, incongruous in a page's cap, standing in a column's shadow. Perception flared then and the sea of faces clarified to reveal clusters of darker types, guards placed by the quality and set for the purpose. The largest group coalesced around Sevire Anargi.

Devyn reached his mark, turned, bowed to the judges and the Prince, glanced at the Prelate, and then fixed his entire attention on the leering arsonist-murderer who smirked down at Devyn from behind the old man's shoulder. He had found Jaryd Corvale in the one place where he could not possibly reach him.

Devyn drew breath to speak; what came out was an amalgam, an extemporaneous blending of both his competition piece and his dirge for Kembril. It came as an instinctive, gut-clenching expression of anger and woe that, even as the words tumbled out, threatened to overwhelm him and break his rhythm. But he took heart from memories, tempered the ashes of his rage, reached for Renia's Grace and found the truth in every syllable and loosed them forth, lashing the genteel mob for their consumptive hypocrisy and exposing all of the Prelate's fraudulent cruelties. Every consonant felt like one of Minuet's darts ripping through the veil of ambivalence and conspiracy's frost. He finished breathless and satisfied.

Good enough to die for.

Stunned silence echoed the end of his poem. Even the Prelate and his covey of priestly attendants gaped wordless. And then a low murmur began to swell that broke the spell and set faces twisting into glares or smiles depending on the conscience of the listener. The Prelate half-rose in wrath, his face a mottled mask of red, splotchy patches and fire-rimmed eyes, his claw-like finger pointed like death's scythe blade directly at Devyn.

And in that moment Devyn existed in his own void, for he heard nothing save the inner rasp of Kembril's contented laugh. He smiled at the Prelate and gave a mocking, half-bow to Corvale, wishing he could get something sharp and at least throw it. But his better sense damped down the urge. The distance was time, place and metaphor, but that did not stop him from giving his enemy a sharp look that promised another meeting. He turned away and barely felt Talyior's light touch on his shoulder when he returned to his seat.

"Well, that has done it," Talyior whispered, leaning close. "No fair changing things up."

Talyior's jest brought Devyn back to the present, and he turned to him and grinned with gallows bravado, quirking one sarcastic eyebrow. "This was never about winning," he responded. "But now that you mention it, it's your turn!"

TALYIOR WAITED FOR THE NOISE TO SUBSIDE before rising to take his turn. Devyn's quip did nothing to dispel his awe at his new friend's power and conviction. He understood what it cost him to present as he did. None better among all the poets, surely, for his own effort might bear a similar cost. When the judges motioned him forward he rose and paced to the center of the hall. The rows of faces served to further muddle his emotions. He stood there, searching for some angle of vision that would make sense of the intemperate innuendoes. His tongue felt heavy, as if tied to an anchor stone from one of his father's ships. He took in the growing number of faces turning from interested to derisive, and almost forgot to breathe.

Demona saved him before he froze completely. He caught her eye as he cast desperately about and saw there, or imagined so, a hint of their former intimacy. Her love looked out at him from beneath a huge cloud of disturbed shadow, lightning framed about the edges, that mostly shrouded it the same way that Sevire's fat arm cupped her naked shoulders. And in that contrast Talyior found his partial salvation.

How tragic a thing is it for the young man of passion to realize the error of his intent? And yet Talyior realized then that words were more substantial than any implied promises of the flesh. He let his gaze linger on Demona for a moment as the noise from the crowd grew to a snarl of disapproval. It was one thing to provide the source of scandal; quite another thing altogether to actually mean it. Here was the poet who would upset the balance of their world, who would tweak the nose of the establish order and rise above his station. Such effrontery had its price.

And as Talyior contemplated the collected scorn of his supposed betters, he decided to pay that price. What else did he have to lose? What else could he do when faced with the emptiness of what he once thought possible? His ears burned. He felt his face flush crimson as the crowd began to jeer. He looked once more at Demona with a glance that spoke of questions doomed to remain unasked. He looked at Sevire and saw there the smug, almost jolly presentiment of one who knows he is—and always will be—superior.

Talyior borrowed some of Devyn's anger and despair and married them with his own, innate sense of romance. The resultant combination lent a tragic attitude to his words when he spoke, and his poem, so sauced, served his purpose.

Noise erupted at his conclusion, a cacophony of rage and warrant. As he made his way towards his seat, he stole a last glance at Demona and saw tears in her eyes.

"Very creditable," Devyn said. "I see you changed yours as well. Cheeky."

Talyior looked at him sidelong then glanced once more at the mob behind and above them. "I had my reasons. So, tell me, which of us do you think won?"

Devyn recoiled as if incredulous. "You are joking, right?"

"I guess it does not matter, does it?"

Talyior settled back in his chair, tipped his head back and closed his eyes. *Farewell, Demona.*

The judges deliberated and made their decision in the wash of sound from the audience, who would have been enraged to know how closely they resembled the crowd at the Cup from two nights previous. Names rained down from velvet throats that had never known the garrulity of the gutter but who nonetheless growled now in an effort to sway the decision. Passion melded to opinion is one of the great levelers, making all sound the same regardless of station. The genteel of Pevana roared like drunken grocers.

After a last consultation, the lead judge took pen and scribbled the name of the winner on a scrap of paper. The Prince came down from his chair to take the folded note and the heavy bag of gold coins that marked the winner's prize. The audience grew louder, its members forgetting their reserve as they roared out the names of those they felt should win. Talyior heard his own name among the shouts. The Prince let them go on for several minutes before raising his hands for silence.

"My friends," he said when things quieted. "Let none of us forget the gifts to our city bestowed by these gentleman! I cannot think of a better way to end the Summer Festival, than by awarding the winner the city's largesse and our eternal respect and admiration. To all the finalists, well done and thank you! As for myself, I thank you with all my heart. There is something in art that works as a suave, a balm to the wounded soul. Your words, my friends, have surmounted the height of the flames of last night. You have all Pevana's gratitude." He looked at both Devyn and Talyior as he spoke, while the smattering of applause died down. Walking over to the poets, who stood to receive judgment, he glanced once at the paper and laughed silently as he stopped in front of Talyior.

"Congratulations, sir," he said quietly. "You are people's poet this season." And he handed him the bag of gold coins.

Chaos flooded the hall as though a damn had burst. Folk filled the floor, some congratulating Talyior and the other poets, others rushing the judges' table to protest the results. Others jostled about, enjoying the tawdry theater of the evening. Talyior and Devyn found themselves back to back in the iddle of the throng, struggling to remain calm despite the surreal quality of the moment. Talyior tightened his grip on the bag of gold and searched the scene for Demona, but found instead, Sevire.

His wrath exploded in a womanish, high pitched keen that cut right through the general noise in the place. He heaved his bulk upright and stumbled and rolled like a ponderous, tidal flood through the crowd. His arms worked like pudgy tumblers, sweeping the hapless out of his way as he rumbled straight for Talyior. Spittle dribbled down his chin in his extremity and his eyes flared, red-rimmed in fury. When he drew close he raised his hands, fingers twitching, reaching to throttle the source of all that affronted him, decorum be damned. Talyior tried to recoil from the attack but the press trapped him, so he did the only thing he could. He swung the bag of gold coins, his winner's prize, in a desperate arc that landed flush on Sevire's forehead. The blow dropped Sevire like a stone, but at impact the bag itself shattered, showering silver and copper coins everywhere. The crowd immediately began scrambling about the floor scooping up markers worth less than the rings many of them sported on their fingers.

Dropping Sevire stunned Talyior less than the awareness that the coins from the bag were not gold. He looked to Devyn who returned it with a frown of his own.

"What?" Talyior began but trailed off as a handful of Sevire's servants rushed forward to aid their fallen master.

"That is trouble, never mind the gold," Devyn said through gritted teeth. "And this way, too." He motioned off toward the dais where the Prelate had accosted the Prince, shaking a boney finger in the man's face while Corvale and another large fellow in priestly vestments advanced menacingly toward the two poets.

They both took a half step backward, tensing to receive what came, but Senden Arolli and Captain Avarran got there first. In seconds they had a screen of guards between the poets and their attackers. Insults were traded, and Talyior had to duck to avoid a thrown goblet. Within seconds the scene was a morass of grunting, gasping combatants making up for their lack of weapons with bare fists and determination. Talyior looked back over at the dais and saw other guards in page livery flanking Donari.

Avarran, his bandaged forehead once again seeping blood spoke to Devyn through gritted teeth. "It seems you cannot stay out of trouble for even one evening. Best you leave now, eh? This bunch will not be put off by words, I think."

At that moment Corvale and the priest joined the fray. Two men in Anargi livery knelt by Sevire's inert form. Corvale snarled and tried to break through. The scene quickly degenerated into a cacophony of screaming women, scrambling forms and the group in the center of the hall intent on blood.

Senden Arolli grabbed Devyn and Talyior by an arm and propelled them bodily backwards towards the doors.

"Go," he rasped. "You have no role here now. Go!"

Talyior hesitated for a moment longer. On the far side of the growing melee he spotted Demona rushing and pushing to where Sevire lay. Talyior took her movements like a body blow, and he staggered backward, following Devyn through the doors and down a side passage. Demona. The promised prize rescinded. But what promise; there had never been. Talyior had no idea what he had won, though he was quite sure of what he had lost: everything but his life, and that was still in doubt.

The doorway from the hall opened onto a servant's passage that led to the kitchens. The sounds of the chaos in the hall faded as Talyior and Devyn padded down the narrow way and out through another door next the hearths that deposited them in the palace simples garden beneath the citadel's western walls.

They stood there breathless and at a loss for a moment before Senden Arolli joined them. He bore several burdens, one of which clinked when he dropped it on the ground. In the semi-darkness of the garden, Talyior saw that he bore a sheathed sword in each hand.

"Your blades," Senden said, holding out the hilts. "My apologies for the unseemly conclusion. Poor payment, I am sure."

Talyior took his sword and swiftly set it so that it hung across his shoulders. Devyn did the same.

"What happened?" Talyior asked.

"Surely you know the answer to that," scoffed Senden, bending down and taking up the bag he had dropped earlier. "Here, the correct prize. I am sure you noticed that the first bag was, how shall we say it, light? Forgive me. I made a switch."

"Why? I do not understand."

"Yes," added Devyn. "Why switch? Surely you could not have known."

Senden stepped back a pace to include both men in his look. "Last night trumped all plans," he answered quietly. "I did not expect this evening to go without incident, as Donari and I told you both earlier. I did not know who the winner would be, but if there was upset, I thought it best to safeguard both the gold and the poet's life. Walking out of here with two hundred gold coins would be certain to get whoever the unlucky fellow was some unwanted attention."

"Yes, but," Talyior began, but Senden stopped him with a raised hand.

"No more *buts.* Take your winnings, and well done to the both of you. If nothing else, you have given the city something to talk about this winter. That mess back in the hall will soon spill out to the lower streets, especially if Sevire comes to. Sadly, I do not think you killed him, but he has long means for a fat fool. And you," he continued, turning his attention to Devyn. "The Prelate already had you a dead man, that bow only put another stone on your grave. Pevana is no safe place for you, either. I do not even think what is left of the Maze could hide you from that one."

"I am not a coward," Devyn grunted, belting his sword to his hip.

"Of course you are no coward," Senden replied. "Both of you are young, foolish, talented, and quite out of options. You have exposed troubles the Prince will be hard put to it to set right. In the end, you have done him a great service. Now he is better placed to deal with what comes next. But you two have now become a distraction neither he nor I can afford. You need to leave. Now. There is a postern gate at the end of the garden that will get you down into the city. After that, you are on your own. And luck to you, until we meet again."

He turned to go but paused to reach into his shirt and pull out a small purse that he tossed to Devyn.

"What is this?"

Senden smiled. "Call it second place prize. Frankly, I liked your poem better."

Then he was gone, and they were alone among the rows of beans and carrots. Talyior looked at Devyn, who returned the look dumbly. So much event in so short a time, and after a festival of words and momentus trial, suddenly, neither of them knew what to say next. Talyior broke the silence by hefting the bag, opening the drawstring and confirming the contents. He smiled as he looked back to Devyn.

"Half?" he asked.

Devyn returned the smile, nodding. "Done."

"We need to get out of here."

"I know where we can get some horses."

"Are we to add theft to our other charges?"

Devyn looked at the purse Senden had given him. "I *could* leave this for Malom to compensate the owners," he said, "but the horses belong to Sevire."

Talyior laughed. "Well that is settled then," he said, turning to go. "Keep your money. Theft it is."

Chapter 15: After

DEMONA SAT COMBING HER HAIR AT HER DRESSING TABLE. A light breeze blew in through her window bringing the scent of the garden and moonlight into her bedroom. She considered herself fortunate. Sevire had only been stunned by the blow Talyior gave him. When things calmed down in the palace, she managed to get him home without further incident. His bloodied forehead had not required stitches.

She switched to a pearl-handled brush; she liked her combs and brushes and the mirrors, unguents and scents Sevire brought to her. She tilted her head, watching how moonlight played upon her face as her hair fell about her shoulders in waves. She ran a painted fingernail down the swell of one breast where it met the lace of her dressing gown. Talyior had liked to do that. She sighed.

Demona brushed the other side, taking care to gentle the tangles. She loved her hair, the way it fell about her shoulders when she let it down. Talyior liked that too.

Setting her brush down, she reached for the etched glass bottle that held her favorite scent, touched the stopper to each wrist and let a drop run down between her breasts. She scrutinized her appearance in the glass; Sevire would be pleased. He was rather easy to please, not like Talyior, who had been as insatiable as she, who had given as much as he gave. Sevire gave her baubles, riches, wealth beyond measure, but those small things like affection and pleasure and love; with those he was stingy.

She moved to the window for a breath of night air. In the distance she could see a dust trail on the southern road rising in the moonlight. She almost fancied she could see horses riding hard, pounding the dust into a haze with their passing.

There came a tapping and Sevire's muffled voice through her door. "Demona, are you ready, sweet?"

She looked again to the south, already the dust was settling back down to the road. She turned away.

"Yes, love," she said. "I am coming."

A STURDY KNOCK ON HER WORKSHOP DOOR the morning after the end of the Summer Festival disturbed Eleni Caralon from her patterns and cloth. She bent back down to continue tracing a line, but the knock came again this time louder and more insistent. She sighed in frustration, spat out the pins she held in her mouth and walked downstairs to open the door, shocked to find a footman in palace livery standing there, bowing.

"Eleni Caralon, the seamstress?" the footman asked.

"Yes," she answered. The footman handed her a small envelope, bowed again and left. Eleni stood there on the doorstep, staring first at the coach and the face of Senden Arolli smiling at her through the window. He gave a slight nod and waved as the carriage departed. She followed its progress until it turned at the intersection before looking down at the envelope. The Prince's seal graced the wax. She opened it. Inside were two pieces of paper. The first, a short note, read:

Mistress Caralon,

I have been told that Pevana has need of all her poets. I heartily agree, especially in these changed times. If you can spare the time from your work, I hope you can put the enclosed to good use.

Yours,

Donari, Prince of Pevana.

Eleni scanned the other, more official document. The words blurred and danced on the page, all but: . . .*hereby granted Royal Appointment to the College of Pevana.*

Tears flowed, her feet flew, and they barely touched the stairs as she sped to share the news with Tomais.

MIDMORNING OF THE DAY AFTER THE SUMMER FESTIVAL found Prince Donari Avedun in his dressing room settling his neck-cloth and staring at his face in the mirror. Business awaited his attention; civic matters, delayed by the festival, affected by the fire, awaited judgement. He stared closely at his reflection, and wondered at his readiness for what loomed ahead. He confessed himself somewhat satisfied with what he had managed to effect: Sevire cowed, Brynard partially checked and revealed. And yet Donari knew he had not *won* anything, not really.

Sevire was still rich, Byrnard was still Prelate, and both of them were still very dangerous. And then there was the King. Roderran was coming, bringing war with him, and Pevana would have to be accommodating to her lord and master. Donari frowned and gazed into his reflected eyes. He saw intelligence there, cunning, and at least a hint, the smallest glint that brought a smile to his lips, of hope.

"Even Kings can be worked," he whispered to the mirror as he turned to leave. "Let Roderran come."

About the Author

Photo credit: Grace Eide-Gabriel

Mark Nelson is a career educator and for the last twenty-two years has been teaching composition and literature at a small high school located in the rain shadow of the Cascade Mountains in eastern Washington State. He is happily married to his best friend and fellow educator and together they have raised three beautiful daughters and one semi-retired cat. Words, music, food and parenting permeate his life and serve as a constant source for inspiration, challenge and reward. To temper such unremitting joy, Mark plays golf: an addiction that provides a healthy dose of humility.

Look for these fantastic fantasies from Hadley Rille Books